# Final Heart

This is a work of fiction. Names, characters, places, and incidents either are the product of the author's imagination or are used fictitiously. Any resemblance to actual persons, living or dead, events, or locales is entirely coincidental.

Copyright © 2024 Whitney Morris

All rights reserved. No part of this book may be reproduced or used in any manner without written permission of the copyright owner except for the use of quotations in a book review. For more information, address: wrlmorris@gmail.com.

First paperback edition April 2023

*Published by WRLMorris Publishing*
*Book design by Whitney Morris*

ISBN 978-1-916935-06-8 (paperback)
ISBN 978-1-916935-07-5 (hardback)
www.wrlmorris.com

For Amaya,

The night rain and bringer of joy

# Prologue

## *Kadon*

The sky was a mishmash of blue, pinks, reds, greens and purple. Kadon hovered above a human city. Below the earth rumbled and cracked. Waves crashed against the shore. The water level rising and gushing past the buildings. He had no idea where he was. The veil that had split the magic world from the human one was gone. As it had come crashing down it had splattered different parts of the magic world on to the human one. Spitting him out in this monstrosity of a place, where the ocean met a heap of land covered in concrete. The world was being reshaped into something new and it was ugly.

Kadon peered down at the city below. Great towers of brick and glass filled the landscape. Paths made of black stone snaked round the buildings, lined with more human contraptions. He had thought the village he had seen when he first escaped the tree of time had been bad, but this city was hideous. The perfect example of what leeches' humans could be. They had been separated from magic for too long and forgotten their place in the world. Humans were magic-less parasites, that needed exterminating. Kadon was the man for the job.

His top lip curled as he looked below at the humans.

They gawked up at him. Pointing and gasping. The earth rumbled and the pavement cracked as water filled the city. Kadon grinned as he watched the natural disaster created by the fall of the veil. He hadn't planned for things to happen like this. Truth be told he hadn't known how the natural order of things would be affected when he destroyed the veil. This was just a delightful side effect, and he would enjoy the show.

Shrill cries pierced Kadon's ears making him snarl. The humans ran around below screaming at the tops of their lungs. They abandoned their vehicles and fled from the buildings. The ground rolled breaking apart and expanding. Grassy land pushed its way up into the gap. Screams echoed around him. The sound made his ears ring. Kadon gritted his teeth as he rained shadow down on the city. Humans dropped like flies as his shadows hit. A smile spread across Kadon's face. Power ran through his veins. He could feel everything around him. Every change in the wind. All the water flowing around the city. With a flick of his wrist, water burst out of the pipes running below the city. Nearby humans cried out. Kadon glared at them and shadow burst from his body, slicing through the humans. He smirked as they slumped to the ground now quiet.

Kadon lowered himself to the ground. Walking down a path littered with body's he grinned. The ground shook. His heart raced as he spun round looking for her. But it wasn't the elf Queen, just the destruction of the veil, still recreating the earth. He clenched his fists as he thought of Mellissa. That annoying hybrid human-elf. She had been nothing but a pain since he met her. He had all this new power, yet he couldn't feel the earth. Not like she could. Freya still held power over him through that girl. Through her descendant. He wouldn't let Freya win. She was long dead, yet she still had something he didn't. She had had an heir. Her bloodline lived on. Kadon would take the legacy Freya had left behind. He would gain the power over the earth she had once wielded. Kadon gritted his teeth. He needed the land stone, and he would take Mellissa for himself.

# 1

# **The New World**

## *Mellissa*

The sun beamed down on us as the wind whistled through the mountains. My heart hammered in my chest as I paced along the craggy mountainside. Harkura and Victoria watched be their eyes darting back and forth with my direction of movement. Greg was stood beside Radius. They were whispering about something, but I didn't care what. We were just outside the camp we had evacuated to after Kadon had destroyed the Capitol and tore down the veil. My mind was racing. There was so much to think about that I couldn't stay still. Or maybe it was still the adrenaline pumping through me that had me unable to stop moving. I had just returned from defending the camp from missiles. Then Radius had kindly informed me a group of human soldiers where at the base of the mountain.

Greg stepped away from the group. He placed himself in my path, so I walked into him. As I turned to go round him, he clasped my arms. "Mellissa, you need to let me heal you."

More forehead creased as I gaped at him. "What? I'm fine."

His brows rose as he tilted his head to the side. "You were just flying around with a dragon to fight off missiles," he replied, "I would rather check that for myself."

"I'm fine."

He cupped my chin in his hands turning my face to the side. "You have a rather large cut on your forehead." He pressed his fingers to my head, and I winced.

"Fine." I huffed over to a large boulder and sat on it. He crouched in front of me and healed the cut on my forehead. As he checked me for any more injuries, I glanced up at the sky. Thoughts of what had just happened filled my mind. Flying with Ignis had been exhilarating. There had been a threat to the camp, and I had just flown into action to protect everyone. I had acted on instinct. Even though I could fly myself, riding on the dragons back had been different. I had felt empowered like I could do anything, but now I was back on solid ground, I was lost.

This was all too much. Now I had finally stopped moving my legs felt like jelly. I was secretly glad Greg had gone into healer mode and I was sat on this rock. It hid my shaking limbs from the others as that adrenaline rush dampened down. My mind reeled as I tried to make sense of everything. Protecting the camp had been the easy part. Now I had to think about what this all meant for us. No veil and the humans attacking in fear. Kadon was no longer our only problem. Ignis had retreated to his cave stating he would leave the humans to me. One moment we had been fighting side by side and the next he had abandoned me on the rocky mountain side. I let out a long breath trying to slow my racing thoughts. I glanced over Greg's shoulder. Just because Ignis had run off, I wasn't alone. Radius, and my two guardians stood huddled together with their arms folded watching Greg's every move.

"All done." Greg leaned forward and pressed a kiss to my forehead. "Apart from that cut on your head, you were all good."

I poked him in the chest. "I told you I was fine."

"Now that we know you really are fine what is the plan?" asked Radius.

"Plan?" I asked peering up at him.

Radius was pale, all warmth drained from his sun kissed skin. He rubbed the back of his neck. "The missiles weren't the only problem. Human soldiers have surrounded the base of the mountains."

I chewed on my bottom lip. Why was I the one who needed to have the plan? I had been hoping one of them were going to tell me what the plan was. Radius was a king and a crystal keeper, he was just as qualified as me to make these decisions. Ignis was too but the sun crystal keeper seemed to like to leave decision making up to others. I clenched my fists that dragon hid is his cave too much. At least Radius was here to work with me. My head was pounding. Magic was no longer a secret. The two separate worlds had remade itself in to one and the humans were looking for answers.

I stood clapping my hands together as I did. "I will talk to them."

Radius's brows drew together. "They fired missiles at us. They do not wish to talk."

My heart was pounding along in tune with my rising anxiety. I tugged at my hair my fingers getting tangled in my curls. Kadon was enough of a problem without adding hostile humans to the mix. "They are just scared because they don't understand what is happening. So, I will go explain it all to them."

Harkura stepped in front of me with his hand out. "No, you will not put yourself in harm's way."

I folded my arms as I jutted my hip out to the side. "Then what do you suggest?"

"What if we put up a glamour charm? That will keep us hidden from prying eyes."

"Thats only if they don't come and physically search the mountains," said Victoria, "A random land mass has appeared out of nowhere I highly doubt they are not going to investigate it."

I put my hand up like a child in school. "Can I just go talk to whoever is in charge and tell them we aren't a threat?"

They all looked at me like I was insane. "No," said both my guardians in unison.

Victoria rubbed the bridge of her nose. "You are so naive. You would think growing up with the humans you would know better." She looked at me one brow risen. "Frightened humans bite first and ask questions later."

Greg cleared his throat. He had been oddly silent for him. "Talking will eventually be out best course of action but not while the humans are still in shock. I suggest we go underground."

"What?" I said.

"As in literally underground." He pointed to the rocky surface at our feet. "Hide within the mountain, like Ignis is in his cave. You and any dwarfs in camp should be able to make that possible."

I nodded as I rubbed my chin. "Okay, that's the plan." A wave of panic hit me. I felt nausea swirl up in me. "What about the others?"

"What others?" Greg asked.

"The other cities. Urbem Folium, Novosvillas and the rest." I clutched my hand over my chest my heart felt like it was about to beat out my body. "They will have popped up randomly as well. The people there could be in danger from the humans as well."

The colour drained from Victoria's face. "But how do we find them? We have no idea where any of our cities are in this new world."

I grabbed Greg's arm steadying myself. "Laxus. I need to find Laxus."

Harkura placed a hand on my shoulder. "Just breathe my queen. Slow breaths." He demonstrated and I synced my breathing with his. "Thats better." I nodded. Having slowed my breathing I didn't feel as dizzy anymore. Harkura rubbed his chin. "Laxus was in the caves they should be well hidden. Out priority should be finding the cities above ground and bring all the residents here."

"And how do you expect us to do that?" asked Victoria throwing her arms in the air.

He pointed at me. "Mellissa is going to."

I frowned scrunching my nose. "I am?"

"Yes, because now Humarya is dead, you can teleport again. Urbem Folium should be the easiest to find as you are very familiar with the area."

"Of course." I thumped my fist down on my hand. "Okay listen up everyone. Greg you're in charge of creating the camp underground. Get Hogan and Caleb to round up any dwarfs to start burrowing. Victoria and Harkura you spread the plan round camp, then keep guard." I pointed at Greg and then to Victoria and Harkura. My gaze landed on Radius. "Radius you put up a temporary glamour, keep us hidden while we work and then fill Ignis in on everything."

Radius nodded. "And you will be gathering the rest of your people." He frowned. "Do you think the mer-folk will be hidden underwater?"

My heart panged with guilt; I hadn't thought about Radius' people just my own. "I believe they will be just like those in the caves but if you want to check in on them."

He placed his arm over his chest like in salute. "No, the immediate danger is here. I will help here first. Now go Queen Mellissa, us four will make sure everything here goes according to plan." He stood tall his broad shoulders tense. I nodded. Shutting my eyes I pictured Urbem Folium, I thought of my people, of Samson and Josh. My powers surged out of me, and I teleported.

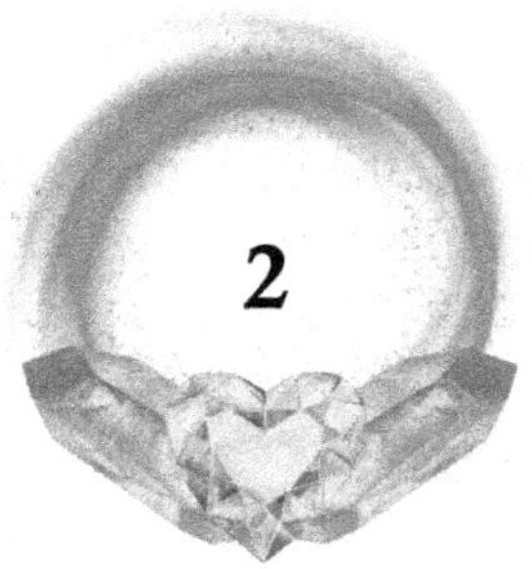

# 2

# **Retreat**

## *Gregory*

Greg and Victoria burst into High Priestess Yuko's tent. She jumped to her feet. "What is the matter with you two?"

Greg swiped sweat from his forehead, as he caught his breath. "The humans" he said, "they just attacked us."

Yuko's eyes went wide. "They what? Is anyone hurt?"

"It's okay Mellissa and the dragon stopped their missiles before they reached the camp," said Victoria.

Yuko rubbed her chin her brow furrowed. "Missiles?"

"Um, think big flying metal cylinders that explode on impact." Victoria waved her hands round trying to illustrate her words.

The corner of Yuko's eyes creased, and her lips twisted into a frown. "Why are they trying to hurt us? We haven't done anything to them".

Greg gritted his teeth. "The why isn't important at the moment. We need to hide in case they try again. Mellissa wants us to get the dwarfs to take us all underground. Can you help me organise them?"

"Maybe they didn't know there were people here." Yuko replied, "Once they see we are a camp of people, families with children." She looked at him with wide hopeful eyes, her blue cheeks rosy.

Greg felt like pulling his hair out. Had she even been listening to him. Victoria brushed past him and grasped Yuko by the shoulders. "I grew up amongst humans, believe me when I say they will see your blue skin and freak. We need to hide now."

Yuko's jaw dropped as she stuttered. "I- I didn't think the humans were that primitive. Mellissa never had any issues with how I look. And all the human elves."

Greg sighed as he pressed his fingers to his forehead. "Mellissa is an exceptional person."

"And all the mixed-race human elves grew up knowing magic existed," said Victoria. "Now can we get on with this?"

Yuko nodded as she bundled up her priestess robes in her hands. "Hogan and Caleb should be in their tents. I will corral them to get the dwarfs moving."

As she marched to the tent exit Harkura almost collided with her. Harkura stepped back panting. "Sorry but it's the humans. They are at the edge of our camp."

Yuko's blue skin paled. "They're already so close."

"Have they spotted us yet?" Greg asked.

Harkura shook his head. "King Radius put up a glamour spell before going to talk with Lord Ignis. It is working so far, but one wrong step and we will be discovered."

"What are we going to do?" Yuko asked her voice had gone up an octave. She looked upwards at the tent ceiling her eyes filled with tears. "Oh, Gabrielle how did you handle this stress?"

Greg's chest tightened at the mention of Lady Gabrielle. She always knew what to do. It wasn't just him that missed her. They were all lost without her. She had been their leader, the one to look to in a time of crisis. Now there was just him and Yuko panicking in a tent. He took a deep breath pushing his emotions down. Thinking like this helped no one. They just needed to execute the original plan but quicker. He took Yukos hands and looked her in the eye. "We are going to take this camp underground."

He looked to Harkura and then Victoria "Can you two alert Radius to the human's movements and then keep an eye on them? Alert us if they get too close. "They both nodded and left the tent, the fabric swishing as they brushed past. Greg turned back to Yuko. "You oversee Hogan and Caleb. I will start gathering everyone else up. We need to make sure the water nymphs are moved first." Yuko and Greg exited the tent and went in opposite directions.

Greg ran from tent to tent, ordering people to evacuate. He told them all to gather where they had held the memorial for Lady Gabrielle. Once people caught wind of what he was doing they began passing the word on themselves. Soon everyone was gathered in one spot.

As Greg looked out at the crowd of people his stomach was in knots. Their lives were a mess. The crowd was a sea of panicked and scared faces. All of them were looking to him like he knew what he was doing. These people were in no shape to fight. Most of them were just normal people who happened to have magic. Hopefully things wouldn't turn into a battle. They would soon be hidden.

Yuko came running over with Caleb and Hogan in tow. She brushed sweat from her brow. "I have briefed the dwarfs on what to do."

Caleb punched one fist into his other hand. "Don't worry we have got this."

Hogan and Caleb took point at the head of a small group of dwarfs. Majority of the dwarfs lived in the caves or the hills which only the Gods now knew where they were. Hopefully the small number that lived in the capitol would be enough for this plan to work. The crowd of people were split into twelve groups. The dwarfs separated into four teams of roughly eight to ten. This meant three trips.

Yuko gripped Greg's forearm. "Are you sure about this?"

"No," Greg ran his finger through his hair. "But this is the best way to avoid a fight."

She gently patted his arm. "I just hope we can keep them all safe."

He gave her a weary smile. "Me to. Now you need to go. You're in one of the first groups with the water nymphs."

She nodded and walked away with her head held high. Greg watched her join a group of water nymphs. Roughly ten dwarfs surrounded them. The other teams of dwarfs gathered round different groups of people. Pushing their hands out in unison and swiping their feet along the ground, the dwarfs cracked the ground under them. Just like Greg had seen Mellissa do on many occasions. The cracks splintered across the rocky surface. The dwarfs pulled their arms back and slammed them down. With a boom, the group disappeared under ground. Gregs blood ran cold at the sound. He peered round hoping the noise didn't draw the humans in quicker.

The dwarfs all lived under ground in the caves and hills. It was an intricate system of tunnels created by their magic. This plan was simply recreating that. Only someone with earth magic would be able to get in or out easily. Something a human definitely wouldn't be able to do. A couple of minutes later the dwarfs reappeared and moved on to the next set of groups. Greg let out a sigh of relief. Things were moving along nicely.

Beatrice hurtled towards him her lips pursed and her brow furrowed. Maybe he had spoken too soon. "Gregory," she said her voice shrill. "Why are the changelings the last group being evacuated?"

Greg pinched the bridge of his nose. "Because as shapeshifters we can escape the easiest by turning into birds or some other animal."

She snorted. "The council members should be prioritised."

"No, we shouldn't. Our powers give us an advantage Beatrice, so those who can't shift go first."

"Who put you in charge anyway? There should have been a vote?"

"You are being ridiculous. There is no time for a vote." Greg gritted his teeth as he tried to stay calm. "Besides this is Mellissa's plan that she came up with before she left."

"Well, no one voted for her."

"You and Lee may not have but Mellissa got the majority vote."

Beatrice crossed her arms as she stuck her nose up in the air. "Of course, you voted for your girlfriend."

Greg chuckled. "You know I didn't vote right?"

Her jaw dropped and her eyes went wide. "Why?"

Greg shrugged. "To be honest, I didn't particularly want Mellissa or Lee in charge, but for very different reasons."

"Well Lee would have never left us in this mess."

"That's because Lee would never put himself in harm's way."

"Gregory," Shouted Lee. Greg groaned as he turned to see Lee marching towards them scowling. "Why have I been lumped in with the rest of the witches? The council should be the first to be evacuated."

"As I was explaining to Beatrice, priority is not based on your job but your ability to escape if attacked. This is why all changelings including myself will go last. The witches will be evacuated with the warlocks before us."

"This is ridiculous," Lee pursed his lips. "And where is Mellissa? She should be helping move people."

Greg's jaw tensed as he fought the urge to shout. "Mellissa is out finding where the rest of us magic folk ended up and checking they haven't come to any harm." Lee opened his mouth to talk but Greg stopped him by putting his hand up in front of his face. He pointed to the group Lee had walked away from. "Look Lee your group is being moved wouldn't want to be left behind."

Lee narrowed his eyes at Greg but hurried back to his group. Greg pressed his fingers to the side of his head. A headache was forming because of those twos' silly demands. The second set of groups were submerged underground. Once the dwarfs came back up the last few people left would all be hidden safely in the mountain. He would wait for Mellissa to return and then she could take over dealing with the idiots.

A loud boom echoed through the mountain side shaking the ground. "What was that?" asked Beatrice in a high pitch squeak.

There was another boom and smoke plumed above the southern edge of camp. Greg's pulse quickened. "Beatrice order, all the changelings to shift. Hopefully the dwarfs won't be long."

Beatrice grabbed his wrist. "What about you?"

"I'm going to find out what that was." Greg pulled away from her and ran towards the explosion. He shifted into a eagle, flapping his wings a fast as he could.  He quickly swerved upwards and circled above a black cloud of smoke. As the smoke cleared Radius was revealed fighting with a pair of humans. Three others were frozen on the spot. Greg gasped as he spotted Harkura. He was laid out on the ground bleeding. Victoria was knelt beside him her hands over his middle. Greg swooped downward. Once he was close enough to the ground, he shifted. He was running as soon as his feet touched the terrain and skidding to a halt by Harkura. Victoria's eyes went wide as she looked up. "Greg," she shouted. "Help him."

Greg knelt beside Harkura. His tunic was soaked in blood. Victoria's hands were pressed firmly down holding pressure. Greg ripped the fabric of Harkura's top revealing his abdomen. "On three move your hands," said Greg. Victoria nodded. "One, two, three." Victoria pulled her hands away and Greg swiftly placed his hands were hers had been. Blood quickly began seeping from the wound. Greg pushed down to create more pressure. With a quick incantation Gregs hands began to glow. His hands were warm with magic as he seeped the spell into the wounds. He felt the spell taking hold and he glanced up at Victoria. "What happened?"

"One idiot human tripped over a rock and fell through the glamour," replied Victoria, "The others followed. Harkura tried to talk to them but the moment they saw him they opened fire." She clenched her fists. "You can heal him, right?"

"That's what I'm doing," Greg's forehead creased. His magic pouring into the wound. The damage ran deep. "But it might take some time."

Radius slid down beside him. His face smudged with dirt. "How is he?"

"He has been in better shape." Greg replied.

Radius frowned. "I don't know how much time we have. One of them managed to radio for help before I knocked them out."

"I don't know if we can move him yet."

Victoria gritted her teeth. "I should have been quicker and frozen them all."

Harkura grunted. "I'm okay." He went to sit up.

Victoria gently placed her hand on his shoulder. "No, you are not."

"I'm okay enough to move." Sweat dripped from his brow and his blue skin was ghastly pale.

"I need to at least stop your bleeding," said Greg.

Harkura grabbed his wrist and looked him dead in the eye unflinching. "There is no time. I am fit enough to move."

"Fine," said Greg, "But I will shift into something large enough to carry you."

Greg shifted into a horse. Radius carefully lifted Harkura and placed him on Greg's back. Victoria walked beside them. Greg tried to hurry but was also aware if he made the wrong move, it could make Harkura's wounds worse. They may not have magic, but these humans and their guns were deadly.

Hogan came running over to them. "I found you." He bent over panting.

"What are you doing here?" Greg asked.

"Everyone is underground." He said, "I came to get you." Hogan's face went pale as he looked at Harkura. A whirling sound thundered above. "What's that?" yelled Hogan.

"A helicopter," said Victoria. "We have to go, before we are spotted."

"Right." Hogan took a wide stance. "Hold tight." Hogan pushed his arms out and stamped his foot. The ground cracked below their feet. Greg's stomach lurched as they plummeted into the mountain.

# 3

# **Urbem Folium**

## *Mellissa*

My body was warm surrounded by the twinkling lights of my magic. It was like I was being launched through space as I teleported.

I materialised in front of Samson. He let out a high-pitched cry. We were in his office in the castle. He lent on his desk with one hand, while clutching his chest with the other. "Your majesty, what's going on?" He asked.

A wave of relief washed over me as I took him in. Samson in a smart grey suit and green tie. His short brown hair neatly slicked back like always. My eyes were damp. "Samson I'm so glad to see you." I stepped forward and hugged him. He was stiff as a board but relaxed into the embrace and patted my back.

"I'm relieved to see you too. I thought something terrible had happened to you."

I gently swept my thumbs below my eye wiping away any tears that threatened to fall. "Something terrible has happened." I stepped away from him so I could clearly see his face. "I lost and now the veil has fallen."

"We noticed." His eyes wouldn't meet mine as he fiddled with his tie.

I clenched my fists as a dark hole of guilt opened inside me. "How is everyone holding up here?"

"When the veil came down, we assumed the worse. Josh and I decided it was best to get everyone moved inside the castle that way everyone was in one place that we could protect. The faeries are also here as well. Lord Ping showed up looking for you."

My heart did a little somersault. All the elves and faeries were safe. Lord ping was here too. He was the only council member to not be in the Capitol. "That's great. It means I'll be able to gather everyone easily." I went to walk out his office when I felt a hand on my arm. He tugged me back.

"Mellissa what happened?" He asked, his tone cold.

My heart felt heavy, and I couldn't bring myself to look at him. "I told you I lost." I yanked my arm from his grip. "I'm sorry I let you down. I let everyone down. I know I'm a rubbish queen."

"That's not what I mean. I thought you were dead," he shouted. His tone shocked me into silence. I looked up at him my mouth a jar. He was shaking as tears rolled down his cheeks. "The veil came down and I was so scared that something had happened to you. And what about Greg? The last time I saw you, you were going to rescue him and then all this happened. You didn't contact me, so of course my mind went to the worse scenario possible." He rubbed his face with the palms of his hands. "I don't think you're a bad Queen you were out there risking your life for all of us." He sighed as he looked up at the ceiling. "I just wish…"

My shoulders sagged. "That I was a better communicator."

He chuckled and gave me a small smile. "Yeah."

"You're not the only one." I took his hand in mine. "I will do better. I promise to keep you in the loop on everything." I sat in one of the chairs by his desk and gestured for him to sit in the other. He sat in the chair one leg crossed over the other and stared at me. I pushed the stray curls that had escaped my braid out my eyes. "Okay so Greg is safe. We rescued him but not before Humarya retrieved the second dark stone. We managed to escape to the Capital but that's when things went really wrong." I fiddled with the hem of my top. "It was Kadon. All of this was his doing, he killed Humarya and took the dark stones for himself. He is more powerful than she ever was. He destroyed the veil. With the help of the Hawklings and the Sun crystal keeper we evacuated the Capital and escaped to the mountains." My chest tightened as I thought of my last battle with Kadon. He had wiped the floor with me. I took as deep breath swallowing the lump in my throat. "Kadon killed Lady Gabrielle."

Samson gasped. I glanced up at him. His hands covered his mouth, and his eyebrows were high on his face. "Lady Gabrielle is dead."

I nodded. I went on to tell him everything that had happened in battle with Kadon. How the last thing Lady Gabrielle did before she died was save me. I also informed him that the sun crystal keeper was a big golden scaled, fire breathing dragon. I went on to explain how the humans had attacked us. He just nodded a long occasionally going "hmm". I told him everything up to what had brought me to him now. When I finished talking, I let out a long breath leaning back in my chair. Rehashing everything had felt like reliving it all. It was like I had lost all over again. "So, you see, I want to gather everyone in a single place because I can't protect you all scattered across the world. The mountains are where I plan to take everyone."

He rubbed his chin. "I get that especially with the humans being so aggressive but why not bring everyone here? Even with the veil gone we are still hidden within a forest."

My forehead creased as I scrunched my nose. "We are?"

"Yes. According to Josh we have appeared just off the coast of the north of England."

I sat up leaning forward. "Wait how does Josh know this?"

He shrugged. "Satellites or something." He stood from his seat and held a handout to me. "It's probably best I show you what Josh has been up to."

I took his hand, and he pulled me to my feet. Samson led me out his office and down the corridor. He stopped outside Joshes office and knocked on the door. "Come in," said Josh.

Samson opened the door, and I followed behind him as he walked inside. "Hey Josh, I was wondering…" Samson started but was cut off by Josh.

"I still haven't found anything on the queen or your cousin yet." Josh was tapping away on a keyboard and hadn't looked up from the large monitor in front of him. I looked around his office, mouth a jar. His office was the same size as Samson's, but I felt like if I moved even a millimetre, I would knock something over. The last time I had been in his office he had an impressive computer set up. Better than what he had installed in mine. But now, the large monitor had the company of three more mounted on the wall above his desk. He had cables running all over the room and what looked like three large hard drives. There was also an open laptop on his desk and three mobile phones.

"Josh," Samson said.

Josh held up his hand to quiet him. He spun sideways in his desk chair, turning from one keyboard to another. "I think I'm on to something. Just give me a minute."

Now that he had moved, I could see him more clearly. His usual nice and bouncy curls were a ratty mess and he had dark circles under his eyes like he hadn't slept in days. Samson looked at me his brown eyes wide and nodded at Josh. I stepped forward placing my hand on Joshes desk. "Josh," I said.

His fingers stopped moving and his hands hovered over his keyboard as he slowly looked up from the monitor. "Queen Mellissa," he said.

I smiled as his eyes met mine. "Yeah, its me."

"Oh my," He scrambled up out his chair tripping over a cable, grabbing his desk just in time to steady himself. "You're here." He clasped my hands in his as his eyes filled with tears. "You're really here."

I nodded as my smile grew wider. "Yeah, I am and I'm so happy to see you." I hugged Josh and he wrapped his arms round me squeezing tight. His stubble was rough against the side of my face.

"We thought that, maybe." His voice caught. "I'm so glad you're okay." He let go of me and turned to Samson. "Why didn't you tell me the Queen was back?"

Samson rolled his shoulders back and huffed. "I tried but you were ignoring me."

Josh rubbed the back of his neck as he wriggled his nose. "Sorry you know how I get when I'm in the zone."

I looked at each monitor in the room. Nothing on the screens made sense to me. "So, Josh, what is all this you're doing?" I pointed to all the computer equipment around the room.

"I was searching for you, but I don't need to do that anymore. But that's not all." He sat back in his desk chair and began typing again. "With the destruction of the veil I knew we would need a way to navigate this new world. I have gained access to certain satellites and been mapping how the land has changed." He pressed the mouse button twice and a map popped up on the largest of the four screens. It was a map of the world, but the land shapes weren't quite right. Josh zoomed in and pointed at a section of the UK. "You see that small island off the northeast coast of the UK." I leant forward peering at the screen. "That's where we are now. I've also used the data I've collected to locate most of the magic cities."

I grabbed his arm and squealed. "That's amazing. I knew you were a tech whiz, but I didn't know you were this good."

Josh smirked as he flexed his fingers. "I don't have a master's degree in computer science for nothing, but I also have the added benefit of dabbling in combining human tech with magic as a hobby."

Samson cleared his throat. "This is why I think Urbem Folium should be our base. While I don't fully understand what Josh is doing, it seems the best way to figure out what the new normal is."

I bit my nails as I tapped my foot. "Maybe but I don't know if I'll be able to get Ignis to leave his cave and we are going to need all three crystal keepers to face Kadon."

"Wait Kadon's back?" asked Josh.

Samson waved a dismissive hand at him. "I'll explain in a bit. Tell the queen what else you have been doing."

"Oh right." Josh slid his chair to the side and began typing on his laptop. "I'm also monitoring the web and news channels for mentions of the new land masses. I have discovered chat about sending in soldiers and even bombing some of the areas. I currently have drones surrounding the forest, so far, no human activity around us."

"The mountains have already been attacked," said Samson, "No doubt they will try again. We have been left alone here."

"From the information I have gathered. The UK government seem more concerned about Novosvillas as its actually connected to the mainland. From an outsider's perspective we appear to be just an island of trees."

My ears twitched at the mention of the changeling city. "What was that about Novosvillas?"

Josh moved his mouse around and the map zoomed out and then in again on a different spot. "The north of Scotland and what were small islands above it are now connected by what we know as Novosvillas." Josh interlaced his fingers as he stretched his arms up above his head. "I have hacked into some very important and supposed to be secret channels. The British government are going to surround the area and make entry by force."

My pulse quickened. "I need to get them all out of there." I rubbed my chin as I narrowed my eyes on the screen.

"Samson you're right. Urbem Folium will be our base." I placed my hand on Joshes back. "Can you print a map of the world with all the new parts?"

He looked up at me one eyebrow high. "Of course." He pressed a few buttons and a machine in the corner buzzed alive. Josh got up and went over to the printer.

"What are you planning?" Samson asked.

"Just what you suggested; bring everyone here." Josh handed me the printed map. "Thanks. I'm also going to have to persuade a dragon to leave his cave. Hopefully this map will help my argument." I looked from Josh to Samson. "Hold down the fort a little longer for me, I'll be back soon."

"Mellissa wait." Samson said holding his hand out in front of me.

"What is it?"

"I know we pretty much are in a state of emergency, but I really think you need to brief Lord Ping."

"Can't you do that for me?"

Samson folded his arms and tilted his head to the side. "It's better coming from you."

I sighed.  Every atom in my body wanted to teleport and it took everything in me to stop myself. "Okay take me to him."

I sat across from Ping. We were in my office sat in front of my desk facing one another. There had been a thin layer of dust on everything due to its lack of use. Ping had a hankie in hand and was dabbing his eyes. "I can't believe she is gone. I should have been there in the Capitol."

I had told him everything that went down in the Capitol and all the events of the last couple days. With how much that had happened it was hard to believe that it had only been days and not weeks or months. I shifted in my seat and twiddled with my fingers not sure what to do with my hands. "There isn't anything you could have done."

"You don't know that. My fairy dust might have made a difference," he cried.

"Kadon is too powerful. You were exactly where you should have been with your heavily pregnant wife, who could give birth any day now. You led the fairies here where they will be safe."

He threw his arms out to the side. "And what sort of world will my child be brought into now?"

I leant forward and patted his hand. "I am working on making this world a safe place, for your child and everyone else."

He clasped my hands. His grip was so tight it felt like my fingers might pop off. "With the help of the other crystal keepers you will stop Kadon and then find a way to make peace with the humans." A wave of relief hit me as Ping let go of my hand. I flinched as he stood. "That Lee already trying to get Lady Gabrielle's seat." He clenched his fists. "Well, I say no. He will not get my vote." Ping looked me up and down. I stiffened under his gaze. "I will nominate you. I have not always agreed with your methods, but you always try to do the right thing."

"Um, thanks."

He linked his thumbs round the braces on his trousers. "Now I must go talk to my people."

"Wait, I would like to talk to everyone together, if that's okay," I said. My stomach churned at the idea, but I was queen. I had been gone too long and my people deserved to know what was happening. I needed to be the one to tell them.

"Of course. We shall debrief our people together, my queen." Ping bowed and then held his arm out to me.

I wiped my clammy palms on my trousers and took his arm. Taking slow breaths as we walked, I tried not to anxiously shake. "I will have to leave straight after, but I'll be back with others."

Ping nodded. "I understand. There are still many others out there in need of your protecting."

I gaped at Ping. He appeared to be serious, there was no indication that he was mocking me. Having other council members look up to and respect my decisions was going to take some getting used to.

# Underground

## *Victoria*

Victoria's stomach was swishing and her ears rang as they plummeted through the rocky mountain. She stumbled forward as they came to a halt inside a dark cavern. Shaking her head Victoria tried to stop the buzzing in her ears.

Radius held his trident up and light burst from the crystal in its centre, illuminating the dark. On either side of them was rocky grey wall and no one else in sight. "This way," said Hogan. He waved his hands at them as he hurried forward. Victoria stepped in line behind Hogan and the others followed her.

Hogan led them through a tunnel. Victoria's heart hammered away. She kept glancing back at Greg in the form of a horse making sure he still had Harkura on his back. They stepped out into a clearing. Victoria's eyes went wide as she looked around at what had been done to the area. On one side the group of dwarfs were still shifting their arms side to side tunnelling into the mountain. The rest of the people were rebuilding their tents from above.

Yuko ran over to them her robes flowing behind her. Her forehead creased as she peered at them. "Gregory is that you? Why are you a horse?"

Victoria stepped in front of him. "Harkura is injured. Is there somewhere we can take him?"

"I've already put my tent up. You can take him there." Yuko took Victoria's arm and walked towards a small bunch of fully erected tents. They entered one of the tents. It looked like Yuko had already started getting comfortable. There was a small table with cushions round it. There was a pile of bags in a corner. But more importantly a camp bed with a sleeping bag laid on it. Victoria pulled the sleeping bag off the camp bed chucking it behind her. Radius lifted Harkura off Greg's back and Greg swiftly shifted back. It felt like everything was moving in slow motion as Harkura was lowered onto the camp bed. Victoria felt a lump forming in her throat. Harkura was unconscious and his body had gone limp. His usually warm blue skin was almost grey.

Greg rushed over and knelt beside the camp bed. He placed his hands back over the wound. "Sodim quid fit." His hands glowed green.

Victoria knelt on the opposite side of the camp bed and took Harkura's hand. Her mind reeled as all forms of awful thoughts shot through her mind. "He feels cold. You are healing him, right? Like your magic is working?"

"Yes, but he lost a lot of blood on the journey here."

"How did this happen?" asked Yuko.

Radius stomped his foot. "Those humans shot him. We weren't doing anything to them, but they attacked us anyway."

Yuko gasped as she shook her head. "They always said the veil was to protect the humans from us but I'm starting to think it was us it was keeping safe."

Victoria's heart felt like it was trapped in a clamp that someone kept tightening. Images of Harkura walking towards the humans flashed through Victoria's mind. She hadn't gone with him because she thought it was pointless. He stopped moving when they had barked orders at him. He put his hands up in way of surrender when they had aimed their weapons at him. He had tried to pose as little threat possible to them yet one trigger happy solider had still shot him. Victoria clenched her fists. She should have gone instead of

Harkura. Outwardly she appeared human. It didn't hurt that she was also a female with blond hair. Women were always deemed as less of a threat. When she had stepped out rage on full show they hadn't been as quick to hold her at gun point. That was their second mistake of the day.

"It's working," exclaimed Greg. Victoria's eyes darted to him. Sweat dripped from Greg's brow. He gritted his teeth and bobbed his head towards the wound. "Look." His hands parted so they were either side of Harkura's stomach. The flesh on Harkura's abdomen twitched. It felt like Victoria's heart had just somersaulted as she smiled.

Yuko knelt beside Greg and dabbed a cloth across his brow. "Is there anything we can do to help?"

"I just need to focus."

Yuko went over to Radius, and they walked out the tent together. Victoria stayed silently holding Harkura's hand, while Greg worked. There was no way she was leaving his side. Harkura was Victoria's partner in crime. They were a team; she couldn't lose him. They stayed this way for the next thirty minutes. Victoria silently gripping Harkura's hand and Greg casting healing spells.

Harkura suddenly shot up right crying out. Victoria jumped startled and Greg fell backwards his spell stopping. Blood poured out the wound as Harkura clasped his admen grunting. "Harkura," yelled Victoria grasping his shoulders. "What are you doing?"

"It feels like my insides are burning," he said through pants.

"It's the healing," Greg said, "It's your internal organs being put back together."

Harkura clasped Victoria's wrist. "Freeze it. You need to cool it, so the pain stops."

"What no I could make things worse." Victoria's brows drew together. Her mind raced trying to think of what to do next, but she didn't know. She was good in a fight. If someone needed protection or defending, she was your girl but injuries like this. She was useless. "Just let Greg heal you."

Harkura's nails dug into her hand as he squeezed it. "Freezing it will be quicker. Just do this for me."

"No don't do that, just give me a sec." Greg scrabbled around the tent pouring out the bags Yuko had left inside. Victoria peered at him her mouth a jar. Had he gone mad? Greg rummaged through some fabric and papers and a bunch of glass jars. He found a bowl and poured in the contents of the jars. Mixing what he had, he muttered a healing incantation. He scurried over to Harkura and thrust the bowl out to him. "Drink this. It'll help."

"Do as he says." Victoria took the bowl from Greg and held it to Harkura's lips. He gulped it down. In a few seconds his eyes rolled back in his head and slumped back onto the camp bed. Victoria chest tightened as panic rose up in her. She got up and was beside Greg in a flash. "What did you do to him?"

"It's a makeshift anaesthetic. It stopped the pain and put him to sleep."

For a moment she had been ready to fight Greg. Tackle him and take him out for hurting Harkura. Logically she knew he wouldn't do anything to hurt Harkura, he was a healer. But when Harkura's eyes rolled back in his head for a brief second, she had seen red. Victoria sighed as she rubbed the sides of her forehead. "Why was he in so much pain? Is there something wrong with your healing abilities?"

"Moving him before he was healed made his injury worse." Greg nudged past her and sat beside Harkura's unconscious body. "I was almost done. That was why it hurt so much." He placed his hands over the wound again. "Sanum quid fit." His hands glowed green as he pushed his magic into the wound. After ten minutes the skin on Harkura's abdomen knit itself back together. Greg let out a long breath as he wiped his forehead with his arm. "All done. He'll be asleep for a while longer."

Victoria sighed with relief. "Thank god."

Greg looked down at his hands. He was covered in blood. "I'm sorry."

"What? You said he was healed. Why are you sorry?"

"Because this never should have happened."

"No, it shouldn't have," Victoria's jaw was tense. "But it did, and we dealt with it. The one who should be sorry is the guy who shot him." Victoria curled her lips at the mention that soldier left a bad taste in her mouth. "But he is now an icicle on a mountainside."

"You are right." Greg's gaze remained low as he got up and walked to the tent exit. "I'm gonna go update Yuko."

"Sure whatever. I'm staying here."

Greg walked out leaving Victoria alone with a sleeping Harkura. He was still pale, but his skin was closer to its usual blue than before. Victoria squeezed his hands. "You've got to stop scaring me like this. I can't lose you." Now that she was alone the tears finally came.

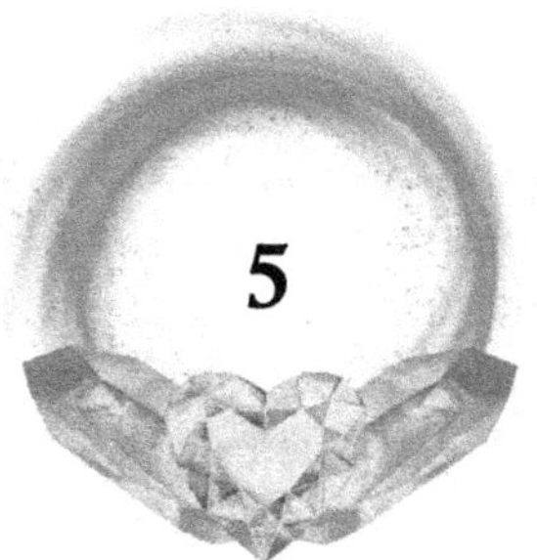

# 5

# New Plan

## *Mellissa*

My heart felt like it had stopped as I took in the sight before me. I had just teleported to Greg covered in blood. The bag I was holding fell from grip to the floor. My mind raced as I took in his appearance. He was hunched over a bowl of water scrubbing at his red hands. I knelt beside him clutching his arms. "Oh god what happened?" My forehead creased as I searched his body for injuries.

"It's not my blood," he said.

"Then who's is it?"

Greg pulled his arms free and dunked them back in the bucket. His gaze remained low as he continued scrubbing blood from his arms. The water had turned a red-brown colour. I grabbed a small towel from the floor beside him and placed my hands over his. Removing them from the water I wrapped his hands in the towel. "Greg what happened?

He swallowed, his gaze not meeting mine. "Harkura was shot."

"What?" My voice was barely a whisper. I couldn't have heard him right. There was no way Harkura had been shot.

"After you left, I went to Yuko to start bringing everyone underground, but the humans were already scouting the mountains." Greg stood turning his back to me. "I sent

Victoria and Harkura to watch them while we evacuated. Radius must have joined them at some point. They were meant to alert us if the humans stumbled through the barrier. According to Victoria they shot Harkura on sight."

"How is he?" I asked.

"He is still out due to the anaesthetic I gave him, but his wounds are all healed."

The tightness in my chest eased. "Good. I assume he is in his tent."

Greg threw the towel he had been holding to the ground. "Is that all you have to say?"

"What more do you want? You told me Harkura was hurt but okay. Now I want to go see him."

Greg spun round finally looking at me. His gaze ran over my whole body. "Did you change while away?"

I fiddled with the skirt of my dress. I was in an emerald, green a-line dress, with my hair up in a high bun and a gold tiara. "Samson made me, he said something about me looking queenly putting people at ease." I shrugged. "I've got to go."

As I walked past him, he grabbed my wrist. "While you were enjoying the comfort of castle life, getting your hair and makeup done, we were risking our lives trying to hide from your humans."

I yanked my wrist free and glared at him. "That isn't what I was doing. I was making plans to find all the displaced magic people. Thanks to my elves we have locations of most of our cities. Our people out there don't have anyone there to lead them. I left the mountains thinking I had someone I could trust in charge." I made sure to emphasis the words 'my' and 'our'. I wouldn't let him turn this round on me. To try other me and lump me in with the humans. My blood boiled as I clenched my fists. I wouldn't let my anger show. I rolled my shoulders and held my head high. "I knew my mixed heritage would be an issue for some, but I didn't think I would hear it from you. I'm dedicated to helping everyone.

That means not just the group here, but all the magic folk lost in this new world."

Greg's shoulder sagged as he took a step back. "I'm sorry I didn't mean that. I know this issue is bigger than the people here." He ran his finger through his hair as he let out a frustrated grunt. "Everything is coming out wrong. I'm just so angry and I don't how to switch it off." Greg gritted his teeth. "Why aren't you angrier?"

"Of course I'm angry," I yelled. Taking a deep breath, I pushed a stray curl behind my ear. "What would be the point of me going and raging at that group of humans? I'm sure Victoria fought them off well enough. Me getting angry would only confirm we are something to fear."

"That's not what I mean. Why aren't you angry with me." He thumped his own chest. "I chose my words purposefully to implicate you cared more about the humans. I know that isn't true, but I want you to be mad."

"You want me to be annoyed with you?"

"Yes, because I deserve it. All this mess is because of me."

I stepped forward grabbing his hands. He tried to pull away, but I held on tight. "This isn't your fault. You couldn't have known this would happen. You gave that task to Harkura because you trusted him."

Greg's chest rose and fell his breathing becoming harsh. "It's not just that. It's everything. The veil falling, Kadon's return. Lady Gabrielle." His voice caught on her name. "It all goes back to me not listening when you told me not to go on that mission to the sea kingdom. Maybe if I had listened Lady Gabrielle would still be alive. She's gone because of me."

A tear rolled down his cheek. Pushing up onto my tiptoes, I pulled him into a hug. "Oh Greg." He buried his face into the crook of my neck. He held me tight his body shaking as he cried. I stroked his back until eventually he went quiet.

Taking a deep breath he rested his forehead on mine. "I'm sorry."

"I know." I stroked his cheek with my thumb. "You can't put all this blame on yourself."

"But I…" he started but I pressed a finger to his lips cutting him off.

"No buts. This mess, this thing with Kadon started long before either of us was even born." I snickered. "What a great inheritance I got from Freya, her psycho ex."

Greg chuckled. "Well, when you put it like that."

"Look there are so many things we could nitpick about and what if I did this different, but it isn't gonna change that this is the situation we find ourselves in. We just gotta keep pushing forward and doing what we can now."

Greg looked at me with wide eyes and smiled. "You're amazing."

I scrunched my nose. "I am?"

"Yeah, and Samson was right. You look very Queenly."

"Well as Queen I really need to go check on Harkura, then go liaise with the other crystal keepers and the council." I placed my hands on his chest and pressed a kiss to his cheek. "And you should get changed because you are really icky." I stepped back looking down at my dress and sighed with relief. "Luckily all that blood seems to be dried in and has not ruined my dress." Picking up the bag I had dropped on arrival, I walked to the tent exit. I turned to look at him. "I'll be back." He nodded but his stare seemed lost. It was like he wasn't fully there.

My heart felt like it was caught in my throat. I had followed the magical auras of my guardians from Gregs tent to the one I had just walked into. What I saw had me frozen on the spot. Victoria was sat beside Harkura's unconscious body, holding his hand. His blue skin was an off shade of grey. A small blanket covered him, but I could see his clothes had been torn up and soaked in blood. Mud and blood were also smeared across what Victoria wore and her hair was a frizzy mess. Dark shadows circled her eyes as she looked up at me. "You're back and looking rather fancy. I assume that means you found home."

"Yeah. Everyone there is okay. I went by your room and Harkura's and brought you a change of clothes." I removed the bag I had brought from my shoulder and held it out to her."

She took it and looked inside. "Thanks."

I sat on the floor by Harkura's head and stroked his cheek. "How did this happen?"

"He was shot."

"I know Greg already told me that." Our eyes met, mine pleading with hers. "But how did that happen?"

Victoria shook her head her eyes filling with tears. "I don't know. We were keeping watch hoping they wouldn't stumble past the glamour when one of the soldiers tripped and fell through. Harkura had his hands up. He tried to speak to them but when he took a step one of them shot him. I lost my shit freezing three of them in one go. Radius jumped out from behind a rock and fought off the other two while I tried to stop the bleeding." She glanced down at her hands. "If Greg hadn't come looking for us when he did, I don't think Harkura would have made it."

I clenched my fist as anger bubbled up inside me. "This is so messed up." I snickered as I thought back to how I had originally wanted to deal with the humans. "And I thought I could just go talk to them, I'm so stupid."

With a shrug Victoria smirked. "Yeah, you're kinda naive but I guess someone needs to be the optimist of the group."

"Well, I have a new plan."

"What is it this time? Have us gather round a fire with the humans singing songs?"

"No," I said my voice going high pitched. I coughed clearing my throat. "I came up with a plan with the help of Josh and Samson."

"Oh, this might actually be a smart plan if they advised you."

"It's fine I don't need your help with this, I'll just take it straight to the other crystal keepers." I stood and turned my back on her.

"Oh, sit back down" she said, "I'll stop teasing." I turned back to her and sat down with my arms crossed. Victoria leaned forward resting her elbows on the side of the camp bed Harkura was laid on. She looked at me with eager eyes. "So, what's the new plan?"

"In the bag I gave you there should be a pile of papers." Victoria opened the bag, rummaged through it, and pulled out a stack of papers. Not bothering to look at them she handed them over.

I took them and held up the map on top. "Josh has already found where all the major magic cities are located, see."

I handed the map to her. She looked at it, bobbing her head as she did. "I'm impressed."

"Now that I know where everyone is I plan to bring them all together in one place so I can protect them."

"You're not gonna bring them all here, are you? There is only so many people you can hide in a mountain."

"No, we are going home to Urbem Folium. Josh is keeping track of the humans' movements. So far, our forest has drawn little attention."

"Really? That's fantastic. No more tents and I'm sure Harkura will recover so much better in his own bed."

I scrunched my nose as I pouted. "I just gotta convince a dragon to leave his cave that he and his ancestors are famous for not leaving."

"Just give me a sec. I'll get changed and I'll be your moral support." Pulling clothes out the bag she stood. "If it comes to it, I'll kick that dragon right out of there." She tugged off her dirty clothes and chucked them on the floor. She slipped into the jeans and sweater I had brought her.

"You don't have to come. It might be best you stay with Harkura in case he wakes."

Victoria ran her fingers through her hair and pulled it up into a high ponytail. "You would have just gone straight to Ignis's cave if you didn't want me to come with you."

"I had to check on Harkura after hearing he got shot." She arched a brow. I threw my arms down beside me. "Fine I want you to come with me but I'm worried that Ignis will judge me for needing you to accompany me."

Victoria waved her hand in the air dismissively. "Who is he to judge? You're already ten times the crystal keeper he is."

She stood beside me and nodded. Together we left the tent and strode through the camp. I hadn't been gone long but there was already rows and rows of tents. A pang of guilt shot through me as I thought of them having to remove them again so soon. As we reached the edge of the cavern that had been dug out, I held my hand out and the heart crystal zoomed into it transformed into staff form. Holding it in front of us the crystal shone brightly lighting our way through the dim tunnel. I glanced at Victoria. Her eyes were focused ahead and face stoic. My stomach churned with every step I took towards the dragon's cave.

As we entered the cave, I saw Ignis wasn't alone. Radius and Rowan were with him. They all stopped talking and turned to look at us. I froze on the spot. Waving I forced myself to smile. "Hey I'm back."

Victoria groaned beside me, and Rowan raised one eyebrow. Radius stepped forward and patted my back. "It's good to see you. Did you find your elves well?"

"Er, yes. They have handled things very well."

"Excellent," said Radius, he puffed out his chest and grinned. "As you can see, we have successfully moved the camp underground and escaped the humans that tried to infiltrate us."

I nodded. "Yeah, I'm impressed how quickly you did all this. Talking of escaping humans-"

"But alas it was not I or Ignis that achieved this." Radius put his arm round my shoulders and waved the other in front of us. "Your courageous land dwellers carved out this space and those wondrous Hawklings are very good at erecting a tent. All I did was help your guardians keep the human soldiers away to give the others time to escape."

I stepped to the side removing myself from his grip. "I have already had the debrief on the events that took place."

Radius frowned. "Oh, well what do you want to discuss?"

"I want to relocate everyone to Urbem Folium."

Radius shrugged. "You are the Queen of the land take your people wherever you want."

I looked at Radius and then to Ignis. "When I say everyone, I mean everyone." I walked past Radius, over to Ignis. "I want you and the hawklings to come as well."

Rowan stepped in front of Ignis his arms wide. "The mountains are our home; we will not abandon them."

"Let Queen Mellissa finish," said Ignis.

Rowan huffed as he folded his arms and stepped aside. I looked up at the dragon. "The threat we face is unlike anything we've dealt with before. The three of us are going to have to work together to defeat Kadon."

"Agreed," said Ignis, "But why do we need to leave our home?"

"My elves have done more than handled this situation they have been proactive." I unrolled the maps Josh had given me and held them up for the others to see. "Josh one of my advisers, has managed to locate most of the magic cities already." I pointed them out on the map. "He has also managed to gather data on the humans' movements in relation to where new land masses have appeared. Urbem Folium is nicely hidden in the forest and so far, hasn't drawn any human attention."

"Something we can't say about the mountains," grumbled Victoria.

Ignis sighed. "You make a convincing argument." He stood his head almost touching the cave ceiling. "Rowan, spread the word. The hawks will be leaving the mountains."

Rowans jaw dropped. "But master."

"Maybe if my ancestor had left his cave all those years ago when Queen Freya had asked him, we wouldn't be in this mess now. I will not repeat his mistake."

Rowan clasped his arm over his chest and bowed. "As you wish."

I turned towards the sea king. "Radius will you come as well?"

Radius nodded. "Of course." He rubbed his chin. "This Josh fellow, does he have any information on the sea kingdom."

"I'm not sure but we can ask him."

He clasped my hand. "Lets get everyone here sorted first." He looked up at Ignis. "Are you able to create those portals again like when you helped us escape the capitol?"

"Yes," replied Ignis, "My portals would be the best way to travel."

I rolled the maps up and tucked them back in my bag. "There is another thing. Once everyone here is in Urbem Folium I want to work on bringing all the other magical beings there too. Will you both help me?"

They both nodded in agreement. Radius clasped my shoulder. "We are in this together." He rolled his shoulders back. "Now let's get this camp evacuated, again."

I stood on top of a rock in a secluded area of the makeshift underground camp. The way the dwarfs had carved out this large cavern in such a short time was impressive. I had gathered Yuko, Beatrice, Lee, Brandon, and Caleb. One leader from each key group here. I didn't want this to turn into a full-blown council meeting, but I needed everyone on broad with our next step. Greg wasn't in the right frame of mind at the moment, so Beatrice was the best replacement.

"I've gathered everyone here to discuss our next steps." I said shuffling a pile of papers. "You can see from the maps I've given you all how the new world looks now, without the veil."

They all looked through the bundle of papers I had handed out. The papers consisted of a map of the world showing everything. The rest where maps of areas highlighting where each of the magical cities were.

"You've found all our cities," said Yuko. "How did you do it so fast?"

"It wasn't me." I interlaced my fingers to stop my fidgeting hands. "My adviser Josh did all of this. It's thanks to him that we will be able navigate this new land."

"What next?" asked Caleb, "Are we all going to gather in this cave?"

Lee folded his arms and snickered. "Are we to become cave people now? Maybe Kadon isn't so wrong about the humans."

Yuko scowled at Lee. "Don't say such terrible things."

"Look what we have become." He flicked his hair back and spread his fingers across his own chest. "We are some of the most important people in the magical world and we have resorted to hiding inside a mountain."

Yuko jabbed her finger in his face. "This isn't ideal, but how could you ever suggest resorting to monstrous behaviour like Kadon."

Lees nostrils flared as his top lip curled. "I did not say I agreed with his methods just that these humans are horrible."

"Not all humans are horrible just like not all magical beings are nice." Yuko waved her hands in his face. "Case in point."

Lee snarled. Just as he opened his mouth to respond, I cut in between them, putting my hands up in front of them. "Stop this. Arguing amongst ourselves achieves nothing."

"But she…," said Lee.

"He is an…," said Yuko.

"Enough," I shouted over them.

Brandon stepped forward and placed a hand on each of their shoulders. "We should listen to the Queen. She gathered us because she has a plan." His grey eyes landed on me. "Isn't that right."

I coughed clearing my throat. "Yes. Lee we are not going to become cave people because we are all moving to Urbem Folium."

"Why the elf city?" said Lee, "The witch city would be much better."

I rolled my eyes. "Because if you look at the maps, can you see Urbem Folium?"

He flicked through the maps; his brows drew together. "Where is it?"

I pointed to the tiny dot next to north England. "Right there. From the information Josh has gathered the bigger cities near human countries are drawing the most attention from the humans. Urben Folium is nicely hidden on an island that looks to just be forest land. The way the elves designed our city makes it blend with the trees."

Lee frowned. "You have a good point."

My jaw dropped. Lee had just agreed with me. Beatrice slid in front of me, so she was almost stepping on my toes. "What about the people in the other cities. How do we know they are safe?"

I stepped back, giving myself some breathing room. "I'm going to evacuate all the cities. They will be brought to Urbem Folium too."

"How you going to do that?" asked Beatrice one brow arched. "Even you can't teleport that many people."

"We are going to do it a city at a time. Josh with the help of my chief of staff Samson are compiling a list of those most at risk. So far, I know Novosvillas and Perluves have had the humans sniffing around, so they are top of the list."

Caleb pointed at the map in his hand. "By the looks of it the caves and hillside dwarfs are well hidden as well."

I nodded. "They are, that's why I think it best they stay put. If Urbem Folium becomes too crowded, they will act as our secondary bases."

"What is the plan exactly?" asked Yuko her hand clasped over her heart. "Beatrice is right you can't teleport everyone."

"The other crystal keepers have agreed to help. Ignis will open a portal for everyone here to get to Urbem Folium. Radius has agreed to assist too." I placed my hand on Yuko's shoulder. "He will open a portal from the river outside Urbem Folium to the bay in Perluves."

Yuko clenched her fists and nodded. "What do you need us to do?"

"Gather everyone here and spread the word that we are leaving. The portal will be in Ignis' cave."

"Got it." Yuko turned round and ushered the others away. They all walked in different directions.

I followed Caleb and tapped his shoulder. "Caleb, do you have a second."

He stood to attention. "Yes, what can I do for you?"

"Are you able to make contact with the caves?"

He stroked his beard. "That is Hogans territory, but it should be doable."

"Can you tell them to stay put and keep Laxus there."

"The pixie boy? Do you think he is still a target?"

"I don't know but I don't want Kadon adding another dark stone to his arsenal. He is strong enough as is."

Caleb grasped my hands forcing me to bend to his height. "Don't worry I'll sort it. Us dwarfs will protect the boy."

"Thank you."

"Don't worry about it." He winked as he bowed. "Your majesty."

I smiled as he walked away. Everyone was listening to me and as long as we worked together this plan would work.

42

# 6

# Evacuation

## *Gregory*

The underground camp was deserted. Greg stood in the middle of the carven inside the mountain. It was dark now that all the floating lights had been put out. He had worked so hard to get them here and they were leaving already. All the people who had been here had neatly lined up and been led to Ignis' cave to be evacuated. Greg shut his eyes taking in the quiet. All he could hear was the sound of his own heart beating in his chest.

"Greg." Came Mellissa's voice causing him to jump. He opened his eyes to see her big brown ones peering up at him. Her forehead creased as she frowned. "What are you still doing here?"

Greg shrugged as he let out a long breath. "I just needed a moment."

"The evacuation has already started." She reached towards him pausing for a second, her hand just hovering away from his face. She bit her bottom lip. "You are coming with us?"

Greg took her hand and pressed a kiss to her knuckles. "Of course. It's just been so chaotic that the quiet of the empty camp is nice."

She interlaced her fingers with his. "If you like, we can skip the crowded portals and teleport."

"Can we? Don't you need to stand next to a dragon looking Queenly?"

Mellissa rolled her eyes. "Naw, Radius is standing pretty beside the Dragon." She winked as she placed her free hand on his chest. "I'm actually meant to be going ahead to make sure Urbem Folium is ready to receive everyone." Pushing up on to her tiptoes she kissed his cheek. "And you're coming with." Greg's stomach lurched as he felt himself yanked forward. Bright light surrounded them. The two of them stumbled as they materialised in the corridors of Mellissa's castle.

"It's going to take some time to get used to that again," Greg said as he steadied himself.

She grinned at him. "Yeah, but it's great being able to teleport again."

"Greg," came Samsons voice behind them. Greg's blood ran cold as he turned towards his cousin. Samson gasped and his eyes went wide. Greg lowered his gaze. His heart was hammering in his ears. A lump stuck in his throat. He didn't have the words to describe what had happened to him if asked. A set of arms wrapped around him as Samson pulled him into a hug. "I'm so happy to see you. Mellissa told me what happened but seeing you okay in real life." Samson squeezed him tighter. "I was so worried and there wasn't anything I could do to help."

"Hey, it was your blood we used for the tracking spell," interjected Mellissa.

"It was?" asked Greg.

Samson stepped back and straightened his tie. "I wasn't sure how much it would help. Just because I think of you as a brother biologically, we are still cousins."

Mellissa placed her hand on Samsons forearm. "It was a lot of help."

"Thanks for worrying about me. Everything has been crazy, so I haven't heard many details of what happened after or how you know…" His words trailed off as he touched the angry red scar on his cheek. The permanent reminder of his failure and how Kadon had made him into a puppet.

Samson placed his arm over Greg's shoulders. "The Queen has ordered me to help settle all the people from the capitol in but once I'm done, we need to catch up."

"Right." Greg smirked. "That boss of yours sure is demanding."

"Hey," said Mellissa. She placed her hands on her hips as she pouted.

Greg laughed. "She is also really cute." He patted her on the head causing her to scowl at him.

"Well, I'll be off." He pointed at Greg. "We'll speak soon."

Greg nodded. He smiled at his cousin and waved as he walked away. Once Samson was gone, Greg's smile fell away. Almost like the weight of it had suddenly become too much for his cheek bones.

Mellissa interlaced her fingers with his and placed her other hand on his chest. "It's alright."

His eyes stayed firmly on the ground unable to meet her gaze. "You saw his face when he saw me."

"That's just because it was the first time he had seen you." She kissed his un-scarred cheek. "I'm sorry I also have to go help with the evacuation and then there's that council meeting about all the other magic cities, but I'll meet you in my living quarters after."

Greg frowned. "Shouldn't I also go?"

Mellissa raised an eyebrow. "Do you really want to attend a council meeting?"

Greg rubbed his chin. What did he want? There was this dark emptiness inside him, He wasn't sure of much lately, but he did know navigating the politics of the council wasn't what he wanted. He shook his head. "No." His response barely a whisper. "It doesn't feel right without Lady Gabrielle." Greg clenched his fists as his body went tense.

"You're right. I still feel the urge to look to her for guidance. You were a lot closer to her than me. I understand this is hard for you." She gently stroked his cheek. Her fingers brushing along the uneven skin of his new scar. "Grieve the loss of Lady Gabrielle as much as you need."

He pulled away from her touch, raking his finger through his hair. "But I'm such a mess. We are on the brink of war, and I can't do my job right."

"Hey, when the camp was in danger, you managed to pull it together and get everyone to safety." She pulled his hands from his hair and held them firmly. "When it really counted you came through and that's what matters."

His eyes met hers and she smiled. "There are those beautiful emeralds that melt my heart."

Greg snorted. "Really even with this ugly thing on my face." He pointed at his scarred cheek.

"Hey, I didn't fall for you because of something so superficial." She cupped his face in her hands. "I love you. The pretty face is just a bonus." She pushed up onto her tip toes and pressed her lips to his. He wrapped his arms round her waist pulling her close. She placed her hands on his chest ending their kiss all too soon. Greg rested his forehead on hers and shut his eyes tight, taking in her sweet cherry blossom scent. Her fingers traced along his jaw line. "I have to go." She kissed his cheek. "Go unwind in my room I'll see you later."

She slowly stepped out of his arms. He watched her walk away his heart in turmoil. A chill swept over his body as if it had been Mellissa that was keeping him warm. He wished everything would just stop. It was all too much. He wasn't the same person anymore. Kadon had broken something inside him. But Mellissa was his one constant. She was still here. Even when he had tried to leave, she had come and brought him back. So, he would try, for her.

Greg laid on the sofa in Mellissa's living room, looking up at the ceiling. He knew there were things he should be doing but for some reason he couldn't get himself to move. He felt numb, like there was a big hole inside him waiting to swallow him up. The room door swung open, and Victoria walked in carrying a box. She glanced in his direction. "What are you doing here?"

"I'm laying on the sofa," replied Greg.

She rolled her eyes. "I can see that. What I meant was, why are you not in the meeting?"

Greg sat up and rested his elbows on his knees. "Because I am not in the mood for the councils rubbish."

"I don't blame you," said Victoria. She put the box down on the coffee table and sat in the arm chair across from him, "but surely Mellissa will need your advice, as majority of them lot are self-serving idiots."

"We are in crisis I'm sure they will put their own interests aside and work towards the greater good."

Victoria laughed. "If you believed that, you would be in the meeting."

"You got me there." Greg sighed and he slouched into the sofa. "Mellissa and I agreed my head isn't in the right place at the moment. So here I am."

"That's understandable."

Greg pointed at the box she had placed on the table. "What's that for?"

"Oh, just some new armour for Mellissa. Once she is done in the meeting, we will be suiting up and heading off to which ever city they have decided is most at risk." Victoria interlaced her fingers. "So how are you holding up?"

"I'm fine," said Greg.

"Yeah, and I'm a fire fairy." She ran her fingers through her long hair and sighed. "What happened to you is messed up no one expects you to be okay."

Greg stared at her his mouth a jar. He didn't know what to say. There were no words to describe the torment Kadon put him through.

The door opened again, and Samson darted in followed by Yuko. Victoria stood. "What's wrong?"

Samson fiddled with his shirt collar. "I just thought you would want to know Mellissa has already left for Novosvillas."

"What?" yelled Victoria. "What about her armour and I'm not with her." She pointed at the box on the table and then to herself.

Samson scratched the side of his head. "I know but she was just very eager to get going. She left with one of Joshes smart watches so they can stay in contact."

"Well Josh better have a watch for me to tell that girl about herself." Victoria marched out the room and Samson followed trying to calm her down.

Yuko strolled across the room and sat in the chair Victoria had just vacated. She sat with her back straight and her hands clasped together in her lap. "And what do you plan to do while Mellissa is gone?"

Greg shrugged. "I don't know."

Yuko tutted. "Very well then." She waved her arms around and the table glowed. A teapot and cups appeared next to the box. "We may as well have a cuppa." She picked up the teapot and poured them both a cup.

"How was the meeting?" asked Greg.

Yuko groaned. "Awful but we got there in the end."

"Novosvillas is the first city to be evacuated? Mellissa didn't choose that because…" Greg didn't finish his sentence, but the way Yuko raised her eyebrows and tilted her head, he was sure she knew he was going to ask, 'because of me'.

"The decisions were made based on the data produced by Josh. He has found the humans are very close to both Novosvillas and Perluves." Yuko took a sip of her tea. "Mellissa will go straight from Novosvillas to Perluves." Greg shifted uncomfortably in his seat. It was weird getting the rundown of Mellissa's plans from Yuko. He should already know these things. Yuko pulled a piece of paper out of the sleeve of her robes. "Here," she said handing it to him, "This is a list of all the cities and their current locations."

Greg looked over the list. "Wow Josh really has found them all, even the caves and sea kingdom."

"I have no idea how he has done it, but it is marvellous."

"Is this the order that the cities are to be evacuated?"

Yuko took another sip of tea. "Yes."

"But the caves are near the bottom. What about Laxus shouldn't we secure him?"

"Caleb has already been in contact with the caves on Mellissa's orders. While the caves remain hidden under ground, we believe Laxus, and the land stone should be safe."

Greg frowned. This didn't feel right to him, but he hadn't gone to the meeting, so he had lost his chance to voice an opinion.

Yuko placed her teacup back on the table next to his untouched one. "The changelings from your city will be arriving through portals by Ignis' cave. Will you be there to greet them?"

"Ignis has a cave here?"

"Yes, it was very recently dug out by the Queen herself. All the hawklings have set up camp amongst the trees in the surrounding area. Now back to my question. Will you be there?"

Greg lent forward resting his elbows on his knees. His fringe fell into his eyes. "I know as their elder I should but none of them have seen me since." He pressed his fingers to his scarred cheek.

Yuko got up and walked round the coffee table. She sat beside Greg on the sofa and placed a hand on his shoulder. "The people of Novosvillas will just be happy to see their leader safe. Your scars show the terrible things you endured and that you survived."

Greg covered his face with his hands. "It's a reminder of how I failed."

Yuko gently rubbed his back. "If you failed then so did I. We were both there in the ocean when the sea stone was found."

Greg turned to her his eyes wide. "But you never could have known what was going to happen. We were taken by surprise."

"Exactly. Give yourself the same grace you give me." Yuko stood and placed her hands inside her robes. "A weaker minded person wouldn't have survived what you did. It is your strong will that made it so Mellissa could expel Kadon's spirit from your body." She looked down at him her indigo eyes misty. "When I see your scar, it reminds me of your strength. I will take my leave and be back when the portals are ready." Yuko walked out the room closing the door behind her.

# 7

# Novosvillas

## *Mellissa*

materialised to the sound of screaming and a book flying at me. I ducked but not fast enough as the book bounced off the top of my head.

"Hey." I yelled rubbing the sore spot. I peered around the area. I appeared to be in an office at city hall. There were two framed diplomas on the wall a leafy plant, two bookcases and a desk. Mary was stood in a chair, with another book over her head, looking like she was ready to throw that at me as well.

"Oh my, Queen Mellissa," said Mary, "I'm so sorry." She put the book down on her desk by a framed picture and climbed down out her chair. She brushed her hands over her blouse working out the creases. "You startled me. I didn't realise you were teleporting again."

"It's a fairly recent repowering thing."

She walked round her desk and stood in front of me. I rolled my shoulders back and stood as tall as I could, but she still towered over me by almost a foot. She sucked in her bottom lip. "May I hug you?"

I blinked a few times as I processed her request. "Um, yes."

She bent down hugging me tightly. It was like all the tension in her body washed away as she squeezed me like I was a cuddly toy. "I'm so glad you're okay. We all thought the worse when the veil fell. I have been so worried about you and Lord Gregory. I haven't heard anything of him in days. How is he? I have been trying my best with running the city, but these circumstances are not something we ever made plans for. Humans are already sniffing around in the outer regions of the city. I don't know what to do if they get any closer."

I backed out of her hug and placed my hands on her forearms. "Mary slow down. That is a lot."

She fiddled with her fingers while her right eye twitched. "I'm used to lord Gregory relying on me but these last few days thinking you and he were dead, have been awful." She stood up tall and looked at me with wide eyes. "Lord Gregory is alive right? I mean you would be a mess if he wasn't, but you look very beautiful so…" She grimaced making a weird humming sound.

I chuckled. "Yes, Greg is alive and yes I would be a mess if he wasn't."

She placed a hand over her heart letting out a long breath. "Thank the gods. So, what do you need from me?"

"Right." I smoothed the sides of my dress down. "I have come to evacuate Novosvillas."

"Are we in danger?"

"Honestly, I don't know. The humans already attacked us in the mountains and Kadon is doing God knows what. When he finally strikes." I winced as I thought of the damage he could cause with the dark stones.

"Kadon's back?" Mary said. I nodded. The colour drained from her face. "And the humans have attacked?"

I nodded again. "I can't protect everyone while we are scattered all over the world. Can you help round everyone up?"

"Of course." She walked past me to take a jacket off a hook on the wall. She put it on and gestured for me to follow. She led the way out her office and down the corridor. "Everyone has already evacuated their homes. We have gathered everyone in the centre of the city, so it shouldn't take long."

I nodded along as she spoke. As we passed a door, I recognised, I paused outside it. I couldn't pinpoint what I was feeling but my heart felt heavy as I traced my fingers along Greg's title and name on the door. It wasn't that long ago that I was visiting him here. How had things become so messed up so fast? "Queen Mellissa," said Mary.

I jumped as she touched my shoulder. "Um, yeah sorry."

She frowned her brows drawing together. "Are you okay?"

"Yeah." I bit my lip. "Um just so you know, when you see Greg again, he looks a bit different."

"Different how?"

"He now has a fairly large burn scar on the left side of his face."

"What happened?"

"While Kadon was still a spirit, he possessed Greg." Mary's eyes went wide as she made a high-pitched squeaking sound. I swallowed the lump in my throat and forced the rest of my words out. "To free him I had to release an enormous amount of light around him. Burning Greg in the process." I ground my teeth as my jaw tensed. Recalling what had happened almost made the lid I had on my anger pop.

"But he is okay now?" Mary asked.

"Physically yes."

Mary clapped her hands together. "Well let's just get everyone out of here, then we will worry about everything else after."

I glanced at Greg's office door. My heart longing for the peaceful life we had been living not so long ago. When my biggest problem was Greg's aunt Josephine hating our relationship. But I couldn't get caught up in thoughts of the past. I pushed it all back down, making sure that lid on my feelings was firmly in place. "Let's get moving."

We continued down the corridor and into the public area of city hall. This part was full of people. We barely made it into the room when I heard someone call out my name. Gasps sounded around us, and the crowd began chattering away. Mary tried to quite them down and shout above them to no avail. I gently pushed off the ground and floated above them. With a click of my fingers a bolt of lightning cracked in my hands. Everyone gasped and looked up at me in awe.

"People of Novosvillas, I know you must have many questions but right now we need to come together to evacuate the city." I looked out at the crowd of faces. All eyes were on me. "Kadon has returned, and the veil has fallen. We are not safe here. I need everyone here to get the word out. Everyone needs to gather at the clock tower in thirty minutes. A portal will appear to take you to Urbem Folium.

A hand shot up from the crowd. I pointed to the man. "Um yes."

"What about Lord Ainsworth? Where is he?"

I smiled at the young man. "He will be waiting for you all on the other side of the portal."

More hands rose in the crowd. Mary climbed on a table. "There will be no more questions for now. You all heard the Queen now go."

The crowd dispersed grumbling and muttering amongst themselves as they did. I set myself back down on the ground. Lifting my left wrist, I looked at my watch. 4:03. I pressed the screen swiped left and hit the call button. "Your majesty." Came Joshes voice from my watch. "Is everyone ready to go in Novosvillas?"

"I've given everyone 30 minutes to gather at the clock tower do you think you can help Ignis locate the area for a portal?"

"I'm not sure. I'll go ask, hold a sec." The line went quiet.

Mary jumped off the table she was standing on landing beside me. She pushed her glasses back up her face. "Are you talking to your watch?"

"Yeah, it's a smartwatch." I held my wrist up so she could see it better. She peered at it. She jumped when Josh started talking again.

"Ignis says it would be easier if you were at the location, but he should be able to do it."

"Okay." I chewed on my bottom lip. Novosvillas was only one of many cities that needed evacuating. "If it doesn't work call me and I'll return. I'm going to Perluves next like planned."

"Radius has already left for the river. Get everyone there to the sea then call him," replied Josh.

"Yeah, I know. I'll be in touch again soon." I ended the call.

Mary looked at my watch her eyes wide. "So, your watch is also a communis device."

"Yes, it's one of our Joshes prototypes of human inspired magic devices."

She nodded as she folded her arms. Tilting her head to the side she frowned. "Can I ask a question?"

"Of course."

"Why is Urbem Folium safer than here? Surely Kadon will expect you to take refuge in your home."

"Oh," I bit my thumb nail. I thought she was going to ask about the watch not that. I interlaced my fingers behind my back to stop me picking at my nails. "It's not Kadon that I'm hiding you all from. Wherever I go he will find me. It's the humans." I snickered. "I resented the council for forcing the elves to create our new city in the forest. Turns out being hidden amongst the trees has its benefits. Currently the humans are more interested in investigating the land masses with obvious buildings and structures. Also helps that Urbem Folium now is an island."

Mary rubbed her chin. "How have you figured this all out?"

"It wasn't me but Josh."

She furrowed her brows. "As in in your adviser Josh, who made those phone things?"

"Yeah. He is like this treasure of brilliance that I didn't know I had. When we get through this Josh can have whatever reward he wants. He will be promoted to whatever position he requests." I looked at the watch on my wrist. "I'll see you back in Urbem Folium."

Mary clasped my hand. "Wait, can't you stay until the portal opens?"

"I'm hoping to at least evacuate Perluves as well today."

"That's a lot of people to move."

"I know. If I can fit in more I will." Before she could ask any more questions, I spun out of her grip and teleported to the water nymph city.

I materialised in the temple of Perluves. It was eerily quiet. I had picked this location as I thought it would be where the water nymphs would gather. Similarly to how the elves had gone to the castle and the changelings, city hall. I walked out the room I was into the hallway. As I walked down the corridor, I tried a few different doors. All the rooms were empty. My head spun as all sort of catastrophic ideas ran through my mind. I ran though the building to the exit. I almost tripped over my own feet as I exited the temple. I gasped. At the bottom of the cliff where the temple stood, Water nymphs were huddled in groups surrounded my human soldiers. I clenched my fists as my blood boiled. My powers surged through me. I was about to launch myself in the air when I heard my name. I spun round. "Queen Mellissa," Came a voice from the bushes.

I narrowed my eyes at the leafy hedges. "Who's there?"

A blue hand emerged from between the leaves, beckoning me over. I walked over, pushing my way through the leafy branches. There was a priestess and a group as water nymph children. The priestess clasped her hands together as she dropped to her knees in front of me. "Praise the gods.

Queen Mellissa, we thought you gone but you have come in our time of need."

I held my hand out to her to take. She looked at it her mouth a small 'o'. She slowly placed her hand in mine, and I pulled her to her feet. She was a couple inches shorter than me. "What happened?" I asked.

"The veil fell."

I put my hand up in front of her. "I know that part. I mean how did you end up hiding in a bush from humans."

The priestess frowned as her forehead creased. "I don't know exactly. We had all decided to gather as close to the temple as possible. I was inside when I heard the screams and bangs." She held one hand close to her heart. "I looked through a window and saw people being rounded up by humans. The priestesses gathered up as many of the children as we could." She opened her arms wide gathering the children to her. "The others distracted the humans and let themselves get taken, while we escaped and hid."

I bit my thumb nail as I looked at the wide-eyed children huddled against the priestess. "Okay, all of you hold on to me, I'm getting you out of here." I held my arms out. The children bundled around me. I shuddered as they placed their little hands on whatever part of my body they could reach.

The priestesses hand hovered just out of reach. "What about the others?"

"Once you are all safe, I'll come back to save them."

The priestess nodded placing her hand on my shoulder. I took a deep breath and shut my eyes. I felt the warmth of my magic running through my body. I had never taken this many people with me on a teleport before. The most I had taken with me was four others. I took a deep breath; it was time to push past my limits. 'I can do this' I thought to myself. Picturing the main hall of the castle in my mind, I teleported.

I hit the cold marble floor with a thud. "Queen Mellissa," Shouted a few of the water nymph kids.

"Mellissa what the hell?" Victoria yelled marching over to me.

"Sorry I've got to get used to landing again." I said rubbing my hip that had been jarred in my fall. I looked around and smiled. At least I had made it to the main hall like I had planned.

Victoria huffed as she held her hands out. I took them and she pulled me to my feet. "Your terrible landing isn't the issue. Why did you leave without me?"

I bit my bottom lip. "Oh, when we finally agreed on which cities to prioritise, I may have got a bit carried away and just started teleporting places." I shook my head and grasped her wrist. "That's not important. I need your help?"

"With what?"

"Where's Greg?" I peered round the room. I had hoped he would be here. Maybe he is what I should have thought of when teleporting.

Victoria yanked her arm away and crossed her arms. "Is that all? He was with Yuko outside by that stupid cave you made that overgrown lizard."

I ushered the children and the priestess together. "I still need you," I said holding my hand out to Victoria. "Walk with me." Victoria rolled her eyes and swatted my hand away. But she fell in line beside me, and we marched out the hall to the exit of the castle. The little group of water nymphs followed us. Victoria nudged me. She looked down at me one eyebrow risen. "Well?"

I pushed a stray piece of hair behind my ear. "When I arrived at Perluves the humans had already infiltrated the area. I got this lot out." I pointed to the group behind us. "But I'm gonna need help rescuing the others."

Victoria's jaw went tense. She wiggled her fingers as I felt her magic flowing to the surface like she was preparing for the fight ahead. "So, what's the plan?"

My heart was pounding in my ears. I took slow breaths. A panicked Queen would be no use to anyone. "We kick some soldiers butts and save the water nymphs." I opened the double doors and exited the castle.

# Portals

## *Gregory*

reg peered at himself in the large mirror in Melissa's dressing room. Before she had left for the meeting, Mellissa had found a pair of black trousers and plain white shirt of his amongst her stuff. Samson had lent him a blue tailored jacket. He was back to looking the part of an elder knight. Well almost. He pressed his fingers to the angry red blotchy part of his left cheek. The burn scar ran down his face towards his neck. This was the first time he would see the people of Novosvillas since the incident. Which was the polite way people referred to his girlfriend burning his face, to make an evil spirit leave his body. That same spirit went on to get a nice new body and send the world into chaos. All of this happened because he wanted to feel useful. He never should have gone on that mission into the ocean. If he hadn't been captured, maybe things would be different. This scar was a reminder of his failure. And now all his people would see it. He clenched his fists resisting the urge to punch his reflection. Plenty of people had seen this horrible thing on his face, so why did it bother him so much now? Greg growled as he threw the blue jacket off and onto the floor. He marched over to a rail with a shelf above it. Clothes fell from the shelf as he rummaged through them. He pulled down a black hoodie. He tugged it on over his shirt and pulled the hood up. The dressing room door opened making Greg jump.

In walked Yuko, she smiled at him. "I didn't mean to startle you."

"It's fine. What do you need?" Greg asked keeping his gaze firmly on his feet.

"Ignis will be opening the portal to Novosvillas soon. You are still coming? Apparently, Mellissa promised Mary you would be waiting to greet everyone."

Greg's heart lurched when he heard his chief of staff's name. He had put her in charge when he left but had been gone a lot longer than planned. What stress had she endured because of him? "Okay I'm coming down."

Yuko stood to the side so Greg could walk past her. He stuffed his hands in his pockets and exited the dressing room. He walked out Mellissa's living quarters and down the corridor to the stairs. Yuko followed behind. They walked down the stairs and once they were on the ground floor she took place beside him. "Ignis will be opening the portal outside by his cave."

Greg altered his course towards the castle exit. "Will Mellissa be with them?"

"No, she has already gone to Perluves to prepare the water nymphs. Once done there, I believe the leprechaun city is next on the list."

Greg nodded keeping his gaze ahead. "Right, I remember." He sighed as they reached the large double doors of the castle entrance. This was it; he was going to be reunited with his people soon. He pushed opened the doors, exited the castle, and strode through the trees to the newly created clearing and cave. Ignis stood with his butch hawkling guardian.

Yuko rushed ahead of Greg, stopping a foot from the dragon. She lowered herself into a curtsy. "Lord Ignis, we are grateful for your assistance in bringing our people here."

Ignis lowered his head, so his snout was almost in front of her. "It is my duty as sun crystal keeper to help in this time of chaos." He turned towards the hawkling man, who stood with his arms crossed and eyes narrowed on Greg. "Have you met my guardian Rowan?" asked Ignis.

"We've met," said Greg.

Ignis lifted his head and tilted it to the side as he took in Greg. "Ah yes young master Gregory, you were with the queen when we first met."

Yuko stepped back and tugged on Greg's arm until he was stood next to her. "Gregory and I have come to assist our people as they come through the portal."

Greg rubbed his left arm. "Is it time to start?"

"It is a little earlier than the Queen stated," said Ignis. The dragon scratched his head with a claw. "But I don't see the harm in starting now. I will open two portals so your people can come through quicker." The dragon sat up tall. He opened his wings wide and flapped once. The strong gust created blew Greg's hood down. He held one arm up in front of his face shielding his eyes. Yuko clung on to her robes as they billowed in the wind. The gust died down and two large portals swirled either side of Ignis.

Rowan stepped forward. He swept his arms towards the portals. "Maybe one of you should go through, so your people know it's safe."

Greg's heart raced. He looked to Yuko. She patted his arm. "It should be you, but if you can't-"

Greg placed his hand over hers. "No, I can do it." She lowered her head as she stepped back. Greg walked over to the portal on the left. Taking a deep breath he stepped through. Greg's chest tightened as his feet crunched into snow. He was stood at the base of the clocktower in Novosvillas. He looked up at the large clock face. His eyes felt wet. He was home.

Gasps sounded behind him. "Lord Gregory," called Mary.

Greg spun round. A big crowd of people were surrounding the clock tower. At the head of the group was

Mary. She ran from the crowd to him and pulled him into a hug. "I'm so happy to see you."

Greg wrapped his arms round her back. "Thank you for protecting everyone in my absence."

Mary pulled back but kept hold of his shoulder. She wiped tears from her eyes with the other hand. "Of course sir, you know you can count on me." She looked at his face and frowned. Greg quickly pulled his hood back up.

"Queen Mellissa told me what happened" she went to touch his cheek, but Greg caught her hand before she could make contact.

"She did?"

"Yes. How are you doing?"

Greg frowned as a pang of anger shot through him. Had Mellissa gone around warning every one of his ugly face. He clenched his fists pushing those thoughts aside. That wasn't the sort of person Mellissa was. He could wallow in self-pity later. Right now, he needed to stay on task. "I just want to focus on getting everyone through these portals."

Marry tugged at the bottom of her coat. "Understood."

Greg stepped round her. He looked out at the crowd of changelings. Swallowing the lump in his throat, he stood tall. "I'm sure you all have a lot of questions. I will answer as many as I can once we are all safely in Urbem Folium. There are two portals so utilise them both. Now everyone follow me." Greg turned, tucking his hands back in his pockets. Mary took place beside him, and they walked through the portal. They stepped off the snow onto wet grass.

Yuko squealed. "They are coming through." Greg went over to her, and they stood to the side as more changelings came through the portal. Mary stood in between the two portals counting people and ticking names off on her tabular.

"It's going well." Yuko said.

"I should call Samson to start taking people into the village." Greg went to get his communis out his trouser pocket when Beatrice came barrelling over. He winced as she said his name in a high pitched shrill.

"Gregory, when will the changelings from my city be coming through?" Beatrice wagged her finger in his face.

"I don't know. Mellissa is the one in charge of these things."

Beatrice placed her hands on her hips and curled her top lip. "Well, you obviously have sway with her. She is evacuating your city first."

Greg pressed his finger to his forehead. "I only knew about the order of the evacuation because Yuko told me."

Yuko stepped in front of Greg. She folded her arms and tensed her jaw. "Beatrice, if you had been paying attention in the meeting. The cities to evacuate first were chosen by their proximity to human settlements. Meaning high risk of them meddling."

Beatrice pressed her lips together. "That may sound like something that was discussed."

"Your city, Highwish is currently its own island far from humans."

Greg rubbed the back of his neck. Maybe he should have attended that meeting. But facing a council meeting with no Lady Gabrielle. Greg clenched his fists. He wasn't ready for that.

"High priestess," cried out a group. A small group of water nymphs came running over. Greg's brow furrowed. They looked to be mostly children. Yuko greeted them all with a large grin and hugging the one grown up in the group.

Mellissa and Victoria approached him. "Are you already done evacuating Perluves?" he asked, "That was quick, the people from Novosvillas are still coming through."

Mellissa grabbed his hand. "I don't have time to explain properly." She pointed at the small group of children surrounding Yuko. "But they are the only ones I got out. I need you and your healing magic to check them over."

"What's going on?" Greg asked.

She shook her head. "I don't have time. Where's Radius?" Greg looked at her his mind going blank. He knew the answer to her question, but his words were not coming to him. Victoria flashed her hand in his face making him blink and step back.

"Hello earth to Greg," Victoria said, "Where is Radius?" She placed her hands on her hips and curled her top lip as she glared at him.

Greg coughed clearing his throat. "He went to the river to open the portal to Perluves for the evacuation."

Mellissa face palmed her hand. "Of course, duh." Mellissa stepped towards him and pushed up onto her tip toes. She kissed his cheek just above his scar. "The priestess I brought with those children can explain. I'm sorry there really isn't time." She grabbed Victoria's hand and disappeared in a flurry of lights. Greg gritted his teeth, remembering why he had sometimes hated that ability of hers. He let out a slow breath. 'Focus on the task at hand,' He thought to himself. That statement seemed to be becoming his new mantra.

# 9

# Perluves

## *Mellissa*

*F*ocusing on the Novos River that ran through the forest I teleported while holding onto Victoria. We were greeted with a giant gold fork in our faces. I yelped as Victoria shoved me behind her.

"Oh, it's only you Mellissa," said Radius lowing his trident.  "You shouldn't sneak up on people like that," His forehead creased as he frowned. "Wait what are you doing here?"

"I need your help." I stepped out from behind Victoria. "The humans have already infiltrated Perluves. They have captured most of the residents."

Radius flexed his muscles as his grip tightened on his trident. "What's the plan?"

"I need you to get the water nymphs out while Victoria and I distract the humans."

Radius nodded and held his hand out. I took his hand and held Victoria's with my other and teleported back to Perluves. I pulled them both down, so we were crouching behind the bushes next to the temple. We had a good view from up on top of the cliff. My blood boiled as I saw what the humans had done in my short absence. The water nymphs were stuffed inside big metal cages with barely any room to move. We didn't have time to spare. I gritted my teeth as I dug my fingers into the earth. My magic surged threw me into the ground. Tremors spread from the cliff top, down to the ground below. I squinted at the space between the cages and the soldiers standing guard. Focusing on the earth below, I pulled my arms up and pushed them out. Sweat dripped from my head. The earth shook more violently as rock shot up from below creating a wall around the cages. Yells sounded below as the humans looked around bewildered.

"Victoria with me." I held my arm out to her. She took hold of me, and I pulled her close. I glanced at Radius, and he nodded. I shot up into the air holding tightly to Victoria's waist and flew us down the cliff. We landed with a thud in front of the rock wall. The humans shouted in a language I didn't understand. They grabbed for the guns slung over their shoulders. Victoria shot from my grip. A frosty mist filled the air. Ice shot from her hands freezing the guns. The humans yelled as they dropped their frozen weapons. Others screamed as their hands became frozen to their guns. I swept my feet across the earth and pushed my hands out. The ground rumbled and holes opened swallowing the soldiers. I ran round the edge of the holes growing vines up and over the top trapping them in. Running to Victoria I took her hand. Holding tight I floated us up and over the rock wall I had made. We landed in the middle of a crowd of water nymphs. Radius had already freed them all.

Radius ran to my side. "If we make our way to the ocean I can open a portal to the river. Unless you can teleport everyone."

I shook my head. "There are way too many people." I looked up at Radius. "You lead the way. Victoria and I will remain at the back of the line in case more soldiers show up."

Radius nodded. I turned swiftly lifting my leg up high. Bringing it back down with force I kicked a hole in the rock wall I'd made. Radius was the first through. He popped his head back through and waved his arm. "Everyone follow me." The water nymphs looked at each other and chatted amongst themselves. They all slowly turned to me.

I dug my nails into my palms but stood tall. "Go with Radius he will lead you to safety. I will follow behind making sure everyone is evacuated."

They all muttered to themselves but walked through the rock barrier. Radius picked up two young children and ran down the path that led to the beach. The water nymphs rushed behind them. Adults carried little kids and supported the elderly along. It only took a few minutes for the area to empty. Victoria and I ran behind them all, keeping an eye out for any human reinforcements.

We were halfway down the path to the beach when my watch buzzed on my wrist. Josh was calling. I pressed on the small phone symbol. "What is it? We are kinda in the middle of running away."

"It's important," said Josh, "I've found Kadon."

I froze on the spot my body going tense. "Where is he?"

"Magnus."

"What is he doing there?"

"From the images I have been able to gather, he appears to be breaking into the prison." My heart raced as my head spun.  He had all this power that I had expected him to wreak havoc with. But since destroying the veil he had been quiet. And now he appears in Magnus. Why was he breaking into a prison? It felt like my blood had gone cold. "To gain followers." I said out loud answering the question I had never actually voiced.

"What?" said Josh.

"I've got to go." I hung up the call.

Victoria stood a few paces away looking at me brows risen. "What's going on?"

"It's Kadon. He is in Magnus."

Her eyes went wide. "Then we need to get Radius and Ignis." She pointed towards the beach.

"There isn't time," I yelled, "I'm going now. Tell Radius what's happening."

"What no." She launched herself forward her arm stretched towards me. I jumped back teleporting as I did. As I materialised, I tripped over a rock falling flat on my face. I sat up on the hard craggy ground rubbing my nose. I wriggled it from side to side, checking it wasn't broken.

"Queen Mellissa," Someone shouted. A teen girl ran towards me. Her brown skin was covered in mud. She dropped to her knees and hugged me. I went stiff as a board in her arms. She pulled away and blushed. "I'm sorry. You don't even know me," She pointed at herself and then to me. "But of course I know you."

I stood up brushing dirt from my clothes. "It's fine. Where is everyone?"

"Most people are hauled up at the cathedral." She jumped to her feet and skipped around me. "My names Daphne by the way."

"What about Kadon?" I asked.

She jumped up and down on the spot. "I knew it. You came to stop him."

I grabbed her shoulders. "You've seen him?"

She brushed some dirt from her face. "Yeah. He came looking for the prison warden. He said if we all behaved, he would spare our lives." She twiddled with her fingers. "He made everyone gather in the cathedral. My parents don't believe him though. They have hidden with a few others on the farm."

"Why aren't you with them?"

"I came looking for my pet cat. They told me not to, but I don't want Kadon to hurt her. I fell in mud and scuffed my knee trying to get her out that tree." She pointed up at a large oak tree. Sure, enough there was a black cat sat amongst the branches. Lifting my arms up I channelled my magic into the tree. The cat meowed as the branches moved towards me. I picked the cat up and handed it to the girl.

Daphne's eyes sparkled. "Oh, thank you Queen Mellissa."

I looked her straight in the eye hoping she would see how serious I was. "You need to go back to your family." She pouted but nodded. "But first can you point me in the direction of the prison?"

"Sure, it over there." She pointed at a tall black tower. "It's awfully ugly."

"Thank you," I said, "Now go quickly."

Daphne gave me a wide toothy grin and skipped off in the direction of a small cottage. I looked over at the black tower. Clenching my fists I ran and pushed off the ground taking flight. I soared through the sky, landing as quietly as I could at the entrance to the black tower. I gasped as I saw a man with his face half burned off, blood seeping from a wound in his chest. I ran over and knelt beside him. Placing two fingers on his wrist I felt for a pulse. It was barely there. He opened his eyes causing me to drop his wrist. "Queen Mellissa is it you?" the man said between harsh breaths.

I took his hand in mine. "It is. I'm so sorry I couldn't help you."

He coughed and blood dripped from the corner of his mouth. "I wouldn't give him the key to enter the prison but that didn't stop him blasting his way in."

My grip tightened on the man's hand. "Kadon did this to you?"

"Yes. Sorry I wasn't strong enough to do anything to stop him."

Tears filled my eyes. "You did everything you could. You are a brave man." His hand went limp in mine. "Sir," I said. There was no response. I felt for his pulse again. Nothing. Anger bubbled up inside me. I stood and called to the Heart crystal. It shone brightly shooting from the chain round my neck into my hand. Light illuminated round it as it transformed into staff form. I ran inside my staff in hand at the ready. I dashed threw a large foyer. There was no one around. I slowed my speed, jogging up to a pair of double doors and went through into a small corridor. I walked down the hall, all the doors connected to rooms hung open. They appeared to be offices. Many had large monitors and cables hanging off the walls. It looked like someone had been through trashing the place.

At the end of the corridor was an elevator. I walked to the left choosing to take the stairs. There was a flight going up and one down. Something inside me told me to descend. I walked down the stairs, listening for any noise. It was all so eerily quiet. At the bottom of the stairs was a single door. Using the bottom of my staff I pushed the door open. Nothing happened so I walked through. I flicked the light switch, but the room stayed dark. Swishing my staff the crystal on top glowed. I held it in front of me lighting the way. Metal bars had been melted and holes blasted through walls. "Hello little lady," said a deep voice.

Jumping back, I swiped my staff round towards the sound. A tall butch man stood grinning at me, his golden tooth reflecting the crystal light. He stepped forward licking his lips. "What brings a pretty little thing like you down here?"

He reached towards me with his oversized hands. I blocked with my staff and pushed him back.

"Feisty." He rolled his shoulders back and his hands glowed with magic. He pressed his arms together shooting a large plasma ball at me.

I swung my staff round deflecting the shot. His jaw dropped as he looked towards were I deflected his attack. He looked down at me and smirked. "You're strong for something so little."

I glared at him, as I tightened my grip on my staff. Shadows lurched forward and wrapped themselves around the man. He was dragged into the darkness. There was a loud bang and suddenly the lights powered on. Kadon hovered at the far end of the room holding the man by his neck. "Now what do you say to the queen?"

Kadon dropped the man. He hit the floor with a thud. He scurried to his feet and bowed. "Sorry your majesty. It is an honour to make your acquaintance."

My jaw dropped as I looked from Kadon to the man. Kadon floated to the ground. He placed his hand on the man's shoulder. "Go join the others while I speak with the little Queen."

The man bowed to Kadon, then ran out a door on the other side of the room. My jaw tightened as Kadon took a step towards me. He smiled. "Hello my elf-ling. It's so good to see you again."

"I can't say the same." He faked shock as he placed a hand over his heart. I glared at him. "What are you doing?"

He shrugged placing his hands behind his back. "Gathering myself a few followers."

"You are now the most powerful being in existence isn't that enough for you?"

"What's the point in being a god, without worshipers?"

"You're not a god, you're a monster."

His nostrils flared as he growled. "I'm no more a monster than those humans that infect the land." He tilted his head and smiled sending chills down my spine. He arched a brow. "Or have they welcomed you all with open arms?"

I gritted my teeth. "They don't understand what's happening yet. They aren't all bad."

"That sort of thinking is what will draw your subjects to me. How long before the magic folk get tired of running and hiding from the humans?"

"We can all live in peace together. Kadon you can still stop this. There is no point to this fight anymore."

Kadon cackled. "You can't have it both ways. You are either a human or an elf. You trying to have it all will leave you the Queen of nothing." He yawned. "Now, I tire of you." He pointed at me, and shadows flew forward. They swirled round me; I cried out as they dug into my skin. "Now it's time for me to destroy this place." Kadon clenched his fists and shot up into the air. He flew straight up smashing through the ceiling. The whole building shook as a loud boom echoed from above. The ceiling began caving in. My powers burst out of me. Light illuminated the room, sizzling away the shadows around me. I teleported to outside the tower.

As I materialised, I was hit by a gush of water and went flying backwards slamming into a building. Kadon swooped down from the sky grabbing my arm, he yanked me into the air. Taking me high up into the sky he spun me round and threw me. I opened my arms out wide stopping myself mid-air. I looked round in time to see balls of shadows flying at me. I swept my staff round shooting rays of light, that dissipated the shadows. Kadon spun his arms and the air swished around me. A funnel formed sending me whirling round. I teleported to the ground skidding along the grass as I landed. Kadon lifted his hand, a ball of water surrounded by wisps of shadow floated above him. Pointing my staff towards him, I channelled my magic into the point. Kadon's smirk turned into a frown, as he looked from side to side. "Where have you gone little elf?" he yelled.

Someone skidded beside me. I turned aiming my staff at them. A man with long white striped, brown hair and a beard stood with his hands up. I peered at him. "Emerson?"

"Yes, my queen." He placed one arm across his chest and bowed his head.

"What do you want?"

"Kadon freed me from my prison, but I will not follow him." He held his hand out to me. "Come quick, it won't take him long to blast through my illusion once he realises what's happening." As Emerson finished his sentence, a gust of wind slammed into us, knocking us off our feet.

"How dare you?" Kadon yelled. A vein on his forehead bulged as he barred his teeth at Emerson. "I freed you and you help her." He jabbed his finger at me.

Emerson rolled himself up off the ground to his feet. He stood in front of me arms wide. "I spent my whole life blindly following Humarya, I will not make the same mistake again."

"Humarya was a fool," shouted Kadon. "I am a true God."

Emerson snickered. "No, you are just a power-hungry maniac."

Kadon shrieked as he unleashed a flurry of black smoke. I launched forward, grabbing Emerson and spinning him behind me. Twirling my staff round, light burst forward cutting through the smoke. I jolted back as Kadon's fist hit my cheek. As his other fist moved towards my face I swept my staff in front of me, blocking him and pushed him back. I placed my staff firmly on the ground and used it as a pole to spin round and kick him in the face. Kadon growled. The wind whipped around slicing my cheek. Rain poured and the sky thundered. Emerson dove at me, knocking me to the ground. Lightning struck.

The ground where I had just stood was singed. Kadon swung a shadow sword round in his right hand. He pointed it at me. "For your disrespect I'm going to kill everyone in this city."

"No," I yelled.

"Don't worry elf-ling. You will be last to die. I'm going to make sure you become the Queen of nothing. Then when you are finally in despair only then will I end you." He shot up into the air, in a loud whoosh and flew towards the cathedral.

My heart hammered so hard it was all I could hear. Letting go of my staff the crystal glowed and zapped back into the form of a necklace round my neck. Grabbing Emersons wrist I teleported to the cathedral. I materialised to the screams of warlocks running from the burning building. My eyes stung as I choked on black smoke. Kadon floated above surrounded in shadows. He grinned when he saw me. His grey skin was cracked by black lines.

"Queen Mellissa, what should we do?" asked Emerson. Sweat dripped from his brow as he tugged at my arm.

"I don't know," I said. My mind was shouting at me to do something. To help these people but my body didn't move. Kadon's dark stare had frozen me to the spot.

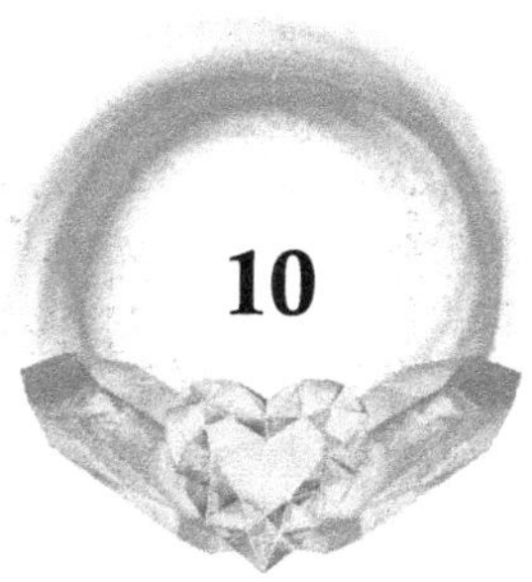

# 10

# Magnus

## *Victoria*

Victoria's hand wrapped around air as Mellissa disappeared. She dropped to her knees and let out a frustrated yell. "That idiot." Ice spread across the stone path as she thumped her fists on the ground. Gritting her teeth Victoria pushed herself up off the floor to her feet. There was no way she would let Mellissa ditch her like that. Running at high-speed Victoria was at the beach in no time. She whooshed past the remaining water nymphs to the edge of the water, shoving in front of a group about to jump into Radius' portal.

Radius held his arms out, holding on to her as she bent over panting. "What's wrong? Where is Mellissa?" he asked.

"She went to face Kadon alone."

Radius' eyes went wide as he gripped is trident tight. "What? I need to go help her."

Victoria gripped his forearm. "Wait. Mellissa would never forgive us if we didn't finish evacuating these people." She stood up to her full height, now almost eye level with the King. "I'm going through now and I'll get Ignis. The evacuation of Novosvillas should be done by now."

Radius rubbed his chin. "I don't like this."

"Neither do I. Which is why I'm not waiting around for approval. There is only one monarch I recognise." Victoria pushed past King Radius and jumped in the portal.

Water surrounded her. She kicked her legs and pushed her arms out. The current swirled round her. She spun round and found herself stood in the middle of the river running through the Novos Forest. The forest that homed Urbem Folium. While her feet reached the bottom of the river her head was only just above water level. She waded her way over to the edge. A couple of water nymphs came over and helped her onto the grass verge. "Thanks," she said. She looked at the group of water nymphs and pointed in the direction of the city. "Urbem Folium is that way, The high priestess is there waiting for you all."

She saw the groups eyes light up at her words. Victoria turned her back on the group and ran the direction she had pointed. As the castle came into view she turned to the left heading to Ignis' cave. She skidded to a halt in the clearing. At the same time Samson came hurtling out of the trees from the other side and collided with her. They both toppled over. Victoria fell on her side with Samson on top of her.

Victoria shoved him away pressing her hand into his face. Samson scurried backwards on the grass. "Sorry, I was in a hurry, and I didn't see you." He frowned as he tilted his head peering at her. "You're soaking wet."

"I don't care I'm in a hurry too." Victoria jumped to her feet.

"Wait I think we are here for the same reason."

"Kadon?" said Victoria. Samson nodded. She waved her hand at him. "Come on then."

Greg, Yuko, and Beatrice along with a small group of changelings stood by a portal. Ignis was a few feet away in front of his cave along with his hawkling guard. "Samson have you already settled that last group in?" asked Yuko, peering at the two of them stood together.

Samson fiddled with the bottom of his tie. "Not exactly."

Victoria grunted and slapped him on the back, jolting him forward. "You fill them in on the Kadon situation and

I'll talk to the lizard." She marched over to the huge scaly dragon stood at the entrance to the cave.

Rowan stepped in front of her as she approached. "How can I help you?"

"I need to speak to your master."

"He is busy right now and needs to focus."

"Mellissa is in danger. Kadon has finally made an appearance."

"What was that?" said Ignis.

"Kadon is in Magnus and Mellissa went after him alone."

"But the queen can just teleport away," said Rowan.

Victoria gritted her teeth. "Mellissa will not leave Magnus while there are still people there for Kadon to hurt." She looked up at Ignis. "Just open a portal and send me to her."

"If he does that the ones to Novosvillas will close."

"But you opened loads of portals when evacuating the capitol."

Rowan pulled at her shoulder. "Do you know how much of my master's power that took?"

Victoria shoved Rowan her anger flaring. "I don't care."

Rowan spread his golden-brown wings wide and glared at her, his fists clenched.

"Hey what's going on?" asked Greg standing between her and Rowan. His back was to her, and his eyes narrowed on hawk man.

Rowan lowered his wings. He pointed at Victoria and curled his top lip. "She is trying to spread my master's power thin. How will we rescue the rest of your people if she does that?"

Victoria folded her arms and looked down her nose at Rowan. "That is exactly what makes my queen a better crystal keeper than your master. She would expend all of her power in order to save lives while your lizard just hides in a cave."

"How dare you," yelled Rowan flexing his fingers as if to summon magic.

"Enough," shouted Ignis. A dragon wing slammed down in between the two of them blowing them away from each other. Victoria stumbled back falling on the grass. Greg landed beside her. Rowan glared at her from his spot on the ground. Ignis held his wings high. His amber eyes glowed as he looked down at them all. "The ice warlock is right."

Rowan's jaw dropped as he looked up at Ignis. "But master."

"I must push past my limits. I have played it safe far too long. Queen Mellissa is in danger because she always puts others before herself." The dragon stomped his front foot causing the ground to shake. "I must do the same. I will go and support her. Rowan stay here and monitor that portal."

Greg stood and approached Ignis. "Everyone is through, it is fine if you close it. Please just go help Mellissa."

Victoria jumped to her feet and ran to stand beside Greg. "I'm going too."

"But Kadon is too powerful even for me," said Ignis.

Victoria placed a hand over her heart. "I don't care, I will fight by Mellissa's side until the end."

"And I also," said Harkura stepping out of the trees.

Victoria hands covered her mouth as tears filled her eyes. "Harkura your awake."

Harkura crossed the clearing and placed a hand on Victoria shoulders. "I woke up a while ago. Josh was just filling me in on everything."

Ignis sighed. "Very well and what of you, young master Gregory?"

Greg opened his mouth to talk but Victoria spoke over him. "He is staying here." She grabbed his arm digging her nails in. "There are a bunch of water nymphs heading this way. The humans had them in cages. I don't know how many are hurt or how bad."

Greg pulled his arm away but nodded. "I'll take care of them. You take care of Mellissa."

Victoria let out a long breath. "Thats my job."

Ignis tucked one wing in and lowered his shoulder. "Get on," he said. Harkura climbed onto the dragons back and held a hand out to Victoria. She took it and he helped her up. They both sat clinging onto the dragons' scales. Ignis shook his head and opened his wings wide. A new portal opened in front of them bigger than the others. "Ready?" asked Ignis.

"Let's go," said Victoria. The dragon lurched forward running through the portal.

They emerged from the portal on a cliff overlooking Magnus. Victoria sat up on the dragons back and looked across the city. Smoke billowed up into the sky. "I would bet my life that the source of that dark smoke is where Mellissa is."

"Agreed." Said Rowan standing beside Ignis on the ground.

Victoria scowled at the winged man. "I thought you were staying behind."

Rowan crossed his arms, his shoulders tense. "I am a guardian. Just like you I will not leave my charges side."

Victoria fell forward as Ignis spread his wings. "Hold tight," grumbled Ignis. Harkura took her hand and squeezed it. With her other hand Victoria dug her fingers into the dragons back clinging on for dear life. Ignis took flight. Rowan flew beside his master, flapping his golden bird like wings. They were over the top of the smoke source in a few wing beats. Screams echoed up into the sky. The cathedral was engulfed in flames. Victoria squinted trying to see what was happening below. Harkura had one arm over his face. "We need to clear the smoke," he yelled.

"On it," said Rowan. He flew in front of them. Rapidly beating his wings, he created a strong gust. He pushed his arms forward and the winds followed his direction. The smoke blew away.

"There," said Harkura pointing. Victoria followed his direction and there was Kadon engulfed in shadow. He was grinning. The look on his face made Victoria shiver. She followed the direction of Kadon's gaze. "Mellissa." Her voice was barely a whisper. She grabbed Harkura's hand. "It's time we were getting off."

The two of them stood, hand in hand. They looked at each other and nodded. The pair jumped off the dragons back in unison. Harkura grasped Victoria round her waist with one arm and propelled them forward by blasting flames with the other. Victoria wrapped her arms round Harkura's neck as the wind swept over them. Her heart raced. Her ears were ringing as all she could think about was getting to Mellissa. As they neared the ground, she pushed one hand out blasting ice. Harkura snuffed out his fire as Victoria's ice took over. As her magic hit the stone path an ice pole shot up to them. Harkura grabbed it swinging them round and sliding down it. Before their feet could touch the ground Victoria redirected her ice sliding them across the path. Just as Kadon fired a hydro-blast at Mellissa, the two guardians slid in front of her. They parted. Victoria ran forward freezing the attack in place. She spun round and swiftly kicked the newly made ice shattering it. Harkura ran back towards Mellissa. As Victoria's ice shards flew at them. Harkura threw his arms wide creating a wall of flames, melting the shards.

"Victoria, Harkura," Mellissa shouted. Victoria turned round to see Mellissa hugging Harkura, tears streaming down her cheeks.

Kadon roared. It was an inhuman sound. "Enjoy this little reunion while you can, Mellissa," shouted Kadon, "Your guardians have just given me two more people to kill." Kadon swirled his hand round creating a shadow sword. He looked like he was about to fly at them when a mighty roar sounded above, and he was engulfed in flames.

"Ignis," said Mellissa looking up at the sky in a daze.

Victoria ran to her side. Grabbing her friends shoulders she shook her. "Snap out of it. We need to figure out how to get everyone out of here."

Another roar echoed above. Ignis was above the cathedral blowing flames while Kadon pushed back at him with streams of water. Mellissa looked on her mouth a jar. Her nose twitched as she looked from Victoria to the chaos around them. "I need to swap places with Ignis." Mellissa rubbed her chin. "I have to hold him off while Ignis opens a portal for everyone to escape."

Victoria shook her head. "You weren't doing great against him when we arrived."

Mellissa winced. "I was just lost for a sec."

Harkura patted Victoria's shoulder. "She is right. Ignis needs to get these people out of here." He looked at Mellissa his face tense. "But we will be coming with you."

Mellissa shook her head. "Ignis will need your help to gather everyone. Once Kadon sees what we are doing, he will push harder against me to try stop you. We will have to be fast."

Someone coughed behind them. A man with shoulder length hair and a bushy beard flecked with Grey, smiled at them. "I could help?"

Victoria narrowed her eyes at the man. Her powers flared as she recognised him. She released an icy wind, freezing him in place. Rage swirled inside her as she snarled. "What the hell do you think you're doing Emerson?"

Mellissa leaped in front of him with her hands up. "Wait. He helped me earlier. I wouldn't exactly call him a good guy but at the moment he is on our side."

Emerson wriggled against the ice. The only part of his body he managed to move was his head and his right hand. "I can help. With my illusions I can make Kadon think Ignis is still fighting."

Mellissa pouted as she rubbed her chin. "It could work."

"At the very least give us enough time to evacuate," said Harkura.

"You two are insane," said Victoria, "Do you not remember how he betrayed us?"

"Of course not," said Mellissa, "But Emerson was loyal to Humarya. Kadon killed her remember. Making Kadon his enemy too."

Emerson raised his free hand. Victoria glared at him. "What?"

"I actually had some time to reflect while in prison. At first it sent me a little crazy but then I had a moment of clarity." His brows drew together as he stuck his bottom lip out. "I would like to apologise for everything I did to you and the Queen. I was misguided."

"Misguided," Victoria yelled.

"Not now," said Harkura his tone flat. "You can sort your differences later. For now, we must focus on Kadon."

Victoria crossed her arms. "Fine."

"Good," said Mellissa flexing her arms. "So, Victoria you start gathering the warlocks. Harkura I'll take you up with me so you can tell Ignis the plan, then you'll assist down here. And Emerson."

"I will make the most amazing dragon illusion you have ever seen," said Emerson sweeping his arm through the air.

"But you also must hide what is happening on the ground. Make it seem like everything is still in chaos. Can you do that?"

He placed a hand on his chest. "They don't call me the illusion master for no reason."

Victoria groaned as she rolled her eyes. Mellissa cringed. "Right. So once everyone's out, you all go through the portals, and I'll teleport."

Everyone nodded in agreement. Mellissa held Harkura's hand and disappeared in a bright light. Victoria marched over to Emerson. She took a deep breath and freed him form the ice. He smiled. "Thank you."

Victoria grabbed the front of his shirt and pulled him in close. She glared at him with gritted teeth. "If you do anything to endanger Mellissa, I will end you." She shoved him away. "This better be a good illusion."

He held his hands in front of himself as if in surrender. "I promise I won't let you down."

"Promises are cheap, Emerson. I only care about your actions. So far, your actions leave me wanting to throw you off a cliff." She pointed at him. "I will be watching you. Now work your magic."

Emerson gulped. He stood waving his arms round in weird shapes and muttering words she didn't understand. Victoria turned on her heel and ran towards the burning building. Her fingers tingled as her magic surged, ice forming. First, she would put out the fire.

# 11

# An Old Friend

## *Mellissa*

e materialised on Ignis' back, stumbling as he pulled his head back breathing fire at Kadon. Harkura and I crouched down, keeping close to the dragon's body. I crawled up onto Ignis's head closer to his ear. "We have a plan," I whispered. His ear twitched. I assumed that meant he heard me. "I'm gonna distract Kadon with a little help of an illusionist on the ground. I need you to open a portal and get these people out of here."

"I don't know," said Ignis.

"Who are you talking to?" shouted Kadon. "Oh, I see." A wide smile spread across his face. "Good of you to join us, my little elf-ling."

I stood up on Ignis's head. "I'm not you're anything." Holding out my right hand, the Heart crystal, zoomed into it, changing into its staff form. I quickly glanced to Harkura. He had climbed up onto Ignis's head as well. He was crouched low and whispering in the dragon's ear.

Kadon chuckled. "Don't you see Mellissa?" He pointed at me and then himself. "You and me. Our destinies have been intertwined from the beginning. Fate wants us to be together."

I snorted. "What sort of crazy are you talking now?"

"Being inside Gregory's head showed me a different side to you." He tilted his head to the side and smirked. "And I liked it."

The air went still. My heart was pounding so hard I was sure the whole world could hear it. Magic surged through me, pointing my staff at him, lightening crashed down on him.  I jumped from Ignis' head and flew after him. I swung my staff towards the sky, then pointed at Kadon. Lightning struck him again. A dark cloud formed around him. I covered my face as the wind direction changed. The air was like knives cutting into my flesh. A gust of wind blew the smoke away, revealing Kadon. His grey skin shimmered with magic, black swirls covered the left side of his face and arm. In a blink of an eye Kadon was in front of me gripping my face in his hand.

"Oh Mellissa," Kadon smiled wide showing off his fangs, "When are you going to stop fighting this?"

"I'll never stop fighting you," I shouted.

Ignis flew towards us. Fire shot at Kadon, but he swatted it away. "Pathetic," said Kadon. He flicked a finger in Ignis' direction. Black water gushed towards him, but it had no effect. Kadon's eyes went wide. "How?"

I pulled my legs up and kicked him away from me. Channelling my magic into my staff, I yelled as light burst forth. It shot at Kadon like rapid fire. Shadows sliced through my light like it was nothing.

I screamed as the shadows slashed at me tearing my clothes and burning my exposed skin. Gritting my teeth I dug deep down finding as much magic as I could within myself. Light burst out of me. My body heated as my magic surged. Shadow and light collided mid-air.

Kadon growled. As he slammed his hands together the wind swirled around me. My body trembled, it felt like my skin was crawling with ants. My light dimmed as my head went dizzy and my throat dry.

"Did you think you could fly through my airs without consequence," shouted Kadon.

I clutched at my throat as the air became thin. I tried to summon magic to keep my light illuminated but I couldn't concentrate, and it fizzled out. My eyesight blurred. Kadon went from a black smudge to a bright orange one.  Fire engulfed Kadon. The heat of it warmed my skin. These flames were the real ones. Kadon pushed against the fire with a swirl of black water. Ignis flapped his wings above us creating a strong wind, putting more force behind his fire. Kadon was pushed back.

Ignis plucked me up out of the sky with his claw and flew away from Kadon. I slumped against the dragons' palm and sucked in air, my mind racing. The Heart returned to a crystal, hanging around my neck.  "Everyone is out," said Ignis, "Do you have the energy to teleport."

I looked below. The scenery was shifting as the illusion fell. The fiery building was now covered in ice. And there was no one in sight. I glanced at the horizon and my blood went cold. "There are still people at that farm."

"Rowan, to that farm," said Ignis. I hadn't realised his guardian was with us. Rowan was flying by Ignis' head. His wings folded in, and he turned towards the farm. He opened his wings wide again flapping hard. I jerked sideways as Ignis changed direction.

"You won't get away from me," cried Kadon. He soared through the air gaining on us rapidly.

"Rowan, go ahead of us," ordered Ignis. Rowan nodded and continued flying ahead. Ignis whirled round. The two of them slashed at each other with wind magic.

Closing my eyes, I focused inwards. Searching for the burning light within me. My heart jolted as I felt the warmth of my magic. I still had some fight left in me. "Drop me," I yelled. Ignis opened his claw and I shot out of his hand. I was a burning light soaring through the sky. I collided with Kadon with a bang. He dropped out the sky to the ground. The ground cracked as he made impact. "Go," I shouted to Ignis. "Once you are all gone, I will teleport away."

He frowned, his facial features creasing. "Are you sure you have enough magic left?"

"I'll be fine." Ignis turned and flew to the farm. I lowered myself to the ground. "It's just you and me now."

"Why would you send your pet away?" He narrowed his eyes at the dragon. "Unless there is something you want to protect." He jumped up and went to fly away but I tackled him back to the ground. We rolled across the grass. I landed on my back, pinned down by Kadon. "Now, now if you wanted some intimate time alone, all you had to was say."

I lurched my head upwards head butting him. He clasped his nose his eye watering. I surrounded myself in light blasting him away. I flipped up onto my feet. Kadon stood across from me his top lip curled. He was shrouded in darkness. The two dark stones round his neck glowed. He ran at me, a shadow whip in each hand. I ran forward illuminating light. Our powers collided in an almighty bang. My feet came out from under me. I fell backwards hitting the earth with a thud. My chest tightened and I struggled to breathe. Kadon stood over me, with his hand stretched above my face. His eyes were pure black. I could see the air moving towards his fingers.

A ball of fire hit Kadon in the abdomen. Knocking him over. He toppled on to the grass. I rolled over, expecting to see a giant dragon but instead there was a young blond man. "You," shouted Kadon. But something was wrong with his voice. I pushed myself up off the ground, to a standing position. Kadon's hand was on the floor, like he was part way through getting up. His body looked like it was twitching. Everything around me was frozen accept this blond guy stood in shadow.

"What on earth?" I pointed my staff at the figure, the Heart Crystal glowing atop it. "Who are you? What have you done to me?"

"Mellissa," said the man.

He stepped closer and I gasped. My arms fell beside me going limp. My jaw dropped. "Matt."

He smiled pushing his long golden locks from his face. "Yeah, that's me."

"What the hell is going on?"

"I slowed time."

I stepped back, raising my staff as I did. It glowed with light energy. "Wait, who are you?"

He patted his body while frowning. "It's me Matt."

"This is a trick; you were trapped in the tree of time and that was destroyed."

"When Kadon destroyed the tree, it freed me." He shrugged, "Well sort of."

A lump caught in my throat as I remembered something Humarya had said to me. 'Only the power of a dark stone could break the seal'. I looked Matt up and down. He still wore the same surfer shorts and t-shirt from the last time I had seen him. He gave me his signature crooked grin. "Matt," I whispered. "It really is you." I ran over to him throwing my arms around him.

He hugged me tight. "It's good to see you but we need to get out of here." He scrunched his nose. "Messing with time is draining."

"But you're a fire warlock."

"Mellissa questions later. Teleport now."

"What about the others?"

He clasped my shoulders. "They have escaped. Now teleport."

Kadon's movements began to speed up, until he was moving at normal speed. He glared at me and snarled. His mouth fell open when his gaze landed on Matt. "How? I killed you."

There was no way Kadon was getting his questions answered. I grabbed Matts hand and teleported.

# 12

# **Reunion**

## *Gregory*

Greg dabbed his face with a wet towel. His magic was drained. He had just finished healing the last water nymph that had needed his help. While there hadn't been any serious wounds, they had all been hurt in some way. Luckily Mellissa had a good team of elf healers to assist him. After Victoria had informed him of Kadon's reappearance, he had busied himself helping the water nymphs. They had met them halfway from the river and brought them all to the main hall in the castle. Focusing on healing their wounds had allowed him not to worry about what Mellissa was doing. But now he was done his mind was going crazy. A part of him wished he had gone with Victoria and the others but at the same time he was glad he hadn't. In a battle with Kadon he would have been in the way, his abilities were best suited to the aftermath. Here was where he was needed. He clenched his fists. This was typical Mellissa running into danger without thinking. She was just so reckless. He sighed, wishing he could know whether she was winning whatever battle she had jumped into.

Yuko walked over to him two cups in hand. She handed him one. "Here, you look like you could use a drink."

Greg looked at the golden liquid. He gulped it down. When it hit the back of his throat, it burned, and he coughed. "What was that?"

Yuko laughed as she took the cup from him. "I should have warned you. It has a bit of a kick to it, but it should calm your nerves."

The doors of the hall flew open banging on the wall behind them. Victoria marched in followed by a large group of warlocks. She looked around the room, when her eyes landed on him, she ran over. She placed a hand on his shoulder and clutched her side panting. "Greg, this is just the first group. Harkura is with the next lot."

"Where's Mellissa?" asked Greg.

"She was still fighting Kadon when I left." She looked at him her brow creased. "I need to get back to her."

Gregs stomach filled with dread. Victoria swayed to the left, her hand falling from his shoulder. Greg caught her, supporting her weight. He moved the hand she had on the side of her stomach. Blood oozed through her clothes. "Victoria your hurt," Greg said.

She waved her hand dismissively. "It's just a scratch. The price of running into a burning building to save people."

Greg's breath caught in his throat. He had no idea what they had been up against in Magnus. "You need a healer."

Victoria slowly lowered herself to the ground. "I'll catch my breath, then I'll go."

Greg pressed his fingers to his forehead. "Yuko a little help."

Yuko swept round behind Victoria and lowered herself to her knees. She placed her hands on the girl's shoulders and made Victoria rest her head on her lap. "Hush young one. You are no use to the Queen injured. Let Gregory heal you."

Victoria let out a frustrated groan. "Fine. Just be quick about it."

Greg knelt beside her. He gently lifted the blood-soaked fabric, revealing a deep cut on her stomach. It looked like something had tried to slice through her. "Sanum quad fit." Greg muttered the healing spell. Her skin slowly knit itself back together. Victoria let out a low sigh. Greg rubbed his brow with the back of his hand. "Quick enough for you?"

Victoria made a rude gesture as she sat up. "Hey, you, where do you think you're going?" yelled Victoria, making Greg jump. She was pointing over his shoulder.

Greg turned and bristled at the sight before him. "Emerson, what the hell are you doing here?" Greg was on his feet in a flash balling his hands in fists.

Emerson bowed. "Why hello Gregory. It is good to see you."

Greg grabbed Emerson by the front of his shirt. "What are you doing here?"

Victoria placed her hand over his. "Hey cool it. He isn't currently being evil. He helped us escape."

Greg stared at her mouth a jar. Victoria pushed her hair from her face. "I know I felt the same when I first saw him. But you know that saying, the enemy of my enemy and all that."

Greg let go of Emerson. "Fine whatever."

Victoria jabbed a finger in Emerson's face. "Stay here where you can be kept an eye on."

Emerson swept into a low bow. "Whatever the lady says."

Victoria let out a disgusted groan. "I gotta get back to Mellissa." Greg went to talk but his words stuck in his throat. He looked up at the ceiling. His heart ached. That magical presence. She was back. He glanced at Yuko who was also looking up at the ceiling. She turned to him. "Go."

Greg walked out the hall. As soon as the door closed behind him, he was running. As fast as he could move, he ran up the stairs. He was halfway up when he realised Victoria was hot on his tail. They both raced down the corridor. He shoved Mellissa's room door open. Greg froze in the doorway. She had one arm draped over a blond guy hanging off him, like she could barely stand. The guy was holding her round the waist, he looked like he was trying to help her sit.

Mellissa looked up at him. Her eyes shone as she smiled. "Greg."

Victoria pushed past and marched over to the pair. She clenched her fist and punched the guy in the face. Greg ran forward with his arms outstretched. He caught Mellissa as she stumbled away from the commotion.

"Who the hell are you?" Victoria had the guy by the scruff of his neck, her eyes glowed an icy blue. "And why are you wearing my brothers face?"

Greg stood straight, holding Mellissa close. He narrowed his eyes at the man. "Matt?"

Victoria shoved Matt to the floor. "That is not my brother." She pointed at the wide-eyed boy on the floor, her eyes filled with tears. "My brother is dead."

Matt stood slowly, keeping his hands up, like he was approaching an injured animal. "It really is me, Vicky."

"Don't call me that, only my brother calls me Vicky."

Mellissa pulled away from Greg and walked over to Victoria. She placed her hand on her lower back. "It really is him."

Tears rolled down Victoria's cheeks. "I don't understand."

Matt approached her with his arms wide open. "I missed you, sis." Victoria fell into his arms.

"Yay, Matt's back." Mellissa wriggled her fingers in the air. "Isn't that great." She turned to Greg and smiled. Her smile turned to a frown as she swayed sideways.

"Mellissa." Greg leapt forward catching her in his arms "Are you okay?"

She placed a hand on his chest. "I'm fine, just a bit lightheaded." She rubbed her head with her other hand. "It's just the adrenaline wearing off."

"She is not fine," said Matt. He rolled his shoulders and pushed his long fringe from his face. "She took some hits that would have killed a normal person. It's a good thing I slowed time when I did."

Victoria gave her brother the side eye. "You did what?"

Greg's heart pounded as he looked down a Mellissa. She was shaking in his arms. He swept her up and walked past the twins laying her across the sofa. Greg knelt in front of her and brushed hair from her face. The braid it had been in was a thing of the past. He stroked her cheek where she had a large purple bruise. Her arms were covered in cuts. "Let me heal you."

"I'm-" She started to say but Greg pressed his finger to her lips.

"You are not fine."

Mellissa wrapped her arms round herself as she continued to shake. "Go on then."

Greg's hand glowed yellow. He ran his hand over her. His heart sank as he detected the amount of damage she had taken. Greg muttered a new spell. He started with internal injuries. Mellissa cried out as something snapped back into place.

She grasped his shoulder resting her head on his. "I was badly hurt, wasn't I?"

"Yes," Greg turned to Victoria. "Can you grab a blanket?"

"Sure." Victoria went through the archway to Mellissa's bedroom. She was gone a few seconds and returned with a pink fluffy blanket. She wrapped it round Mellissa's shoulders. Victoria glanced at Greg. "She looks pale."

"Can you get her some hot tea?" Greg asked.

"Of course." She walked to the door. Turning to her brother and clicked her fingers. "You with me." Matt followed Victoria out the room, leaving Greg alone with Mellissa.

"Sanam quad fit," Gregs hand glowed green as he cupped Mellissa's cheek. She shut her eyes and leaned into his touch. Her bruise disappeared leaving her brown skin clear. He pressed a kiss to her cheek. "Now let me see those arms."

She held her arms out in front of her. He slowly ran his hands over her cuts, healing them one at a time. When her arms where healed, he rested his head on her shoulder. "I was so worried about you."

"I'm sorry everything was happening so fast I didn't have time to stop. It's all kind of a blur now." She wrapped her arms round his neck, weaving her fingers in his hair. "I fought off human soldiers and battled Kadon within hours of each other." Her voice cracked. "But I couldn't save them all."

Greg sat on the sofa next to her pulling her into his arms. She snuggled her face on his chest as tears rolled down her cheeks. He rubbed her back. "Don't think like that. Think about all the people you saved today. I should know I healed a bunch of them."

She looked up at him her eyes glistening. "You're amazing."

He brushed her tears away with his thumb. "I think you're confused. You're the amazing one."

With her hands placed on his chest she leaned into him. He closed the gap pressing his lips on hers.  Her fingers brushed his scarred cheek making him flinch. She pulled away. Looking at him with wide eyes. "I'm sorry did I hurt you."

"No, it's just…" He lowered his gaze.

She cupped his face in her hands. Running her fingers across his scar. He sat frozen to the spot. She leaned in and kissed his scarred cheek. "I love you, scars and all."

He turned his face, his lips meeting hers. She kissed him fiercely. He pulled her body to his. Her fingers ran through his hair, down the side of his face and under his shirt. She gasped as their lips parted. He trailed kisses down her neck making her giggle. She shoved his chest and straddled him, pinning him down on the sofa. She lowered her face to his. He pushed his head up catching her lips with his.

"Hey," said Victoria. "You could have just asked for some alone time instead of tea if this is what you wanted to do."

Greg groaned as Mellissa sat up, quickly getting off his lap. He sat up. Victoria walked over to the coffee table, placing a tray with a pot of tea and biscuits on it. She sat in one of the armchairs and picked up a chocolate biscuit. Matt sat in the other armchair with a wide toothy grin. "I guess that means Mellissa is all healed or were you just giving her a thorough exam."

Mellissa's face turned rosy. Greg grumbled as he picked up a biscuit. Victoria smirked. "We can go if you wanna get back to it."

"It's fine," blurted Mellissa.

Victoria shrugged. "We're in the middle of a crisis you gotta get it in when you can."

"I'm just gonna pour the tea." Mellissa picked up the tea pot and poured the hot liquid in to the four cups on the tray. Victoria laughed as Mellissa placed a cup in front of her. Mellissa huffed as she picked up her own cup. She added milk and two spoons of sugar.

"So, what's everyone been up to while I was stuck in a tree?" asked Matt. He pointed between Mellissa and Greg. "I mean apart from that obviously. I mean I was totally routing for you two."

The door burst open and in charged Harkura. "Here you all are. Is everyone okay?"

Mellissa leapt to her feet. She marched over to Harkura meeting him halfway and hugging him. "I'm so happy you're okay. I can't believe you just reappeared after being injured in battle like that."

"Why hello beautiful." Matt got up and went to walk over to Mellissa and Harkura. Victoria grabbed his arm, making him sit back down.

"Don't start," said Victoria.

Matt leaned on the arm of his chair. "Vicky there is a water nymph over there and you're not even going to let me say hello."

Greg burst out laughing. "Please, Victoria let him."

"Not today." Victoria folded her arms as she glared at Matt. "You can crash and burn another day."

Mellissa peered at the three of them. She placed an arm around Harkura's shoulders and guided him out the room. Victoria picked up the milk jug and poured some in her tea. She stirred in a spoon of sugar. She picked up her cup and blew on it. "How badly hurt was she?"

"Bad."

Victoria sipped her tea. "You know she left to go fight Kadon alone, even after we went there specifically to help her.

Gregs jaw tensed. "Yes."

"What are we gonna do with her?"

"Well, we know what Greg wants to do." Matt chuckled.

Greg peered at Matt. "Sorry to be blunt but how are you alive?"

"Nah bro totally cool," said Matt. He picked up a biscuit and stuffed it in his mouth. "While I was in the tree of time we sort of bonded. Its magic protected me when Kadon destroyed it. Now we are one."

"Wait you mean you are the tree of time?"

Matt nodded, picking up another biscuit. "Yep. It left my head a mess. When you see so many things at once it makes it hard to focus. It's why it took me awhile to find you again."

Greg placed his elbows on his knees and pressed his thumbs together. "Well, er, Thanks, for waking me up."

Matt clicked his fingers and pointed at him. "No problem."

Victoria looked between the two of them. "What are you on about?"

"When I was in my coma, Matt helped guide me back," said Greg.

Victoria put her hands up between the two of them. "Wait a minute. So, you contacted him in his coma?" Matt nodded, his blue eyes wide like saucers. Victoria rubbed her forehead. "Was that really you warning Mellissa in her dreams?"

"Yeah, I tried to tell her about this whole Kadon thing, but the tree wasn't used to having a voice then and well fate wanted this to happen."

"Why only Mellissa?" Victoria looked down at the table. "Why no one else?"

"Because the tree was coated in her magic. It gave me a pathway to latch onto."

She pointed at Greg. "But you woke him up."

"It was Mellissa's connection to him that allowed me to do that." He looked Greg straight in the eye. The intensity of his gaze made Greg lean away from him. "You and Mellissa are meant to be. The two of you together like this." Matt crossed his fingers and smiled.

Greg raised an eyebrow as he sat up straight in the sofa. "Okay, glad to know you approve of our relationship."

"Dude I was like the original Greg and Mellissa shipper." Greg opened his mouth to say something but decided against it. He distinctly remembered Matt not being overly fond of him but thought it better not to mention it. If that's how Matt wanted to remember things he would let him. At least he wasn't going to try break him and Mellissa up. His head and heart couldn't deal with that sort of drama.

Victoria snickered. "So, me being your twin sister wasn't a strong enough connection? You just left me in the dark thinking you were lost to that tree."

"It wasn't about who I was close to but the person whose magic had created the seal." Matt leaned over placing his hand on Victoria's arm.

She jerked away from him and stood. "I can't do this right now." She stormed out the room slamming the door behind her.

Greg stared at the spot Victoria had just vacated for a second then turned to Matt. "Aren't you going to go after her?"

"And say what?" Matt rested his elbows on his knees, hanging his head so his face was covered by his long hair. "I don't want to hurt her more than I already have."

"You claim you could only contact Mellissa because it was her magic on the tree, but you helped wake me."

"I already explained that."

"Yeah, but Victoria is Mellissa's guardian and best friend. Those two are attached to each other just as deeply as I am to Mellissa."

"Don't you think I tried." Matt stood stamping his feet and throwing his arms out to the side. "She's my sister of course I wanted to talk to her, but I didn't get a say in how things worked then." He paced the length of the living room tugging at his hair. "When I said you and Mellissa were meant to be. I really mean it. In every version I saw of how things could have played out, you and Mellissa are together. But Victoria and her are not always friends."

Greg frowned as he rubbed his chin. "Every version? As in different timelines?"

"Sort of." Matt stopped pacing and stared at the wall behind Greg. "The tree of time exists at every point in time. Before the future becomes the present there are many routes it could take, and the tree sees them all. After I was accidentally sealed in the tree, I saw all the possibilities of what could have happened between you all." Matt sat in the armchair with a sigh. "In all versions you and Mellissa are a couple. But in some Victoria was angry and blamed Mellissa for what happened."

Greg massaged the sides of his head trying to make sense of what Matt had just said. "So because mine and

Mellissa relationship was a certainty but her's and Victoria's could have been different it makes the bonds weaker?"

Matt nodded. "Pretty much."

Greg clicked his finger and pointed at Matt. "Do not tell Victoria that."

"That's why I didn't go after her. I don't know how to explain myself without hurting her feelings."

"I think your just gonna have to let her feel whatever it is she feels. When my mum returned, I had a lot of conflicting emotions. At least you haven't come back to try spy on us and manipulate the situation to help our enemy." Greg frowned as he arched a brow. "You haven't returned to just betray us later, have you?"

Matt put his hands up in front of his chest. "No of course not." He grimaced. "I saw that whole mess with your mum from inside the tree. That was rough dude."

The door swung open and Mellissa marched in. "Mathew Street, go and talk to your sister right now."

Matt sat up straight in his seat with wide eyes. "You just used my full name."

Mellissa placed her hands on her hips. "Yes, I did. Now don't make me repeat myself."

Matt rubbed the back of his neck. "But I upset her."

"That's exactly why you need to talk to her. Forget about the technicality of what the tree allowed you to do. Just be there for her and acknowledge how shitty the whole situation was."

Matt stood and hurried out the room, closing the door behind him. Mellissa let out a long breath as she rubbed the bridge of her nose. "I really hope he doesn't try to chat up Harkura because Victoria just might kill him."

Greg got up and walked over to Mellissa. "From what he said to me I think he will be focused on fixing things with his sister."

"Should I go back? Make sure everything is alright."

"I think you should let them sort things out for themselves." Greg wrapped his arms round her waist and kissed the top of her head. "Besides I think they interrupted us earlier."

Mellissa turned in his arms, so she was facing him and arched a brow. "Oh, really and what exactly were we doing?" Greg leaned in and she pushed up onto her tip toes, her lips meeting his.

# 13

# Reconnecting

## *Victoria*

The door slammed shut as Mellissa stormed out. Victoria sighed. "She's not gonna have a go at Matt, is she?"

Harkura sat beside her on the large double bed. He patted her hand. "Mellissa cares about you just as much as you do her. What would you do in this situation?"

"I would kill the person who upset her, but I don't want her to kill my brother."

Harkura laughed. "Mellissa won't harm Matt she will just try fix things."

Victoria threw herself back on the bed sprawling herself out across her plush bedding. "She can't change the fact my brother chose her over me."

Harkura laid beside her resting his head on his elbow. "I don't think he chose Mellissa over you. It sounds like the tree's ability's had limits much like our own magic does."

Victoria sighed as she looked up at the ceiling. What Harkura said made sense. It was what Matt had said himself but for some reason her heart ached. While Matt had been explaining why he had only communicated with Mellissa, it had felt like someone had been tightening a vice around her chest. She had missed Matt so much so why wasn't she overjoyed by this. Her mind ran over all the times Mellissa had told her about her dreams of Matt. She had put it down to guilt weighing on the girl's mind. Even when Mellissa had insisted they felt real, she had dismissed her. It was because whenever she had dreamed of her brother that was what she had been feeling. Guilt that she had gone on without him. That she continued to be a guardian. That she had stolen his best friend. She should be overjoyed that Matt had returned but if she was being real with herself it scared her. She was scared that the life she had built in his absence would be taken away. Matt had always been the more likable out of the two of them. He had been Mellissa's best friend first. What if now he was back, she was no longer needed. Victoria rubbed at her eyes as tears threatened to fall.

Harkura traced circles with his finger on the duvet. "If Matt was going to replace someone in this equation it would be me." Victoria jolted up right. She stared at Harkura her mouth a jar. It was like he had just read her mind and pulled her concerns out her head. "You are worried you will be pushed aside now your brother has returned. Him communicating with Mellissa reminded you of their bond." Harkura sat up. He crossed his legs and faced her. "But I was only called on after Matt was no longer able to serve as guardian."

Victoria clutched Harkura's hand. "No. Mellissa needs you. I mean Greg and I tried to train her. We did okay but when you took over, you took her to the next level." Victoria peered at Harkura making sure their eyes met. "I need you. We're a team."

There was a knock on the door and in walked Matt. "Hey sis."

Victoria sat up straight and tried to make her face a neutral wall. "What do you want?"

"I'm sorry." He stepped closer stopping at the edge of the bed. "I wanted to talk to you. When you used to visit the tree, I tried to talk to you but I couldn't." His gaze lowered as he fidgeted on the spot. "But you stopped visiting and I found a way to contact someone."

Victoria felt like he had just stabbed her. She swallowed the lump in her throat. "I stopped visiting because I had seen no sign that you could hear me when I spoke to you."

Matt smiled. "I heard you."

Harkura slid to the edge of the bed. "I'll leave you so you can catch up."

Victoria put her arm out in front of him. "Wait." She looked up at Matt. "Have you returned to be a guardian again?"

Matt's head shot up his gaze landing on her. "What no. Once I became trapped that bond was broken and passed on to another." He chuckled as he ruffled his hair. "Besides you two are both better guardians than I ever was. I think the crystal just chose me because of my close proximity to it's keeper."

"That's not true." Victoria interlaced her fingers digging her nails into the backs of her hands. "I mean now you have weird time powers. What does Mellissa need me for? I freeze things but you literally stop time."

Matt looked between her and Harkura. "Neither of you have to worry I'm not gonna try steal your jobs. I just want to help but I'm not a guardian anymore." He looked down at his hands as he opened them wide. "The tree of time made me something else."

His words made Victoria's stomach churn. Something about his tone was unsettling. She got off the bed and hugged her brother. "Please don't leave us again."

Matt wrapped his arms round her squeezing tight. "I came to help so that's what I plan to do."

She stepped back looking him over. It still didn't feel real having him here. He looked just as she remembered. From when he was sealed away to now, he hadn't changed at all. Victoria gasped. "Oh my god you haven't aged." She placed her hands on his shoulders and starred into his blue eyes. "I'm a year older than you are now."

Matt wriggled his nose and smiled. "You always acted like you were my older sister and now you are."

Victoria backed away from Matt as she let out a shrill cry. "Now that you are out of the tree of time you are going to age, right?" She jabbed her fingers in her brother's direction. "Cos I can't have you staying like that while I get old."

"I don't know."

"What do you mean you don't know," she yelled.

"The tree and I are now one. So I don't know."

Victoria turned to Harkura her eyes wide. "Tell me he is going to age."

Harkura placed his hands up in front of his chest. "I can't. What has happened to Matt is unprecedented. We have no idea what affects the trees power has had on him." Harkura shrugged. "Only time will tell."

Victoria groaned. "You did not just say that."

"I couldn't help it." Patting his chin with a finger Harkura looked up at the ceiling. "Once we are no longer in the middle of this crisis, we can persuade Gregory to research this subject for us."

A wide grin spread across Matt's face. Victoria nudged him. "What's so funny?"

"Nothing. It's just nice how you guys are all like this happy family."

Victoria cringed. She opened her mouth to make a retort, but her bedroom door flew open. Greg ran in his face looked grim. Harkura was at his side in a flash. "What is it?"

"Kadon is attacking the Caves."

Victoria's pulse quickened. "Where's Mellissa?"

"Gone to the other crystal keepers." Greg ran his finger through his hair. "At least I think that's where she went. She said something about Ignis and teleported."

Harkura grabbed Victoria's hand. "Come on we gotta be quick if we want to catch her."

The pair ran out the room. Victoria's heart hammered so loudly it was all she could hear. They raced through the castle. Hoping that they made it in time to back Mellissa up in this fight.

# 14

# The Caves

## *Mellissa*

As soon as Samson had alerted me of the reappearance of Kadon, my magic had surged through me. I had teleported and landed face first in the dirt. My heart had been racing and panic had made me jittery. As soon as I had said, 'I need to alert Ignis and Radius.' The dragons cave had popped into my mind and my teleporting power had activated. When Humarya had used some unknown magic to block this ability of mine, I had thought it gone forever. Now I had it back it was like I was learning to use it all over again. Whenever I teleported, it felt like a force was yanking me forward at high speed and when I rematerialized it was like someone had suddenly put the brakes on. It had taken a lot of training with Harkura to master my landings. Now I was back to falling flat on my face wherever I materialised.

I grumbled as I pushed myself up off the grass. Brushing dirt off my jumper, I walked into the cave. Inside I was greeted by a giant pair of amber eyes. "Queen Mellissa," said Ignis, "What brings you to my cave?"

"It's Kadon," I said, "He is attacking the dwarf caves."

Warm air hit me as Ignis huffed. "But you said they were safely hidden under ground."

"Safely hidden from the humans but not from Kadon." I clenched my fists. I had been stupid to think

Kadon wouldn't easily find where the third and final dark stone was. "We need to stop him. I can teleport us."

"We should also request the sea king's assistance this time," said Ignis.

I looked round the cave, suddenly realising it was just me and the dragon here. I sighed. "I should have bought Radius with me."

"It's all right, I am here," said Radius. I turned to see him at the entrance to the cave with my guardians and Rowan. Radius rolled his shoulders back, puffing out his chest. "Your guardians filled me in. What is the plan of attack?"

I scrunched my nose as I rubbed my chin. "We split up."

"What?" Victoria stepped forward jabbing her finger in my direction. "You are not fighting alone again."

I put my hands up in front of me. "No, I'm not, just here me out."

She folded her arms and pouted. "Fine."

"You all go through a portal with Ignis and engage Kadon," I said.

"And what will you be doing?" asked Harkura his forehead creased as he frowned.

I rolled my eyes. "I was getting to that. While Kadon is distracted. I teleport straight to Laxus and get him straight out."

Harkura nodded. "That is a good plan." He narrowed his eyes on me. "Just make sure you are in and out."

I put my hand over my heart and held the other up like I was making an oath. "I will be in and out in seconds. I'll join the battle once Laxus is safe."

"Very well," boomed Ignis' voice. "Let's get to it." We all walked out the cave. Once in the open space outside Ignis flapped his wings opening a portal. He lowered a wing so the others could climb on his back. Rowan was the first up, followed by Radius and my guardians. They pressed closely to the dragons back as he ran through the portal.

I shut my eyes. Taking slow breaths, I pushed my panic down. Letting my magic flow, sprinkles of my power spread through the earth. My pulse quickened as I sensed him. Focusing on Laxus' aura, I teleported.

I materialised in an underground tunnel illuminated by small orbs of light. My heart warmed as I sensed Laxus. Dwarfs ran around shouting at one another. The earth above shook.  I heard his voice before I saw him. "Mellissa," cried Laxus. His blue curls bounced as he ran into my arms. His pink eyes filled with tears as he looked up at me. "I was so worried something had happened to you. When the veil fell-" his voice caught as tears rolled down his cheeks.

I gently dried his wet cheeks with the pads of my fingers. "I'm so glad I found you. I was worried Kadon would find you first."

His eyes widened. "Kadon?"

"I have so much to tell you but first I need to get you out of here."

He wiped his face with the back of his hand and nodded as his lips pressed into a thin line. I took his hand in mine and teleported again.

"Mellissa what's going on?" asked Greg.  He stood up from the sofa in my living quarters. Matt was sat in the arm chair across from him.

"I'm sorry there isn't time. Please take care of him." I gently guided Laxus towards Greg.

Greg's eyebrows drew together. "What about the others?"

"Later," I said. Shutting my eyes I focused on finding the other crystal keepers' energy. Once I had a lock I dematerialised.

I screamed as I fell through the clouds. Clasping the heart crystal round my neck magic seared through me. I spun round mid-air and stopped my descent. Wisps of shadow slithered through the sky. I grimaced as one brushed my arm. My skin sizzled where it had made contact. Dodging the shadows, I flew upwards. The heat was overbearing. Sweat dripped down my back. Ignis's fire lit up the sky. I threw up a light barrier to protect myself. When the smoke cleared Kadon smirked. He hovered in the sky without a scratch on him. Radius and Ignis both flew around him blasting him with fire and light. Kadon swiped his arm down sending their attack billowing back at them. I flew over to join them as they steadied themselves.

"Are you okay?" I asked.

Radius panted blood dripped from a cut under his eye. "We got him away from the tunnels, but he is too strong."

"Where are Victoria and Harkura?"

"They are with Rowan fighting off the ground forces," replied Ignis, "while helping the dwarfs escape through a portal I opened."

"What ground forces?" I asked.

"He is using the ex-prisoners he freed as soldiers." said Ignis.

Shadows shot at us, causing us to part. I flew upwards avoiding the strike. Ignis roared as he was struck by flurries of shadow. Kadon grinned showing off his fangs. "Sorry to break up your little crystal keeper meeting." His eyes turned dark as he shot black lightning from his fingers. Ignis let out an ear-piercing roar as he was struck.

Radius and I nodded at each other. We flew around Kadon and struck in unison. Kadon met our blasts of water and light with a gust of wind and shadow. Our magic collided. We pushed more power into our attacks, but Kadon countered. The power built up causing an enormous bang. All four of us hurtled towards the ground. Ignis opened his wings wide catching the wind. He glided round stopping his fall. Radius and I crashed onto his back. I gasped as I looked down at the ground. Kadon cackled. "Do you like what I've done with the place?"

My heart felt like it had been sliced open. The hillside was on fire. The tunnels had collapsed in on themselves creating a giant cavernous whole in the earth. Smoke and grit covered the whole area. Victoria and Harkura where pushing back a group of attacks while Rowan helped the last few dwarves through the portal.

Kadon smirked. "Now kneel before your new king."

Radius pointed his trident at him. "You are no king."

"Have it your way." Kadon tilted his head and his eyes turned black. Swirls of shadow burst from his body. Ignis' swirled round mid-air knocking Radius and myself off his back. Radius grabbed my hand flying away from the dragon as his body burst into flames. The shadows slammed into him but sizzled away as they made contact with the flames. Kadon yelled and rain plummeted us. Ignis' fires went out. He roared as shadows wrapped round him. His flesh sizzled. "Ignis," I shouted as he crashed to the ground. I flew after him.

"Master," yelled Rowan. He went to run towards us.

"No," shouted Ignis, "Get out before the portal closes."

Rowan clenched his fists but turned on his heel he hurried the last of the dwarfs through. He created a mini tornado sweeping up Victoria and Harkura. He chucked them through the portal and flew through after them. Ignis's body slumped on the ground as his magic fizzled out. I landed and ran towards the dragon but fell face first into the dirt as something wrapped around my legs. Shadows snaked up my body. I screamed as pain seared through me. My skin burned where the shadows had hold. It felt like my skin was being peeled off. I closed my eyes tight searching for the warmth of my light within. With a yell I released as much light as I could. My body suddenly felt lighter. Panting I opened my eyes. I jumped to my feet and froze.

"Don't move," shouted an armed man. We were surrounded by human soldiers. Majority of them had their guns aimed at Ignis.

I held my hands up. "Please we mean you no harm."

The man's finger hovered over the trigger. "I said don't move." He nodded his head in the direction of Ignis on the ground. "What sort of monster have you got over there?"

"He isn't a monster." I said, "Please you don't understand the danger you're in."

"Is that a threat little missy?"

The man's body suddenly went limp. Shadows burst through his body. I screamed as I was splattered with his blood. Radius ran to my side and grabbed my hand. "We need to get out of here."

The soldiers were dropping fast as shadows blasted through them. Kadon flew through the area like he was a shadow, slicing up the humans. His new army of ex-prisoners were wreaking havoc in his wake.

"We have to help them," I said.

"He's too strong. Ignis is hurt." Radius shook me by the shoulders. "We need to escape so we can fight another day."

Radius took my hand and dragged me over to Ignis. I gritted my teeth as I took hold of the dragon and teleported.

We materialised inside his cave. I pulled away from Radius. "I need to go back. Try save who I can."

Radius grabbed my wrist holding tight. "No, we need a healer for Ignis."

Not moving a muscle, I just stood staring at Radius. He was also covered head to toe in blood. Images of the carnage we had just left flashed through my mind. My hand shot to my chest. "There's no one to go save is there?"

Radius's eyes turned down. "No but we can still help Ignis. Go find Gregory."

"No," said Ignis. His voice was gruff. "Find Faizah, my other guardian. She is a healer."

"As you wish." Radius ran out the cave.

My ears rang as I stood looking at nothing in particular. Radius returned with Rowan and a hawkling woman. I recognised her. She was the healer who had healed me when I had first went looking for the Hawks. They busied themselves round Ignis. They spoke words but I didn't hear what they said. It was all just noise. Slowly I stepped backwards. Making sure I wasn't making contact with anyone, I teleported.

# Fractured Heart

## *Gregory*

As fast as Mellissa had appeared she was gone. Laxus ran across the room and wrapped Greg in a hug. "I never thought I would be so happy to see you, Gregory."

Greg patted the boy's blue curls. "It's good to see you too."

Laxus walked across the room and back again. "You have no idea how awful it was being stuck in those caves. I mean the facilities are very nice, but the not knowing what was going on with you guys." Laxus continued to pace while dramatically waving his arms around. "But the dwarfs had their orders because even with this whole veil mess the caves were still the safest place for me. Well guess what they aren't safe anymore." Laxus stopped in front of the coffee table and slammed his hands down on it. "And was anyone ever going to tell me that Kadon had returned and had two dark stones."

Greg scratched the side of his head. "To be honest I didn't realise you didn't know."

Laxus pointed at Greg. "Also, what happened to your face?"

Greg waved his hand away. "Don't point at people like that, its rude." He pulled his hood up and scowled at the pixie boy.

Laxus winced. "Sorry, sore subject huh."

Matt draped an arm round Greg. "He's a little touchy about the scar," said Matt, "But I think it makes him look ruggedly handsome. Like one of those rogue heroes, you see in films."

Laxus arched an eyebrow and gestured to Matt with his thumb. "Who is he?"

"Right, you never met Matt," said Greg as he stepped out of the warlock's grip.

Laxus' eyes went wide. "Matt as in Mellissa's original guardian with fire powers before Harkura."

Matt made a gun motion with his hands and clicked his tongue as he winked. "That's me."

Laxus groaned. "No wonder he got trapped."

"Hey," said Matt. Greg coughed as he tried not to laugh. The building shook as a loud snap sound rang through the air. The room went silent as all three boys looked at each other. Samson burst through the door. "Er Greg, we have a problem."

Greg marched over to his cousin and grasped his shoulder. "What's wrong?"

Samsons eye was twitching. "There are glass creatures surrounding the castle. We have locked and barricaded the entrances, but I'm not sure who exactly is in charge with Mellissa gone." Samson fanned his face with his hands. "I left Mary in command of the guards we have and came to get you. Most people inside are not fighters."

"Don't worry," said Matt. He slammed one hand into the other and smirked. "I'll shatter those glass creatures in no time."

Samson frowned as he took in Matt. His forehead creased as he tilted his head. "Matt," His face lit up with recognition. "Oh Matt, yes come get rid of the glass things."

Samson waved Matt over to the door. Greg's mind raced as he processed the information. This wasn't right. "Wait," said Greg. The two men stopped just outside the room and looked back. A strong gust blew through the room slamming the door in their faces. The door glowed as a sealing spell took hold on it.  He heard banging from the other side. Greg paid them no notice. He spun round and reached his hand out to Laxus. The boys' pink eyes went wide like saucers. A bird swept through the room as if materialising out of thin air. It shifted into a red-haired woman. She wrapped her arm round Laxus' neck holding a dagger to the side of his head.

Greg froze on the spot gritting his teeth. "Of course you would find a new master to serve. Can't ever think for yourself can you."

Gwendolyn swished her head back her red locks flowing behind her. "Hello to you too son."

"I'm not your son," he yelled.

Her nostrils flared. "Make the boy hand over the land stone and nobody needs to get hurt."

"Why would I believe anything you say?"

"Fine, I can't grantee no one will get hurt." She ran her fingers along Laxus' cheeks. "Unfortunately, the pixie has no hope. Sorry masters' orders but you Gregory do." She waved her arm across the room. "Kadon has promised me a new life with you. And I don't think he plans to kill your girlfriend either." She shrugged putting both arms up in the air.  "For some reason he is kind of obsessed with her. I think he sees her as a plaything."

Laxus elbowed Gwendolyn in the stomach. She stumbled back clutching the area he'd hit. The boy dived away from her and as he did, he shrunk, taking flight. He flew over to Greg and landed on his shoulder.

"You little brat," shouted Gwendolyn.

"Hide," Greg whispered. Laxus flew from Greg's shoulder and into the dressing room. Gwendolyn ran after him. Greg pushed his hands forward, summoning magic. He created a barrier in front of the dressing room door.

Gwendolyn screeched as she slammed into it. A vein on her forehead bulged, looking like it was about to burst. "Why do you have to make everything so hard Gregory?"

"Why do you have to be a traitorous shrew?"

Gwendolyn dove to the right shifting as she did. Greg scanned the room. He couldn't see what she had turned into. A blur shot up from the floor at him. He put his arms up just in time to catch the snake his mother had transformed into. The creature was the same grey as the carpet. He cried out as she sunk her fangs into his hand and stumbled back. His throat went tight as the snake wrapped round his neck.  He grabbed at its scaly skin.  Greg's eyes watered as his lungs burned for air. Anger bubbled up inside him. He remembered this. But he had been the snake. This was the move Kadon had pulled on Mellissa while he had control of his body. He dropped to his knees and transformed into a mouse, then swiftly into an elephant and then a tiger. The snake was flung up in the air with all the quick shape changes. Greg lunged at it, aiming to catch her with his claw. The snake shifted mid-air into a red kite. Swooping round, dodging his big paw, and scratching at his eyes with its talons. Greg rolled across the ground changing back to human form. He kicked up making contact with the bird.  She dropped onto the sofa. Greg jumped to his feet. The bird's body shook, and it shifted into a leopard. It pounced from the sofa. There was a loud bang, and the room door flew off its hinges, hitting the leopard mid-air.  She crashed into the coffee table shattering it.

Gwendolyn shifted back to human form. Greg swiftly whirled his arms round pushing a domed barrier around his mother. She laid dazed with the broken door on top of her.

Matt ran into the room, fists at the ready. He halted beside Greg. "Where's the bad guy?"

Greg pointed at the barrier. "She's in there."

Matt patted Gregs shoulder and nodded approvingly. "Good work buddy."

"You sent that door flying off its hinges at a very convenient time."

Gwendoyln shrieked as she pushed the broken door off of herself.  She ran at the barrier thumping her fists against it. "When I get out of this, you'll be sorry boy."

Anger rolled through Greg. "You better hope you don't escape for your own good."

She sneered at him. "Is that a threat Gregory?"

Greg stood inches away from her only the barrier protecting her from his temper. "If I see you again, I will not hesitate to end you."

She folded her arms and pouted. "You're a terrible son."

Greg snickered. "That's rich coming from you."

There was another bang like earlier and the castle shook. An alarm blared, the sound coming from all directions. "That alarm," shouted Samson. He was stood braced against the door frame. "It means the castle has been breached."

Gwendolyn smiled with her hands on her hips. "You didn't think I came alone. My master has put me in charge of a team."

Greg's heart raced. Holding his hand out Greg called out, "Laxus with me."

What looked like a butterfly fluttered into his hand. A mini Laxus stood in his palm scowling with his arms crossed. "I don't like being ordered about."

"Save it for later. I need you close, so I know you haven't been captured. In my pocket now." He placed the small pixie in his shirt pocket under the hoddie he was wearing.

Greg ran out the room grabbing Samson's wrist on the way past dragging him behind him. Matt dashed after them, following him down the stairs and into the foyer. A butch man, covered in tattoos had hold of an elf solider. He threw the elf into a wall. Matt leaped in front of them. "He's mine." He ran at the man his hands engulfed in flames. The man countered his fire with plasma blasts.

Glass creatures funnelled in through the broken doors. Samson trembled beside him. "What is the plan?"

"Don't get sliced and diced," replied Greg.

Samson gulped and took a deep breath. He stopped shaking and took up a fighting stance, his back against Greg's. "Right."

The two moved in unison as the creatures swarmed them. Magic tingled along Greg's fingertips. He cut through the creatures by creating barriers though them. Glass shards scattered along the ground. Shifting into a tiger Greg swatted a creature with his claws. As he went to strike another creature, the ground below rumbled, and a small man jumped out and punched him in the jaw. Greg stumbled back as pain sored across his face. A dwarf snickered at him and dropped into the earth. The ground rumbled again. The dwarf man popped up again, right underneath Greg. He punched him in the gut and popped back into the ground. Greg hit the ground with a thud and shifted back to human form. The ground around him grumbled again. With gritted teeth he carefully watched the grounds movements. This time when the dwarf popped up, Greg dove on him. He gripped the man's wrists and yanked at him with all his strength. Greg fell backwards as the dwarf was pulled out the ground. The dwarf man punched Greg in the face making him see stars. As the dwarf turned to try tunnel again Greg spun round on the floor swinging his legs. He kicked the guy in the chest and swiftly followed with another kick from his other leg. The dwarf hit the marble floor with a thud. Samson swiftly waved his arms over the man binding his hands and feet together. "Try tunnelling like that," Samson said smugly.

There was an explosion beside them. Greg flinched as Matt lit the big butch guy on fire. He fell to the floor with a thud, smoke coming off him. Matt walked over rubbing his hands together. "Told you, piece of cake."

What remained of the castle doors shattered as a swarm of glass creatures burst in. Greg narrowed his eyes at Matt. "You were saying."

Matt shrugged. "We still got this."

A huge wave of water swept up over them and crashed into the creatures. They were all swept up and forced out.

Yuko and Kai stood behind them pushing and pulling their arms controlling the water. The floor rumbled. It cracked in two lines heading to the entrance. Caleb and Hogan popped up from the ground. They landed in wide stances. They brushed their feet across the floor cracking the marble and hurling it in chunks at the creatures caught in the funnel of water. Brandon leapt past them. The super tall leprechaun punched his fist into the water. As he opened his hand Ping grew to full size. The fairy leader scattered fairy dust. Ping grabbed Brandon's hand and he was tugged out of the current.

"Now," yelled Ping. Kai and Yuko pushed forward swirling the water, spreading the fairy dust around. Any creatures that tried to break free of the water were pushed back by the two dwarfs hurling chunks of marble or Brandon's fists. When the fairy dust was scattered throughout ping clicked his fingers activating it. All the glass creatures shattered into pieces in one go.

Greg watched his fellow council members with his mouth wide open. He rubbed his eyes to check he wasn't seeing things. Matt bounced beside him. "I told you we had this." Matt held his hand up. "High five."

Greg rolled his eyes but slapped his hand to Matts. Laxus wriggled in his pocket. "Can I come out now?" Greg unzipped his hoodie and let Laxus fly out of his shirt pocket. Laxus grew back to full size. He shook his arms out in front of him. "Let's not do that again."

Greg burst out laughing. He wasn't sure what came over him, but he couldn't help himself. He had just become content with not fighting and acting as support but somehow, he had wound up in a battle. He should have learned by now, that his true role was to be adaptable.

Greg punched the wall as he let out a frustrated yell. She was gone. He had made his way back up to Mellissa's room with

Laxus and Matt to find it empty. During the commotion in the foyer his mother had somehow escaped the barrier he had put her in.

"I never should have taken my eyes off her," Greg said through gritted teeth.

"Dude don't be so hard on yourself," said Matt, "We had other pressing matters to see to."

Greg ran his fingers through his hair. "You don't understand all the damage she has caused is my fault."

Matt shook his head as he leaned against the dresser. "Your mother is bat shit crazy, her bad deeds are her own and nothing to do with you."

Laxus gently placed his hand on Greg's arm. "Don't be so harsh on yourself. You kept me safe and those others who attacked the castle have been detained."

"You're right." Greg clenched his fists and kicked the air. "That woman just gets under my skin."

"That is understandable," said Laxus shifting back and forth on the balls of his heels. "What that woman has put you through is unforgivable. She has no right to call herself your mother."

"What now?" asked Matt.

Greg shrugged. "I don't know. I guess we wait for Mellissa to return."

The room door opened and Victoria marched in with Harkura. "There you are?" she said. "At least we know your safe Laxus."

"We heard about the attack," said Harkura, "It seems you handled it well."

"Where's Mellissa?" asked Greg.

Victoria gritted her teeth as her body went tense. Harkura clenched his fists. "We were forced through a portal by Rowan. The crystal keepers were still battling Kadon."

Victoria sighed. "At least she wasn't fighting alone this time."

A flurry of lights appeared in between the group. Mellissa materialised, covered in blood and her hair a matted mess. Her eyes were red and puffy. "Greg," she shouted as she ran into his arms.

"Oh my god Mellissa," said Victoria.

"Are you hurt?" asked Greg.

Mellissa shook her head keeping her face against his chest. "It's not my blood."

"Who's is it? Do they need a healer?"

Her body went still, and her voice became monotone. "It's alright. Faizah, a hawklings healer is seeing to Ignis's wounds."

"So, this is Ignis's blood?"

"No but there's no helping them now." She looked down at her blood-soaked hands. Turning them over like she was inspecting them.

"We will give you two a minute," Said Harkura. He ushered Matt and Laxus out the room. Holding hands with Victoria the two guardians left glancing back at their Queen with worried looks.

"Let's get you cleaned up and you can tell me what happened." Mellissa nodded and Greg guided her into the bathroom. He turned the shower on. She stood staring at the tiles on the wall. He helped her out her blood-soaked clothes, tossing them on the floor. Holding her hands he guided her to the shower. She stepped into the water letting it pour over her. The water washed away the blood. Rummaging through the bathroom cupboard Greg found Mellissa's shampoo and conditioner. He brought it over to her, but she didn't take it. She stared blankly at the shower drain. He poured shampoo in her hair and rubbed it in. Once the water had rinsed it out, he did the same with her conditioner. She still didn't move or say anything. Greg's heart felt like it was being stepped on. He looked down at his shirt. Blood was smeared across it and his sleeves were now damp. His head throbbed as he tried to think of what to do. How could he help her when he didn't know what had happened to leave her in such a state?

Greg jumped as; Mellissa suddenly burst into tears. She wrapped her arms round herself as she sobbed. "It was awful Greg." Her voice was strained as she spoke. "We were fighting Kadon, Ignis was already hurt when a group of human soldiers surrounded us, guns at the ready." Her breathing became harsh. "They were scared of Ignis. I tried to tell them he wasn't a threat but what Kadon did. He slaughtered all of them." Letting out a disgruntled yell she slammed her hand against the tiles. "And we ran away. I wanted to help them, but Radius insisted I teleported us to safety." Pressing her back to the shower wall, Mellissa slid down it until she was sat on the floor. She pulled her knees up to her chest and stared blankly ahead. "I ran away."

Greg's heart felt like it was breaking as he watched her fall apart. He stepped into the shower and sat beside her. He scooped her up in his arms hugging her tight. "It's okay."

"No, it's not." She spluttered through tears. "Too many people have died." She clutched tight to his wet clothes. "I can't do this. Going from one fight to another. Failing to prevent deaths."

He brushed her wet hair from her face. "Even the life crystals can't stop people from dying." He cupped her face in his hands. "But think of those you have saved. Everyone in this castle wouldn't be here now if it wasn't for you."

Mellissa flung her arms round his neck, burying her face in his chest. Greg wasn't sure how long they sat there with the warm water running over them. He held her while she cried until there was nothing left.

She rubbed her face with her palms. "I'm sorry I made a mess of your shirt and now you're soaked."

Greg pulled his shirt off and threw it out the shower. It made a splat sound as it hit the tiled floor. He smirked and winked at her. "It's my own fault. I should have joined you in the shower without my clothes on."

She rested her head on his shoulder. "I love you."

"I love you too." Greg pressed a kiss to her forehead. "Now let me take a look at those burns on your legs because it doesn't look like you were as uninjured as you claimed."

"I just meant it wasn't a bad injury."

"I'll get us some towels." He stood and stepped out the shower. He walked over to the cupboard and opened it. He draped a towel round himself and grabbed two more for Mellissa. He held the biggest one out to her and she stepped into it, and he wrapped it round her. She took the smaller one and twisted it round her hair. Interlacing his fingers with hers, he led her out of the bathroom. He knew the moment she was called on again to fight she would jump straight into it all again. This was why she had shut down like this. Being forced to run went against every instinct she had. Greg's heart ached as he thought of the damage this war was doing to her fragile soul.

# 16

# Interlude

## *Victoria*

Victoria paced the length of her bedroom as she chewed at her thumb nail. Laxus was sat in the middle of the double bed eating a bag of sweets. Matt sat at her dressing table rummaging through her jewellery box. Victoria huffed. "Maybe I should go back and check on her."

Matt scrunched his nose. "Don't you think it better we leave this to Gregory? Don't want to over crowd her."

"But she looked so broken." Said Victoria, "What happened after we left?"

"That's what Harkura went to find out," replied Laxus.

"I know but what is taking him so long?"

"Well by the few details we got from Mellissa sounds like Ignis was hurt so it may take some time before everyone feels like story time."

Victoria threw her arms up in the air. "That's it I'm going back."

She marched over to the door, but it opened before she touched it. Harkura almost collided with her. Victoria stepped back letting him in. He arched a brow. "I see you were getting impatient waiting for my return."

Victoria crossed her arms as she pursed her lips. "Well, what the hell happened to our Queen?"

Harkura sat on the edge of the bed and interlaced his fingers. "After we were forced through the portal, Kadon continued to dominate the fight. Ignis was on the ground out of action. Radius and Mellissa were knocked out the sky when a group of human soldiers tried to detain them at gun point."

Victoria's brows rouse. "What the hell is wrong with these people?"

Harkura held his hand up. "I'm not done. Kadon slaughtered them all and Radius insisted Mellissa teleport the three of them to safety."

"She didn't help them," whispered Victoria. Harkura shook his head.

Matt slammed the lid of the jewellery box, making her jump. "So what? You expect Mellissa to save everyone?" Matt asked. "She's one person. It was either die trying to save those people or live to fight another day."

"We know that" snapped Victoria, "but Mellissa."

"Not staying and helping will have broken a small part of her," said Harkura finishing her sentence.

Victoria sat on the edge of the bed next to him. "I'm scared that this war is going to break her."

"How do you know it hasn't already?" said Laxus. Victoria turned to stare at the boy. His pink eyes were turned down as he frowned. "She's been through much more than any person should."

Victoria took the boys hand in hers. "She'll be alright. Mellissa is strong." Laxus squeezed her hand and smiled but his eyes were still sad. Victoria gulped as she pushed away the creeping feeling of dread inside her. "Mellissa will be fine." She said out loud to the room, mostly for herself.

"I swear if I ever see Gwendolyn again, I'm gonna freeze her fingers off one by one." Victoria's grip on her cards tightened.

She was sat on the floor across from Matt, with Harkura, and Laxus on either side of her. They had started a group game of cards a couple hours ago. Placing bets with sweets they had found in the kitchen. As they played Matt and Laxus had given them a rundown of the events that happened in the castle while they were gone.

Harkura slammed a card down with more force than necessary. "You'll have to beat me to her."

Matt whistled as he picked up a card. "This woman seems to have a queue of people wanting her dead. Greg said something similar."

"Well, she is the Queen of bad mothers," said Laxus placing down a card.

Victoria peered at her hand of cards, then to the one in the centre. She chewed on her bottom lip as she thought about the best next move. "Come on Vicky," said Matt, "It's your turn."

She batted her hand at her brother. "Shh, I'm trying to concentrate. I'm not losing again."

The door flew open, and Mellissa rushed in, followed closely by Greg. "Where is he?" Mellissa asked looking round the room franticly.

Victoria dropped her cards as she stood. Harkura also threw his cards down and was by Mellissa's side in a flash. His forehead creased as he gripped her arm. "What's wrong?"

"It's Laxus. Where is he?"

Laxus raised his hand. "I'm here."

Mellissa sighed. "You're okay? Greg just told me about Gwendolyn's attack."

"I'm fine. Greg and Matt protected me well."

Greg put his arm round Mellissa's shoulders. "Just like I said."

She jerked away from him. "You should have told me sooner."

His forehead creased. "You weren't in the best way when you first got back."

Victoria stepped between them placing her hands on Mellissa's shoulders. "Laxus is fine."

"But they attacked the castle." Mellissa's bottom lip trembled. "And I wasn't here to protect everyone."

Victoria bent her knees lowing herself down to Mellissa's height. Their eyes met. "Everyone is okay that's all that matters. You're good right?" Mellissa sucked in her bottom lip as she tilted her head side to side. Looking like she was trying to form a response but couldn't find the right words. Victoria embraced her hugging her tight. "You don't have to take all the burden on yourself."

"I know. It's just..." Mellissa words trailed off.

Victoria stepped back and wriggled her nose. "Today was hard."

"Yeah." Mellissa clenched her fists as her jaw tensed. "I swear when I get my hands on Gwendolyn."

"There's a queue," interjected Matt, "Want me to add your name to the list."

"Let me guess Harkura's top of the list followed by Victoria and Greg."

Matt smiled his crooked grin. "Actually, Greg put his name down first."

Mellissa looked over at Greg. He shrugged. "She did almost kill me and serve me up to Kadon."

Victoria clicked her finger and pointed to Greg. "You know what I'll allow you to stay at the front of that queue."

Harkura flexed his fingers sparking flames as he did. "I on the other hand am not above pushing to the front."

Mellissa burst into a fit of laughter and everyone stared at her. She coughed as her giggling ended. "I'm sorry. Today has been awful but watching you guys argue about who gets to take the first shot at Gwendoyln." She shrugged. "I dunno but I'm just glad I've got you guys."

Victoria slung her arm over Mellissa's shoulder. "You know we've always got ya back."

Harkura yawned as he stretched. "Now I think it's past my bedtime." He clicked his fingers and beckoned to

Laxus. "Come on you are bunking with me." Harkura squeezed Mellissa's hand and she nodded.

Laxus pouted. "I do not like being ordered around." But the boy stood and followed Harkura out the room.

"We should be going too." Greg held his hand out to Mellissa. She looked to Victoria.

"Go get some sleep," Victoria said taking a step back.

"Night." Mellissa took Greg's hand and he led her away.

Matt stood in the middle of the room rubbing the back of his neck. "I don't have anywhere to go."

Victoria huffed as she snapped her fingers at her brother. "You can sleep at the end of my bed. I'll see if there is a guest room available for you in the morning."

Matt grinned. "Thanks sis." Victoria found Matt an oversized t-shirt and shorts of hers to were. They were too big for her but only just fit him. She went to the bathroom and got herself ready for bed. Removing her makeup and putting on fluffy pyjamas. As she walked back into the room she smiled. The site of him sat on the end of her bed with a blanket warmed her heart. Everything had been so chaotic that she hadn't really taken a moment to take in the fact her brother was back. Her other half had been returned to her. She sat on the other end of the bed and got comfy. The pair ended up talking about anything and everything until eventually they fell asleep in the early hours of the morning.

# 17

# Ultimatum

## *Mellissa*

I laid with my head on Greg's chest, listening to his heartbeat. The steady rhythm thrumming away tamed the turmoil of my mind. We were snuggled up in my bed, surrounded by pillows. The morning sun gleamed in through a crack in the curtains. Somehow, we had made it through the rest of the night without me being called on to fight. I'm not sure how many times I had cried during the night. I had gone from one battle to another in such a short amount of time. That final fight yesterday had just made my bucket overflow and it all just burst out of me. When I had finally got all of those tears out those feelings were replaced by fear for Laxus after hearing about Gwendolyn's attack. Kadon had planned things well. He had known I would just teleport Laxus away from him. So, he had sent in his little birdie.

Greg ran his fingers through my hair, tangling his fingers in my curls. I traced a circle with my finger on his bare chest. "I wish we could stay like this forever," I said.

"That would be nice," he said, his breath warm on the top of my head. "Just to lay here in our own little bubble."

"Hidden from the outside world." I curled my legs round his and tilted my head upwards. "It sucks having to be responsible."

"You have done so well leading during this crisis."

"It doesn't really feel like I have a choice. I haven't had time to stop and think. I'm just reacting because if I don't do anything who will?" My voice caught in my throat as my lips trembled. "Because when I do slow down and think about everything that's happening." I squeezed my eyes shut trying to force out the images of last night's battle with Kadon. All that blood. So many lost lives.

"It's normal to be shaken by the horrific things you witnessed."

I shook my head. "But I can't show it, not when everyone is looking to me to solve their problems. If anyone else had seen the way I was last night."

Greg stroked my cheek with his thumb. "When it's just the two of us you can fall apart as much as you want."

I shimmied myself up the mattress, so my face was across from his. "Thank you for just being there last night."

He turned so our noses where touching. "You don't have to shoulder this burden alone." I ran my fingers softly along his jawline and then his cheek. When I had felt myself starting to shut down in that cave, he was who I had teleported too. He was my safe place. Resting my hand at the back of his neck, I closed the small gap between us. Pressing my lips to his. I'm not sure where this sudden urgency came from, but I was kissing him like our lives depended on it. I breathed in his scent. He smelled of my shampoo which sent me wild. It's like it was marking him as mine. He pushed me back and rolled on top of me. My fingers grip his hair pulling him closer.  My lips parted against his and groaned as his tongue explored further. It was as if he felt the same urgency I did. I couldn't get enough. I never wanted him to stop kissing me. To stay in this bliss and forget reality.

Screams and yells sounded from outside the castle. We were both up off the bed in a flash, pulling on any items of clothing we found on the floor.

"My fellow magic folk," echoed Kadon's voice. The sound had me calling to the heart crystal and transforming it into staff form. I ran out onto the balcony wearing Greg's hoodie and a pair of shorts. The cold air made me shiver but it was the sight before me that chilled me to my core. A giant shadowy image of Kadon's face hovered above Urbem Folium. The people below were cowering in fear.

"I mean you no harm, for now." The image of Kadon smirked. "By now you have all seen how welcoming the humans are of our kind. These savages think they can cage us like animals. They should bow to us like the gods we are." The shadow turned its head making me shudder. I could feel him staring at me through the projection. "Queen Mellissa wants to befriend these beasts; she will be the end of us all. Join me and we will rule over the humans.  All you have to do is call out the phrase 'Kadon the almighty, we pledge allegiance to you' and a portal will appear to bring you to your true King. Stay with her and die." Kadon shouted the last word and the shadow swooped down towards me. I thrust my staff in front of me releasing light. The shadow disintegrated leaving behind a tiny wisp of darkness.

My chest felt tight, and my breathing became rapid. Greg linked his arms undermine just before my legs gave way and pulled me back inside. My head was spinning, and the room was a blur. "He wants them to join him. You don't think…" I clasped the sides of my head gripping my hair. "They wouldn't."

Greg grasped my shoulders and crouched so he was eye level with me. "No one is going to join Kadon." He pulled me close, hugging me tight. I rested my head on his chest while he rubbed my back. I shut my eyes, slowing my breathing by pacing it to the sounds of his heartbeat.

I heard the door to my living room open and shut. A moment later Victoria and Harkura rushed into the bedroom. Harkura went straight into my dressing room and Victoria marched over to us. "I'm so sorry about this but we don't have much time."

"What's wrong?" I asked as a new panic began to rise up in me.

Harkura came out the dressing room with an emerald dress and a pair of knee high boots. "Samson is holding them off for now, but they won't be put off for long."

"Who is coming?" I asked.

Harkura and Victoria exchanged a glance. "Pretty much the whole council," Said Harkura.

"What?" I said.

"Why are they all coming here?" asked Greg.

"For Mellissa duh," replied Victoria.

Harkura removed the dress from its hanger and handed it to Victoria. Harkura narrowed his eyes at Greg and then walked back into the dressing room. Victoria tugged at my clothes. "Get that thing off."

I removed the hoodie I was wearing. She knelt, holding the dress unzipped out to me. I stepped into it and as she stood, she pulled it up and over my arms. It's cascading ruffled skirt tickling my legs. She spun me round and zipped the dress up. Victoria tugged at my hair finger combing it out. "This will have to do." She patted my back. "Quick get the boots on."

I grabbed the boots Harkura had left on the floor and slipped them on just as I heard a bang on my door. Harkura darted out the dressing room and threw some clothes at Greg. "Fresh shirt and tie quick."

Greg swiftly redressed himself in the items Harkura had picked out. I walked out the bedroom into the living room as the door flew open. Samson was stood by the door with his arms up in front of his chest. "We should wait for the queen to answer."

"We've waited long enough," snapped Beatrice as she marched in with Lee by her side. They were followed by the rest of the council. The last person to enter was King Radius. My living quarters was now filled with people. Some of whom had never been here before and I really wished weren't right now. They were all speaking at once and I couldn't make out what any of them were saying. My head was spinning. All I could hear was buzzing like a bee was hovering in my ear canal. I clasped my ears trying to shut the noise out. I couldn't focus. A warm hand slid into mine. I opened my eyes and looked up a Greg. He squeezed my hand and nodded. I took a deep breath.

"That's enough," I shouted, "I can barely hear myself think." They all quietened down and stared at me mouths a jar. "I get that you are all worried but talking over each other solves nothing. One person at a time." I pointed to the back of the crowd. "King Radius, you are first."

Radius stepped forward and cleared his throat. "Right. Ignis and I just want to know what you think our next steps should be." He looked awkwardly at the others in the room. "We also wanted to assess the risk."

My brows drew together as I scrunched my nose. "Risk?" My eyes went wide as understanding dawned on me. He was worried about the same thing I had been. "No one is joining Kadon." I said repeating the words Greg had said to me.

Radius frowned. "How can you be so sure?"

"Because I have faith."

Beatrice stepped forward, barging in front of Radius. "But Kadon wasn't wrong. Those humans had the water nymphs in cages." She glanced at Yuko, Kai and Akito and curled her top lip. "Are you sure they can be trusted?"

"Yuko would never betray me."

"That is right," said Yuko glaring a Beatrice. "When the people of Perluves were caged, it was Queen Mellissa who saved them. Kadon was nowhere in sight." Yuko clenched her fists. "He proclaims himself a King but never lifts a finger to help his would be subjects."

Beatrice crossed her arms and pursed her lips. "Fine but what about him. "She nodded her head at Brandon. "They are his kind."

Brandon growled. "The leprechauns will never associate with that monster again. Yuko is right. Kadon just wants power and to be worshiped. He does not have what it takes to be a good King. Anyone who flocks to him will be used and disposed of when no longer useful."

"I think that answers the risk question," I said. Kate raised her hand. I stared at her for a moment, as she very rarely voiced an opinion. I pointed to her. "Yes Kate."

"While we all agree Kadon is a monster, he isn't wrong about the human issue. What do you plan to do about that?"

I bit my bottom lip as I tried to think of what to say. Greg stroked the back of my hand with his thumb. His gentle touch was enough reassurance. "I am going to talk to them and show them that we are not a threat."

Kate's forehead creased. "Really that's your plan?"

"I know it doesn't sound like much but defending against two threats is spreading us thin. If we can get them to back off even just temporary, we can focus on stopping Kadon for good. Kadon's actions are just fuelling this fear. We need to show them we are not all like him."

Kate folded her arms. "Thats sounds wonderful in theory but how do you plan on actually making it happen?"

"By talking directly to their leaders. Josh is already working on a way for me to get direct access. I just need them to see that we are not the same as Kadon."

"I suppose you are having faith in those human leaders too," Kate glanced at Beatrice and then back to me. "Like you are all of us."

Lee shuffled forward to stand by Kate. "Are we meant to just rely on your advisor to deal with something this important," he said with a scoff.

"That adviser of mine is the reason we found all our cities, he is the reason we are able to track Kadon and the humans' movements." I tightened my grip on Greg's hand. "So yeah, I think Josh is pretty damn reliable."

Lee pressed his lips together into a thin line. "I suppose."

I rolled my eyes at him and looked out at the others in my room. "Anyone else got something to say?"

Caleb walked forward with his hand raised. I tilted my head to the side. "What is it?"

"It's about the people." Caleb interlaced his fingers. "I think they will be just as worried as we were after Kadon's grand announcement. Urbem Folium was meant to be a safe haven. I just think we need to do something to reassure them."

I nodded. "You're right. If we gather everyone in front of the castle I will address them from my balcony." I looked to Radius. "Can you and Ignis be in attendance? We need to show them a united front. Our three crystals together should overpower Kadon's two dark stones."

"I will make sure the dragon is in attendance," said Radius, "Even if I have to drag him out that cave myself." He held his arm across his chest and bowed his head. The council members looked at him stunned. They all scurried about and copied the sea kings' actions. Greg tugged at my hand as he also bowed. My body wanted to squirm away, but I forced myself to stay still and stand tall.

They all slowly left. Samson stood holding the door watching each of them go. When the last person had walked out, Samson bowed and left the room shutting the door behind him.

My legs turned to jelly as I leaned into Greg. "That was awful."

"But you did amazing." Greg picked me up and spun me round. I clung onto him wrapping my arms round his neck. He kissed both my cheeks and then his lips met mine. I gripped his hair in my fingers, pulling his face closer to mine.

"Ahem," coughed Victoria, "We are still here."

Greg placed me back on the ground. My face felt warm, and I was still giddy. "You guys did great with that quick outfit change." Greg said. He pointed at Harkura, "Good choice on the dress."

"Yes, but we forgot to put a tiara on her." Harkura frowned as he rubbed his chin.

Victoria waved her hands dismissively. "Hey, we only had a couple minutes to work with. I think we pulled it off. Even got them matching as a couple." She arched an eyebrow and gestured at Greg. "You did good as the supporting boyfriend. Man, you must have bit your tongue a lot. I know I did."

Greg brushed his hand through his hair. "Oh, there were so many times I wanted to cut in and say something, but I didn't want to undermine Mellissa's authority." He wrapped his arms around my waist pulling me close. "And you did great all on your own." He kissed the top of my head.

I pouted. "You know I would rather let you and Victoria deal with them lot."

Victoria chuckled. "They would probably still all be here arguing if you had."

"Why not add Harkura to the mix as well?" said Greg.

I laughed. "Harkura only gets called on as a last resort. Isn't that right."

I looked over at Harkura. He flexed his fingers and grinned. "Those who mess with my Queen do not get to walk away intact."

Greg gulped. Victoria slung her arm over the fire nymph shoulders. "Oh, Harkura you are always so serious."

Harkura shrugged. "That is why I'm the last resort." He glanced my way and pointed to the door. "I will go find Samson and get him to come back. He can help you decide what to say when you address the citizens."

"Yes, thank you, that's a great idea," I said. Harkura tugged Victoria along and out my room. I chewed at my thumb nail. I had agreed it was a good idea to address everyone but now my stomach was full of butterflies just from thinking about it.

Greg took my hands in his. "It'll be fine."

"I don't know."

"You handled the council fantastically; you will handle this just as well."

"You say that, but it doesn't feel that way to me. If I hadn't been holding your hand I would have crumbled."

"All I did was support you. You were in the middle of your own panic when Victoria and Harkura burst in here, but you pulled it together when it counted." He cupped my face in his hands. "You have been amazing since the start of this crisis. You have become the Queen you were always destined to be." He rested his forehead on mine. "I will be by your side through it all."

I nodded, wrapping my arms round his body pulling him close. I rested my head on his chest wishing I could stay safe in his arms like this forever.

Sunlight glistened on the tops of the trees, the green leaves blowing on the wind. The cold air pricked my cheeks as I stepped out onto my balcony. Clutching my staff close to my chest, I took slow steady breaths. My heart pounded as I looked out at all the people gathered below murmuring to one another. Greg interlaced his fingers with mine and gave my hand a gentle squeeze. I looked up into his emerald eyes, his stare grounding me in the moment. Looking out at the crowd below I addressed my subjects.

"Thank you all for coming." As I spoke, they stopped their chatting and looked up at me. "I know these are troublesome times. The world we knew is no more and now we find ourselves stranded in this new one. I want to assure you all that I will find us a place in this new world. Be it Kadon or the humans I will keep you all safe. Kadon's announcement is worrisome but as you can see all three crystal keepers are here." I gestured below to Radius and Ignis stood on the ground below the balcony. "Something that hasn't happened in thousands of years. This is why Kadon didn't appear here himself and only sent a projection. He wants to lure people out of the safety of this forest. He knows he is no match for the three life crystals combined power. If we all remain united, we will weather this storm."

The forest was silent except for the rustle of leaves in the wind. The crowd erupted into cheers and cries of solidarity. I smiled my heart feeling less burdened. They were with me. No one seemed to have considered Kadon's offer. I had had faith and they had delivered.

# 18

# Casualty

## *Mellissa*

I tied my hair up into a ponytail. Victoria pouted behind me as she sat on my bed with her arms crossed. "I should be coming with you."

"Harkura will be with me." I pulled my black armoured jacket on. It seemed like over kill but with how yesterday had unfolded I understood my guardians insisting on me being more cautious.

Victoria handed me my silver gauntlets. "Matt and Greg did a pretty good job babysitting Laxus yesterday."

I placed my gauntlets on my wrists. "Victoria please I need you to do this. After Gwendolyn and co attacking as soon as I had dropped Laxus off here." My stomach churned as I thought of what could have happened if their plan had succeeded. I shook my head pushing those images out my mind. "I just want the odds to be more skewed towards us."

"You know Harkura has a better relationship with Laxus. So maybe he should stay with him."

I arched a brow as I placed my hands on my hips. "I don't need two fire wielders protecting Laxus. Your abilities are better suited to this."

Victoria sighed. "Fine."

Harkura strode into my room, dressed in an identical black outfit to me. "You ready?"

I patted myself down. Nothing seemed to be missing. "Yep."

"Good." He flicked his wrist and a blade extended from the gauntlets he was wearing. My set didn't have that feature.

I raised an eyebrow. "Do you really need those for evacuating the next set of cities?"

"Considering how the last set of evacuations went I think it best to be prepared." He flicked his wrist back and the blade went back into the gauntlet. He smiled. "Besides one can never have too many knives."

Victoria bobbed her head side to side. "You know he has a point."

I grumbled as I didn't have a response. They were both right. Yesterday had been the longest day in my life. I linked arms with Harkura. "We'll see you when we get back."

"May your day be uneventful." Victoria said with a wave.

Harkura and I walked out my room and through the castle to the exit. We strolled into the clearing in front of Ignis' cave. A small group was already there talking amongst themselves. I clapped my hands together. "Good you are all here."

Lee curled his top lip. "Why exactly have you made us come out here so early in the morning for?"

I smiled sweetly ignoring Lee. I looked at the others gathered here. Beatrice was stood huddled up in a fur coat. Brandon had his hands stuffed in the pockets of his coat, while Caleb tried to persuade him to drink from his metal flask he was dangling in front of him. Rowan stood with his wings pulled in beside Ignis. Radius was in a long fleece robe on the other side of the Dragon. "The aim of the day is to get the rest of our people into the safety of the forest," I said, "Kadon's dramatics made me realise I had been too focused on hiding from the humans that I forgot that nowhere is safe from him. The sooner we start the quicker we finish."

"I did say Highwish should have been a top priority," said Beatrice crossing her arms. "But what exactly do you want me to do now that you have realised your mistake?"

I gritted my teeth. "I was getting to that." Taking slow breaths, I refocused my mind back to the plan. "To try make this go quicker, I'm going to teleport each of you to your cities." I pointed at each council member here separately. "Your task will to be to get everyone ready to evacuate. Lee I'll be taking you first. You'll have ten minutes before Ignis opens a portal. Will that be enough time?"

Lee waved his hand in the air dismissively. "I'll only need five. The witches are respectful people and know how to follow orders."

"Very well." I looked up at the dragon. "Ignis, do you think you can open the portal in five minutes after Lee and I leave."

Ignis bowed his head to me. "As you wish Queen Mellissa."

I held my hand out to Lee. He scrunched his nose and pursed his lips as he placed his hand in mine. I looked over at Beatrice. "You come too and Radius. I'll take you two straight to Highwish after."

Beatrice raised an eyebrow. "Why is the sea King coming to Highwish?"

"Because your city is now an island much like this forest. You'll be going through a water portal, created by Radius."

Her eyes went wide as she gasped. "You mean I'll have to get wet on my return?"

I sighed. "Yes. It's the most efficient way. Divide and concur and all that." I waved my hand at her. "Now come on."

She huffed over to my side and took my other hand. Radius walked over and placed a hand on my shoulder. In a flurry of lights, we teleported and rematerialized in the tower in the witches fortress.

I let go of Lee's hand. "Are you okay from here?"

Lee gripped the sides of his jacket and stood up straight tilting his nose upwards. "Of course."

"Remember to call me if you need anything."

He rolled his eyes. "I know but I won't need to."

"Well see you back in Urbem Folium." I turned back to Beatrice and Radius. Holding each of their hands I teleported again.

We materialised in the centre of the city. A commotion broke out as the changelings saw us. Shouts and cries of joy. Others praised the gods for sending us to them. I let go of Beatrice and Radius' hands. "Well, I'll let you two handle this. I've two other cities to get to." Taking a step back I teleported back to Urbem Folium.

I materialised in the same spot I had left from. "Okay so Caleb, I'll drop you off at the hills. Get the dwarfs there prepared once all the witches are in Ignis will open a portal for you. And Brandon we are going to start teleporting leprechauns here."

I went to take their hands, but Harkura stood in front of Brandon blocking me. His indigo eyes were serious as he folded his arms. "I'm coming with you."

"But your meant to greet people as they come through and guide them to the castle."

"And what happens if you encounter trouble again."

"I'll come get you and we'll deal with it together." He narrowed his eyes at me. I placed my hand over my heart and the other on his shoulder. "I promise I won't go into a fight without you."

"No, you won't because I'm coming with you." He linked his arm through mine locking onto to me tight and glanced at Rowan. "I've already sent a message to Samson he should be here soon but if the witches arrive before then just point them to the castle."

Rowan nodded in response. Harkura took Brandons hand with his free one and I held Calebs with my hand that was not death locked against my guardian. With a sigh I teleported to the hillside. We dropped off Caleb and went straight to Leath, the leprechaun city.

In next to no time Brandon had rounded up all the leprechauns and we were ready to start teleporting. While initially everyone had been a mix of panic and joy to see us. Brandon had swiftly calmed everyone and spread the word quickly about evacuating. Somehow neither Kadon nor the humans had made any contact with the leprechauns. It appeared that even Kadon knew that his former people wanted nothing to do with him. Brandon had sorted everything that I had been left with nothing to do until now.

"Queen Mellissa, how many people do you think you can teleport at once?" asked Brandon.

I rubbed my chin. "I'm not sure." I looked out at the crowd gathered. It would take a lot of teleports if I took them in groups of four. I clicked my fingers and pointed at the crowd. "Let's try twenty at a time."

"She'll take groups of ten," said Harkura beside me, his voice stern.

Brandon looked at Harkura and then me his mouth a jar. I gave a thumbs up. "Groups of ten it is." Brandon nodded and walked over to the Leprechauns and began splitting them into groups.

Placing my hands on my hips I frowned at my guardian. "Why did you do that? It'll take longer going in smaller groups."

Harkura crossed his arms as he tutted. "More trips are better than the risk of taking too many people and loosing someone mid teleport."

I cringed at the thought. What happened to the person if this occurred was not something I wanted to discover. Brandon came back over with the first group of ten. I stepped forward. "Okay everyone stand in a circle and hold hands." I took the hands of the two closest to me. Everyone clasped onto the person next to them until we were all linked. "Do not let go of each other until I say." They all responded affirmatively. "Let's do this." I shut my eyes pushing my magic out through my fingertips. I felt it surge along each person until it made a full circle. I opened my eyes to lights dancing around the group. With a small smile I thought of where I wanted to be and, in a flash, we appeared in Urbem Folium outside the castle.

I let go of the two leprechauns' hand I was holding and wiped sweat from my forehead with the back of my hand. "You can all let go now." They released each other's hands and looked round at the castle gasping. "If you all go inside my staff will be waiting to greet you." I pointed to the entrance.

A leprechaun women clasped my hand. "Thank you, Queen Mellissa. We were so scared before, but you have given us hope."

My heart ached at her words, but I smiled through it. "I'll be back soon with the rest."

She nodded and went back to the group. They walked towards the castle entrance, and I teleported again. I repeated the process, teleporting back and forth. I could feel my magic draining but I pushed forward. All the women and children where safely in Urbem Folium now I just had the last group of men. We were stood in a circle. Harkura and Brandon either side of me. We teleported and arrived back. I let out a sigh of relief and leaned into Harkura. He put his arm round my back and under my arm supporting my weight.

Brandon peered at me. "Your majesty are you alright?"

"Yeah, just tired. Take them all inside and go reunite with the rest of your people." His forehead creased and he looked worried, but he nodded and did as I suggested. I patted Harkura's hand. "Right, we should go check how the others got on."

"I think you should rest. You used a lot of energy and your looking peaky." I was about to protest when the watch on my wrist buzzed. Swiping my finger across the screen I answered the call. "Hello"

"Queen Mellissa," came Radius' voice. He sounded strained. "Come quick I need help."

"What's wrong?" I asked, "Are you still in Highwish?"

"Yes, it's the humans-" The call cut off. Dread swirled around my stomach. Thinking of Radius I teleported.

We materialised on the outskirts of the city engulfed in flames. My pulse quickened as I scanned the area. Someone shouted my name. A man was knelt on the floor beside a body waving his arms and two more people huddled beside him. I gasped. The body on the ground was Radius.  I ran to him skidding down on my knees beside Radius's body. Blood was seeping from I don't know where. The man who had waved us down was trying to stop the bleeding with what looked to be his own shirt. I held my hands over Radius's body not sure what to do. It looked like something had sliced a chunk from his side and singed his body at the same time. There was so much blood. Harkura pulled off his jacket and wrapped it round Radius' body pulling it tight.

I turned to the man. "What happened?" No response. I leaned forward and touched his shoulder. The man startled at my touch. I drew my hand back. "I'm sorry but can you tell us what happened?"

"Yes, um, Lady Beatrice and the king were seeing us through the portals." He was pale and shaking. "There was only a few of us remaining, when suddenly these aircrafts flew over and dropped objects into the city." He looked up at the sky and then towards the burning city. "Suddenly the city exploded. King Radius created a barrier protecting us. He shouted for us all to hurry through the portal, but those planes circled round dropping more explosives. Radius was hit by debris. When he went down the portal shut." He looked down at the sea king and then into my eyes. "Somehow he found the strength to call you before passing out."

I looked around the area. There was a women and boy huddled together sat behind the man and another man stood by the water looking dazed.  "Is anyone else hurt?" I asked.

Before anyone could respond a loud boom echoed around us. A building crumbled and debris went flying. As I stood, I summoned my magic. Pushing light out I created a barrier deflecting the debris back towards the collapsed building. As the dust cleared, I lowered my barrier.

"Mellissa," shouted Harkura, "We need to get out of here."

I dug my nails into my palms, trying to stop myself from panicking. "Everyone gather round." I beckoned them over. They all huddled round except the man by the water. He remained stood staring at the city in flames. I ran over to him. He didn't acknowledge me or say anything, but he let me guide him over to the others. Once I had the small group gathered, I made sure everyone had hold of someone.

Harkura locked eyes with me. "Straight to Greg," he said. I nodded. He didn't need to tell me. That was already where I was heading.

# 19

# Healing

## *Gregory*

Greg sat in the main hall at his healer's station flicking through his tabular looking at nothing in particular.
So far, his day had been uneventful. The witches and leprechauns had started arriving at the castle but so far no one needed healing. This should have been a relief. It meant no one was hurt but it was really boring. What was a healer to do when no one was wounded? Just a few minor injuries would do.

"There you are," said Samson making Greg jump.

He placed his tabular down expecting a patient. But it was just Samson on his own, looking smart in his suit not an injury in sight. Greg frowned. "Is something wrong?"

"No actually I think it's something pretty good." The smile on Samson face grew wider. "Queen Mellissa isn't back yet so I thought you were the next best person to share it with."

"Okay what is it?"

"You've gotta come to Joshes office he explains it better." Samson gestured for Greg to follow him, and he obliged. They went upstairs to the first floor where the offices were. They walked down the corridor side by side. "So, how's everything going with you?"

Greg rubbed the back of his neck. "I'm fine."

"Everything with you and Mellissa is good then?"

"Yeah, why wouldn't it be?"

"Just after she you know." Samson pointed at his own face. Anger bubbled up in Greg, but he pushed back down. Instead, he decided to address the elephant in the room that was his face.

"Oh, you mean are me and my girlfriend still on good terms after she burned my face scarring me." Samson winced. Greg wafted his hand in the air dismissively. "Yeah, we are totally cool. Did you know I also have a burn scar on my left arm."

Samson's forehead creased as his brows drew close. "No, I didn't."

"That one's easier to hide with my clothes but the face makes me a walking side show."

"No that's not what I meant. It's just what you went though was pretty traumatic we haven't really spoke since you returned." Samson's eye twitched as he fiddled with his shirt collar. "It's like there is still a lot going on, so I just wanted to make sure you are actually fine and not just outwardly fine." He scrunched his nose. "You know the whole putting on the display of a happy couple to just not worry the people. Does that make sense?"

Greg wasn't sure he could put into words what was going on in his head. He was not fine. Just moments ago, he had been longing for someone to come in injured to cure his boredom. That was a little messed up, but he and Mellissa were good. She was the only thing keeping him sane. Greg sighed as he ran his fingers through his hair. "I never blamed Mellissa for what happened. I have always been madder at myself about it all. So yeah, Mellissa and I are good. We are really good." Greg shoulders sagged. "But I wouldn't say either of us is okay."

"You know no one thinks what happened is your fault."

"I know but my brain doesn't want to accept that."

They stopped walking outside Joshes office. Samson placed a hand on Greg's shoulder. "Just know I am here if you need anything."

"I know." Greg pointed at the office door. "Now what is this good thing Josh has found?"

"You'll see." Samson knocked on the door. He didn't wait for a response before letting himself in. They walked into the office.

Josh peered up at them from his computer and his smile turned to a frown. "You're not the queen."

Samson stepped forward interlacing his fingers. "The Queen is still out but Greg…"

"So, you brought me her boyfriend."

"Greg is more than just the Queens boyfriend." Samson pressed both his hands down on Joshes desk. "He is a changeling elder, a member of the council and an adviser to the Queen. He is also really good at planning things, so if he likes your plan, it's highly likely the Queen will too."

Josh leaned to the side looking at Greg round Samson. "I didn't mean to come off as rude. I was just expecting to talk with Queen Mellissa." He looked up at Samson with stern eyes. "Because that's who I asked Samson to get." He glanced back to Greg. "But I'm happy to share what I've found with you. I love talking about my discoveries."

Greg walked past Samson and sat in the chair at the end of Joshes desk. He interlaced his fingers and rested his elbows on the edge of the desk. "So, what have you discovered?"

"I was tasked with finding the Queen a way to contact all the world leaders. I started by getting all of their personal details, addresses, phone numbers and email but I thought that was too individual." Josh waved his hands around illustrating his words with his hand gestures. "I was like hey what about a UN meeting. Leaders from around the world gather for those things so I did a deep dive, and I found an even better opportunity." A big grin spread across his face as he leaned forward. His brows rose. "A united nations security meeting is being held in three days to discuss the issues of the new land masses and strange being." He waved his hands between them. "I figured they wanna have a meeting about us, we should show up. I already know the date, time, and location."

Greg stared at Josh. He had been nodding along as he spoke but now he was just awe struck. "That's brilliant. Mellissa is gonna be ecstatic."

Josh grinned as he bounced in his seat. "Good because I have worked really hard on this." He turned back to his computer and began typing. "I've just downloaded the building blueprints so we should be able to make a proper plan."

"Can you print them off?" asked Greg.

"Sure thing." Josh tapped away on his keyboard. A juddering noise sounded in the corner as the printer started up.

Samson was leaned against a wall and smiled. "I told you it was good."

The smile fell from Greg's face as someone screamed his name. "Greg." Shouted Mellissa's voice from just outside the door. Greg was on his feet in flash. Samson threw the door open, and they both fumbled out the room.

Mellissa was crouched on the floor in the corridor. In her arms was an unconscious Radius. Harkura had a hand on her back, and he was holding onto three changelings. Blood and muck swirled together covering them all. Mellissa looked up at him, tears in her eyes. "Greg quick Radius is badly hurt."

Greg ran over to her and knelt. He took Radius from her arms and laid him flat on the ground.  Peeling away the fabric wrapped around Radius body, Greg examined the wound. His skin was a murky grey colour and he looked to be missing a chunk of flesh. In the short amount of time, they had been here, the floor had become covered in his blood. "Sanam quad fit." Gregs hands glowed green. His magic seeped into the open wound. The damage ran deep. "This is bad. What happened?" he asked.

"I don't really know. He called me for help but was already unconscious when I arrived." Mellissa's lips trembled as she clutched the sea king's hand. "I think humans bombed Highwish."

Greg looked up at the others who had arrived with them. "Was anyone else hurt?"

A man shook his head. "We only have minor injuries. The King shielded us from the worst of it."

Greg nodded to Samson. "Take them to the main hall. There are other healers who can see to them." Samson nodded. He gathered up the small group of changelings and ushered them down the corridor.

"Hey, can you two assists please?" said Greg.

"What do you need?" asked Harkura.

"I've managed to stop the bleeding but I'm going to need to use healing stones for the rest," explained Greg, "The three of us need to very carefully roll Radius." Greg turned back to the door he had come out of. "Josh."

The elf appeared in the doorway. His eyes went wide as the colour drained from his face. "Yes."

"I need your assistance."

"What can I do? I'm the tech guy you're the healing guy."

"While we lift Radius can you place four stones under him."

Josh came over and knelt beside Greg. "Sure, where are the stones?"

Greg slammed his hands together focusing on the object he wanted to summon. He always theorised this was similar to how Mellissa's teleporting worked. He pictured his set of healing stones. The draw they were in and the navy pouch that housed them. As he pulled his hands apart, the navy pouch appeared in his hands. He pulled four stones out the bag and handed them to Josh. They all lined up on their knees beside the sea king's body. Greg rubbed his hands together. "Ready." The other three nodded. "Okay now." With the help of Harkura and Mellissa, he heaved Radius' body up as carefully as possible. Josh swiftly placed the stones, and they rolled him back down. Greg placed four more stones from the bag, on top of Radius' body. With a click of his fingers the stones activated. Greg smiled as he felt the warmth of their magic. Weaving his fingers back and forth like he was tugging on invisible wires, he pulled at the stones magic directing it round Radius's body. Sweat dripped from his forehead.

Mellissa bit her bottom lip. "Is he going to be okay?"

"I can't say, this is going to take time," replied Greg. He gritted his teeth his arms aching from the repetitive motions.

Victoria came hurtling down the corridor. "Oh my god. This is bad if he dies we are done for. He needs to survive."

"That is the goal of my healing," snapped Greg.

Harkura paced the width of the corridor. "If Kadon gets wind of this. Knowing we are down a crystal keeper he won't hesitate to attack."

Victoria hovered over Greg. "Do you think I should get another healer to help?"

"I am very aware of how important my patient is," shouted Greg. "You would think I had proved my competence with the number of times I've healed my own girlfriend who has come to me in worse condition than this." Greg inhaled slowly. "Now shut up and let me work." Returning his attention to his patent Greg channelled the healing magic to the right places.

Mellissa stood and ushered her guardians to her. "Could you two clear the area and make sure no one else comes down this corridor." Victoria and Harkura walked down the corridor. With them gone the pressure weighing on Greg shoulders eased slightly.

"Can I go back in my office?" asked Josh.

"Yes," said Mellissa. Footsteps and then the sound of a door closing. Mellissa knelt beside Greg. "It's just us now." She rubbed his back. "I know that you've got this."

Sweat dripped down the back of Greg's neck. Shutting his eyes he pushed out the thoughts of who he was treating and focused on the magic. He let his senses take over and followed the healing stones lead.

# 20

# The Way Forward

## *Mellissa*

My heart felt heavy as I watched Radius being placed down on the bed in the guest room. This was where he had been staying since arriving at the castle. Greg's hands glowed yellow as he checked Radius over again.

I looked round the room, but he didn't have much in here. This wasn't his home. Radius home was in the ocean. That's where his family was. I knew he was in contact with them but how would I have been able to communicate with them if something happened to him. What would I have done if he hadn't survived? If I hadn't got to him in time. Shaking my head I forced myself not to think of these what ifs. Radius was healed.

Greg walked over to me. "He's going to be fine." He interlaced his fingers with mine. "Come, let's get out of these blood-soaked clothes." I nodded and followed him out of the room. We walked in silence up the stairs and down the corridor to my room.

Once in my room, Greg headed towards the bathroom but I stopped in the middle of the room. Greg turned back to me and frowned. "What's wrong?"

My chest felt tight. "Is Radius really going to be alright?"

Greg nodded. "Yes, but he may have a scar."

My fingers shot to my stomach feeling for the uneven skin there. I could feel the raised line through my clothes. The scars left behind from being stabbed. Had I looked as awful as Radius had? Or what about the first time I had faced Kadon. I had almost died. I would have died if Greg hadn't been there to heal me. My eyes filled with tears. I strode across the room and threw my arms round Gregs neck. He hugged me as I buried my face in his chest. "I'm sorry."

He stroked my hair. "What for?"

"All the times I looked like that, and you had to heal me." I shook my head as tears rolled down my cheeks. "That was awful. I thought he was dead, and you said that you've had to heal me from worse."

"I didn't say that to guilt you. They were just making it hard to focus."

"I know that, but it just made me think. Seeing Radius like that was hard enough but if that had been you." Shacking my head I pushed those thoughts away. "I couldn't do what you do."

"It's a good thing that I'm the healer then." Greg cupped my face in his hands, stroking my cheeks with his thumbs. "But seriously focusing on my healing skills is what gets me through those situations. It would feel a lot worse having your fate in someone else's hands." He kissed my forehead. "Now let's get in the shower." I slid my hand into his and let him lead me into the bathroom.

Knocking at my door had me moving. I grabbed a towel and wrapped my wet hair as I walked. I entered the living room to find Josh and Greg chatting. Josh handed a pile of papers to Greg, pointing to things as he spoke.

"What's going on?" I asked.

Josh waved awkwardly. "Gregory let me in. Sorry I thought I had left a reasonable amount of time after the whole

Radius thing before coming up here." He flashed his hands around as he spoke. "But if you still need more time."

"Josh it's fine," I said putting my hand out as I stepped in front of him. "Have you found something?"

"But you have a towel on your head," he said pointing at my head.

I raised a brow as I crossed my arms. "You know how long it takes for curls like ours to dry."

He bobbed his head side to side. "True."

"Josh just tell her," interjected Greg.

"I think I have the solution you were looking for." He grinned as he rolled back and forth on his heels. "You wanted to talk to the world leaders, right?" I nodded and Josh smile grew wider. He grabbed the papers from Greg and began laying them out on the floor. It looked like he was doing a puzzle. I knelt down to get a closer look. Combined the pages looked to be the blueprints of a building. Once he was done laying the pages out, he pointed to a spot on the page. "I was thinking if you teleport in here, you can crash their meeting to plead our case and get the humans off our back."

"I really think you have skipped a couple steps in this plan of yours. What meeting?" I pointed at the blueprints. "Where is this place?

"Oh, right I did miss out a few details." Josh let out a nervous laugh and his curls fell in his eyes.

"Josh when was the last time you slept?"

He shrugged, as he flicked his curly hair from his face. Dark circles rimmed his eyes. "I forget. Anyway, that's not important. The United Nations security council is meeting in three days' time. This is your chance to get some talk time with representatives who make important decisions in times of crisis."

"How do you know about this?"

Josh smirked. "I have my ways. Which involves a lot of caffeine and not sleeping."

I grasped his arm and squealed. "This is perfect Josh."

I jumped up and ran back into my bedroom. Roughly ringing the towel round my hair, I squeezed as much water out as I could. I threw the towel down and brushed my hair up into a ponytail. Pulling on a fluffy jumper I went back out into the living room. "Follow me. You can explain all this to me and Ignis at the same time."

"You want me to talk to the dragon," said Josh.

"Yep. It'll save time going over it twice." I helped Josh gather the papers up off the floor. I kissed Greg on the cheek. "Back in a bit." Linking arms with Josh, I led him out the room, down the corridor and the stairs. As we entered the foyer a shrill voice called my name. I winced at the sound and turned round to see Beatrice marching towards me.

"There you are," Beatrice yelled, "It's about time you showed your face."

I took a deep breath and relaxed my face trying to show no emotion. "What can I do for you Beatrice?"

"You can tell me what you are going to do about those humans. They bombed Highwish."

"Funny you should say that" I said, "Josh and I were just on our way to discuss that very issue with Ignis. You are free to tag along."

Beatrice marched to the castle doors and threw them open. "Come on then." We walked out the castle and through the trees. The cold air prickled my skin. The wet grass squelched beneath our feet as we walked. Beatrice huffed. "I told you my city should have been a priority, but you said it would be fine because it was an island. Yet it has now burned to the ground."

"I'm sorry about what happened to Highwish," I stuffed my hands in my jumpers' pockets lowing my gaze. "At least no lives were lost."

"Yes, but Radius was injured."

My chest tightened and I felt my eyes sting at her words. "But Greg healed him."

Beatrice pursed her lips. "My city is ash and rubble."

We stepped out of the trees and into the clearing. "Oh look we are here." I walked ahead into Ignis' cave. There was a small fire burning Rowan was sat warming his hands beside it.

"Queen Mellissa," said Ignis from the back of the cave, "I hope you bring us good news. How is Radius?"

"He is all healed up and resting. I have brought Josh with me," I ushered Josh forward. "He has an idea of how to communicate with the humans."

"You mean the amazing adviser of yours that you keep talking about."

"I don't know about amazing," stuttered Josh, "but yes that's me."

I placed my hand on his shoulder. "You are pretty amazing." Joshes cheeks went red. I pointed behind me. "Beatrice is here too."

Ignis came closer to the fire, his auburn eyes glowing in the light. "What is this idea of yours?"

I patted Josh on the back encouraging him forward. We moved closer to the fire. Josh placed the pieces of the blueprints on the floor. Rowan peered at them. "What are these?"

"They are the blueprints of a building," replied Josh Rowan frowned. "A blue what?"

"Think of them as a map of a particular building."

"Why is this building important?"

"This is where the United Nations security council will be having a meeting," explained Josh, "A group of very important humans will be meeting about the current crisis we face. Well, their view on it."

"This is the opportunity we have needed." I said, "World leaders in one place so I can-"

"We can bomb that place," interjected Beatrice. She shoved past me and jabbed her finger at the plans on the ground. "Take them out in one go. See how they like having their cities burnt to the ground."

"What no," I said. "I want to reason with them. Show them that we are not the threat they think we are."

She glared at me as her top lip curled. "And let them get away with what they did to Highwish."

"What happened in Highwish was awful, but no lives were lost. If we retaliate with force, we are only proving them right. That we are something to fear."

"They started this fight," snarled Beatrice, "I say we fight fire with fire."

"And then we all get burned," I yelled.

Beatrice sucked her teeth making a 'tsk' sound. "I'm sure the dragon knows what I'm talking about. Fire is his specialty."

"I do know a lot about fire," said Ignis, "Which is why we have to at least try a peaceful approach first. We haven't been able to communicate properly with the humans since the veil was destroyed." He huffed and a plume of smoke filled the cave. "We must give talking a chance and only if that fails," Ignis shook his head. "We will cross that bridge only if we have to."

Beatrice growled. As she clenched her fists the vein on her forehead bulged. "You are both ridiculous."

Ignis sighed. "No I just do not want a never ending war. If we retaliate with force what then? They retaliate right back and the loop continues."

"No one wins," I said, "We've gotta give peace a chance."

"Whatever, you go talk things out with your humans." Beatrice scowled at me. "But I will not hesitate to say I told you so, when your little plan backfires."

"I wouldn't expect anything less." I gritted my teeth and turned back to Josh, who was staring at us with a bewildered expression. "This building they are meeting in where is it?" I asked.

"Oh New York," replied Josh, "It is gonna have a hell of a lot of security, but they don't have any measures to stop your teleporting." Josh continued to explain the lay out. We had three days to prepare ourselves. As we spoke a sinking feeling of dread absorbed me. Beatrice kept glaring at me. Even when I wasn't looking at her, I could feel her stare boring into the back of me. I had made a mistake bringing her with me.

*My head is spinning. Memories of the past reel through my mind. I'm at a ball dancing with a prince. He bows and kisses my hand, "I'm prince Kadon."*

*The images blurs and we are together walking through a market. I pick up a pastry and we talk. The image shatters and now we are facing each other in battle.*

*It feels like my brain is on fire, as the scene changes again. I'm by the tree of time. I place my hand on its trunk my magic is seeping into it. I fall to the ground my power drained. Forcing myself up I take the heart crystal into my hands. My eyes sting as I feel them filling with tears. The Crystal shines brightly. "I am doing this for you. I am sending this message with the Heart, so you understand why I did this." The image splinters and suddenly there are two of me. No that's not it. I'm no longer seeing this memory from Freya's perspective. Freya is sat beside me. Talking to the crystal. "I am not the light of hope this world needs. You are my child. You will bring peace to this world in a way I never could." She repeats the line again. "I love you, Marissa."*

*Freya's image begins to blur but her voice rings loudly all around me. "You are my child- bring peace to this world - I love you." Clasping my ears I try to dull the pain in my mind. "You are the light of hope," says Freya so clearly like she is talking directly to my soul.*

*My heart feels like it is being smashed to pieces and my head is throbbing. I cry out forcing myself awake.*

Sweat dripped down my back as I bolted up into a sitting position. My heart raced as I gasped for air.

"Mellissa, what's wrong?" asked Greg. He placed his hand on my shoulder, and I flinched away. He pulled his hand back and put his hands up in front of him like he is surrendering. "I'm sorry, I didn't mean to startle you."

"It's fine." Taking a deep breath, I rubbed my head with my arm. "It was a dream."

"A dream that seems to have spooked you."

"It wasn't a normal dream." I pulled my legs up to my chest and wrapped my arms round my knees. "I saw Freya's memories. They are ones I have seen before, but they were disjointed and all over the place."

"Did you gleam anything new?"

I pressed my fingers to the side of my head. "At first it was just glimpses of parts of her life but the end- It felt like Freya herself was trying to talk to me."

"Is that possible?"

"I dunno." I said shrugging. "If I'm gonna get messages from people who are dead, I'd prefer to talk to my dad." Tears rolled down my cheeks. The thought of my dad had me blubbering. I brushed at my face with my palms. Those feeling about him had been pushed down deep and locked away but my mention if him opened a flood gate of emotions. "His advice would be so much more useful to me than these garbled memories of Freya. My dad always knew just the right thing to say." Greg shuffled closer, placing his arm round my shoulders, and pulling me close. Curling myself into his arms, I rested my head on his chest. I snivelled as I dried my eyes with the back of my hand. "I'm sorry."

"You have nothing to apologise for." His breath was warm on the top of my head as he traced circles along my arm. A wave of dread suddenly swept through me. My body went tense as I pushed away from Greg. "What's wrong?" he asked.

"Don't you feel that?" I got out of bed and stood in the middle of my room. Taking slow breaths, I focused on the eerie aura in the air.

Greg got up and stood beside me. "What are you sensing?"

"I don't know. Something isn't right." A jolt shot through my body and I ran out the room, through my living room and out the door into the corridor.

Greg followed close behind. "What's going on?"

"Someone is or was up here that shouldn't be." We ran down the corridor and turned right towards Victoria and Harkura's rooms. Laxus was bunking with Harkura, and that was where my senses told me I needed to be. I gasped as I saw Harkura's room door hung open. We both slowed down and entered the room on high alert.

The room was dark and both beds empty. It felt like my heart stopped as my eyes landed on Harkura sprawled out on the floor. "Harkura," I cried. Tears filled my eyes as I ran to his side. I dropped to my knees and went to touch him but my hands froze, hovering above him just out of reach.

Greg knelt on the floor on the opposite side of Harkura. "Vulnere," he muttered. His hand glowed yellow and he hovered them over Harkura's body. "It's okay he has just been dosed with sleeping powder."

Tears streamed down my cheeks. My chest heaved as breathing became hard. Greg leaned over and grabbed my shoulders. He looked me in the eye. "Mellissa," he said firmly. "He is alive."

I stared into his emerald eyes. His gaze pulled me out of my panic. "He's just asleep?"

"Yes." Greg let go of me and looked down at Harkura. Now that I wasn't panicking, I could see the slight rise and fall of his chest as he took a breath. "But someone did this to him," said Greg with a frown.

My pulse quickened as I jumped to my feet and looked around the room. "Laxus," I shouted. He wasn't in the room.

"Laxus," I shouted louder running into the en-suite. The bathroom was empty. I ran back into the room. "He's gone."

Victoria walked in rubbing her eyes. "What is all the noise about?" Her jaw dropped as she saw Harkura on the floor and she was at his side in a flash. "Oh my god what happened?"

"Laxus is missing." I yelled tugging at my hair. "We need to find him."

Greg placed his hand on Victoria's shoulder. "Harkura is fine. I'll stay with him. You two go."

Victoria nodded. She marched over to me and clasped my hand. "Mellissa, teleport."

"But where?" I yelled. My face felt warm as my heart raced.

"Calm down," she said, "Just think of Laxus."

She was right I was too worked up to be of any use at the moment. Taking slow breaths I steadied my reeling mind. Closing my eyes I focused on Laxus. I let thoughts of the blue hair pixie fill my mind. The heart glowed as my magic latched onto his aura and I teleported.

We materialised in front of Beatrice. Her eyes went wide as her nostrils flared. We were on the edge of the forest, a few steps away from the city's barrier. Beatrice was dressed all in black. Behind her was a small group of changelings from Highwish. Two of them had Laxus laid out on a stretcher.

"What is this?" I asked.

Victoria put her arm out in front of me. "They're traitors."

A chill spread through the air as her hands glowed. Ice smashed into the two holding Laxus. They screamed dropping him. Victoria ran at them firing more ice. The group scattered. Beatrice launched at her and threw a vial. Victoria whirled round and created a barrier of ice. The vial shattered and dust filled the air around it. Thrusting her arms forward, Victoria shifted the ice forward slamming it into Beatrice. As Victoria went to attack again, a gush of water slammed into her from within the forest. She crashed to the ground. Beatrice scrabbled over smashing another vial in Victoria's face. Her eyelids drooped and she passed out.

I ran to her side sliding to the floor beside her. I shook her shoulders, but she was fast asleep. "What did you do?"

The group of changelings ran through the barrier. Beatrice waved her hands around frantically. "Quick get the boy while Mellissa is still dazed."

Kai and Akito emerged from the trees. They ran to where Laxus lay and bent to pick him up. Anger rolled through me. My magic surged. "No," I screamed. The earth rumbled knocking them away from Laxus. Power surged through me as I glowed, filling the area with light. They staggered to Beatrice and grabbed her arms. "We are no match for the Queen," yelled Kai.

"But we need him as an offering," shouted Akito.

I stamped my foot and the earth shifted rolling Laxus over to me. "You won't be taking him anywhere." I gritted my teeth as I plunged my magic into the soil beneath my feet. "In fact, you won't be going anywhere." Vines shot up from the ground and launched at the three of them.

"Run," cried Kai. He and Akito slashed at the vines with water whips. They ran but my plants followed them. As they ran through the barrier Beatrice chanted. "Kadon the almighty, we pledged allegiance to you."

A portal opened. My pulse quickened and I launched forward. As I crossed the barrier a flurry of shadows burst out the portal and slammed into me hurling me back into city limits. I was back on my feet in a flash, but they were gone. The portal had closed as if it had never been there.

I scanned the area. Laxus and Victoria were both laid on the ground beside each other. I knelt beside them and felt for their pulses. I sighed with relief as I felt strong beats from them both. At least they were safe. Placing a hand on each of them I teleported back to the castle. We materialised back in Harkura's bedroom.

Greg had moved Harkura into bed and was just tucking him in. His eyes widened as he saw us. "You found him but what happened?"

"I think it's the same sleeping powder."

He ran round the bed and over to us on the bedroom floor. Gregs hands glowed yellow and he placed one over each of them. He nodded. "Your correct. It's sleeping powder. It'll be a few hours before they wake." With a flick of his wrists his hands stopped glowing. His forehead creased as he cupped my face in his hands. "What happened? Who took Laxus?"

My mouth moved but no words came. I gritted my teeth as the reality of what just happened sunk in. They had betrayed us. Beatrice, Kai and Akito had tried to take Laxus to Kadon. My chest felt tight. I didn't know whose betrayal hurt most. Even when we had disagreed, I had always thought ultimately our goals had been the same. I was so stupid. Beatrice had been waving red flags in my face for days. But Kai and Akito, I hadn't seen that coming. I had been so sure Yuko wouldn't betray me that I assumed the same applied to them, but the truth was I didn't know them as well as I did her. Digging my nails into my palms I forced the lump in my throat down. "It was Beatrice," I said forcing the words out. "Kai and Akito too."

The colour drained from his face as he too seemed to lose his words. We just sat there on the floor staring at each other. With no words available to describe the pain of this betrayal.

# 21

# Betrayal

## *Gregory*

reg clenched his fists and unclenched them as he paced the length of Mellissa's living room. He knew not everyone was happy with their current situation, but he hadn't expected this. How could they choose Kadon after everything he had done? Kadon had murdered Lady Gabrielle. Rage swirled around inside him. He didn't know what to do with it, so he just kept pacing.

Lee sat resting against the small table. "I can't believe she betrayed me." He muttered to himself for what must have been the hundredth time. He sipped his glass of whiskey. Hogan had placed it in front of the man fifteen minutes ago. It had been a full bottle, and it was already half empty. Yuko was hunched over sat on the floor beside an armchair. Mellissa had her arms round the high priestess, as the women cried uncontrollably.

Once Victoria and Laxus were comfortable in bed, they had called guards to watch their doors and gone back to Mellissa's rooms. From here they had requested the presence of the council. None of them had known what the others had done. Upon hearing about Kai and Akito's betrayal Yuko had collapsed to the floor where she had been stood. Lee was next to buckle. The others had left to do head counts to see if anyone else was missing.

"I should have been able to stop them," Yuko cried out. "If I was a better high priestess_"

Mellissa gently rubbed her back. "You are not to blame." Yuko threw her arms round Mellissa' neck and cried on her shoulder. Mellissa's face was tight. Her eyes burned with anger, but she gently cooed and comforted Yuko.

Greg gritted his teeth as he tried to keep the bubbling anger inside him at bay. He had been so stupid telling Mellissa that no one would join Kadon. And of all people it had to be Beatrice. *'What was wrong with the changeling leadership?'* he thought to himself. First Emerson had sold them out to Humarya and now Beatrice had joined Kadon. They had both been a challenge to work with at times, but he had trusted them both.

The door to the room opened and in walked Kate. Greg turned and looked at her expectantly. "I have done a head count, and all witches are accounted for," announced Kate. "Not one has left."

"At least my subjects are loyal," said Lee. He hiccupped as he poured himself another glass. "My ex-wife is probably loving this."

Kate sat on the floor beside Lee and placed her hand over his. "Don't think like that. No one would take any glee in this."

"But I picked Beatrice. She was my bumble Bea," stuttered Lee. "I thought she felt the same but she just up and left without a word."

Greg sighed as he sat in the armchair beside where they were on the floor. "I never thought she would do this either."

Lee shook the remains of the bottle of whiskey at Greg. "Want some?"

Greg's forehead creased as he looked at the drunk man. His feelings were real, he felt just as betrayed maybe more so than Greg did. "You know what I think I will." Greg took the whiskey and took a swig straight from the bottle. As the liquid hit the back of his throat he felt the welcome burn. He took another sip and handed it back to Lee.

Lee swayed as he pointed at Greg. "That's how it's done."

Brandon coughed. He stood in the doorway to the room. "Your Majesty." His chiselled grey features were serious.

Mellissa stood and waved him in. "Brandon, what have you got to report?"

He walked over to Mellissa and took a knee, placing his arm across his chest. "Not one Leprechaun has left our campsite. I counted them myself. As I told you before, we are loyal only to you. We will not follow Kadon ever again." Mellissa gestured for him to stand, and he did. He peered round the room. "Kadon promises the world but all he brings is destruction. He knew people would be angry about Perluves and Highwish, so he gave them an option of revenge."

Mellissa's forehead creased. "We need to convince the humans to stand down. When they see peaceful methods working maybe…" She didn't finish her sentence as her gaze lowered to the ground.

Brandon frowned. "Even if we get the humans to stand down, I do not think it will win our people back."

The air was thick with the tension. Mary walked in through the open door, followed by Hogan and Caleb. "What is it Mary?" asked Greg standing and walking over to them.

"All the fairies are accounted for. Lord Ping sends his apologies for not noticing the movement in the forest." Mary gripped her tabular tightly to her chest as she gulped. "However, there are forty changelings missing." Greg's chest tightened as he ground his teeth. Mary placed her hand on his shoulder. "All the missing changelings are from Highwish. Not one person from our city left." The tension in Greg's body eased slightly but it didn't completely go away.

Mellissa joined the group, standing beside Greg. "What of the dwarfs and water nymphs?" she asked.

Hogan and Caleb glanced at each other. "All the dwarfs are present," replied Hogan.

Caleb coughed as he tugged at the neck of his top. "Over a hundred water nymphs are gone." Caleb looked at the clip board he was holding and ran his finger down the page. "Only 64 remain mostly children, 65 including the High priestess."

A high pitch shriek filled the room as Yuko burst into hysterical crying. She burrowed her face in her hands. Hogan ran over to Yuko and hugged her tight, his face a wash with worry. Mellissa took the clipboard from Caleb. "How have so many left? I only saw maybe ten people with Beatrice." Mellissa's small frame began to shake as she gripped tightly to the board looking over the checklist Caleb had made.

Greg put his arms round her and rubbed her shoulders. "We'll figure this out." Mellissa leaned into him as all her energy seemed to drain from her. The anger he had felt from her seemed to have dissipated.

"Is there anything we can do to get them back?" asked Mary.

"It's not like they've been captured," replied Greg. "They chose to leave."

The room was silent for a moment accept Yuko's sobs. Brandon stomped his foot as he clenched his fists. "This isn't right. Did Freya not fore see this? Surely, she knew her veil couldn't last forever?"

Mellissa gasped. "That's it." She clasped Brandons hand causing him to blush. "Freya had some sort of plan; I saw it in a dream. I just need to figure out how to see the rest of that memory." She lifted the heart crystal from around her neck and peered at it. "Ignis said I could access all the memories of the keepers before me if I asked the right questions." She peered at Greg. "Our new task is to figure out what the right question is."

Greg put his hands round hers. "I think right now everyone needs to rest."

She glanced around the room. "You're right. Everyone go get some rest. Tonight has been hard."

Slowly everyone left. Brandon supported Yuko in her distressed state and vowed to stay with her as long as she needed. Kate was almost carrying a drunken Lee as they staggered out. Caleb and Hogan bowed and left.

Mary gripped Greg's hand. "You know where I am if you need me."

"I know thank you." Greg shut the door once she left. He turned round to see Mellissa sat on the coffee table the heart crystal hovering in front of her.

"What was Freya's plan to deal with the humans?" She peered at the crystal, but nothing happened. "What is the message Freya left for her daughter?" She groaned as the crystal didn't respond. She snatched the crystal out of the air.

Greg walked over and sat on the sofa behind her. "I thought we were all getting some rest."

She glanced back at him. "No, I told everyone else to get rest I never said I was."

"Mellissa, you need to sleep too."

She shook her head. "If I go to bed now, I will just lay there awake my mind reeling about everything that has happened. I need to do this." Her voice shook as she rolled her shoulders. "If there is a chance that Freya did leave a message with the Heart I need to know."

Greg laid back on the sofa getting comfortable "Then what would be the right question?"

"If I knew that I would have already asked it."

Greg rubbed his chin. "One of your dreams before showed you Freya never meant for the veil to be permanent."

"Yeah, she believed her daughter once grown could bring balance between those with magic and those without it."

"Why go to the trouble of using up the last of her magic to create the veil just to have it destroyed?"

Mellissa shrugged. "To protect Marissa. She was only a baby." Mellissa gasped. "That's it." She straightened her back and focused on the Heart crystal.  She opened her fist and the crystal floated up in front of her.  "Heart crystal, why did Freya create the veil?"  The Crystal hummed and shined brightly. Greg sat up as the crystal shone brighter. He leaned forward peering at the crystal floating in front of her. They both flinched as rays shot from it and Freya was stood in front of the coffee table. Her dark brown skin was smeared with blood and ash. Her hair was pulled up into a ponytail her long curls hanging down her back. Mellissa reached out to her, but her hand went through her. Greg walked round the table staring at the image in front of them. "It's a hologram," he said.

Freya smiled sweetly; her eyes glistened with tears. Her gaze low. "I am doing this for you. I am sending this message with the Heart, so you understand why I did this. So that you will know what to do next." She looked up her eyes filled with tears. "I am not the light of hope this world needs. You are my child. You will bring peace to this world in a way I never could." She placed her hand over her heart. "I have failed to defeat the darkness. Kadon is too powerful for me. My plan to seal him away won't last forever, which is why I'm creating the veil. You and the elves will be protected on the other side with the humans. This will give your father time to train you. Once you are ready to return, the crystal will give you the power to bring the veil down and re-join our worlds. Be the light in the dark my darling child. Be the ray of hope that re-joins our worlds and leads us to a better united future. Hopefully, the time I give you now will be enough for you to find a way to defeat Kadon for good. I wish so much I could be with you. To guide you." Tears rolled down her cheeks. "I love you, Marissa."

The image disappeared and the crystal stopped shining. A loud thud snapped Greg out of his trance. He turned to see the crystal fallen on the coffee table and Mellissa on the floor in tears. Greg knelt down and pulled her into a hug. "What's wrong? You did it. You accessed the message like you wanted."

Mellissa snorted as she wiped her eyes with the back of her hand. "Don't you see.  I am Freya's plan and I've royally screwed everything up."

A lumped formed in Greg's throat. She was right. Freya's plan had been to entrust the future of the world to the next generation. Greg stroked Mellissa's damp cheek.  "You didn't screw this up. Freya was the one who put up the veil and separated us all but forgot to make sure the Heart Crystal actually made it to her daughter."

"She didn't know that would happen."

Greg gritted his teeth. "That doesn't matter. She is the reason the humans were separated from magic for so long that they are now scared of us."

"She never meant for this to happen."

"And neither did you or any of us for that matter. We were just born into this world and expected to deal with what our ancestors left behind."

Mellissa giggled through her tears. "When you put it like that it is kinda sucky."

Greg brushed her hair from her face. "You were not raised to rule like Freya was." He kissed her forehead. "But you have risen up every time you have needed to. And I know you would never willingly pass the task on to anyone else especially not a child."

"She was dying Greg."

"She had no right to make such a big decision for us all."

Mellissa brows furrowed as she pouted. "Maybe your right. Even with Kadon's return things would have been easier if the world had never been divided."

"I believe you can unite our world once again. Not because of some prophecy but because of who you are." Greg rested his forehead on hers. "From the moment I met you I knew you were like no one I had met before. You bring hope wherever you go."

"We'll find our own way through this together." Mellissa tilted her head upwards and kissed him. Her lips tasted of her salty tears. She pressed closer to him and wrapped her arms round his neck. He held her tight because she was everything to him. With all his heart he believed that Mellissa truly was the light of hope.

# 22

# A Guardians Responsibility

## *Victoria*

"I swear when I get my hands on Beatrice," Victoria yelled as she paced the length of her room. "I'm gonna turn her into an icicle and shatter her into tiny pieces."

"Not if I get to her first," said Harkura. He was sat in the middle of her bed with his legs crossed and a scowl on his face. "She'll be ash in seconds." He clicked his fingers, a plume of smoke drifted up from his hand.

Laxus was curled in a ball on the end of the bed. "Do you guys have to be so loud? My head still hurts. It feels like they whacked me over the head instead of sleeping powder."

Mellissa peered at the pixie with sad eyes, from her seat at the dressing table. "Greg said it was highly concentrated to make it work quicker."

A new wave of anger shot though Victoria. She knew exactly how Laxus was feeling. When she had woke that morning, she felt like she had been on an all-night bender. Her head had been pounding and her throat sore. But then as she had recalled last night's events rage had consumed her. She had just been about to go in search for Mellissa when the girl had appeared at her door along with Harkura and Laxus. Images of last night in the forest flashed though Victoria's mind. She would have beat Beatrice if those other two hadn't been hiding in the trees. "And what Kai and Akito did. The next time I see them." Victoria stopped pacing and started punching the air envisioning the two water nymphs. "Somehow what they did feels worse."

"Even water magic users will succumb to my flames," said Harkura.

"Guy's this isn't what I wanted to talk about," interjected Mellissa.

Victoria arched a brow. "Wait, you didn't call this little meeting in my bedroom to discuss how to destroy those traitorous snakes?"

Harkura flicked a small dagger between his fingers. "Just give the word and I'll go hunt them down." He looked at Mellissa is features sharp and serious.

"No, I don't want you to do that." She narrowed her eyes at him. "Where did you even get that dagger from?"

Continuing to flick the blade back and forth he smirked. "I told you before I'm always armed." He flicked the wrist of his empty hand and produced another blade. Mellissa grumbled as she leaned on the dressing table and rested her head on her hands. Shaking her hands out Victoria began pacing again. She had so much anger building up in her that she couldn't stay still. She was itching for a fight. "What is the plan then?"

"I don't know," Mellissa shrugged as she shook her head. "A council meeting is scheduled later today about that." Her shoulders sagged as her gaze lowered. "Well, what is left of the council."

Victoria's heart felt tight as she took in Mellissa small frame. Her warm brown skin had lost its usual glow and her gaze seemed distant. It was like she was staring down at something through the floor that Victoria had no hope of seeing. Placing her hand on Mellissa's shoulder Victoria sighed. "Are you okay?"

Mellissa shook her head. "No, I need to talk to you guys before bringing this up at the meeting. To check I'm not being crazy." Mellissa finally looked up from the carpet. Her big eyes full of worry. "Last night made me realise that Laxus can't stay here any longer."

Victoria's jaw went slack. "You're gonna send him away." Mellissa nodded as her jaw tensed.

Laxus shot up into a seated position at the end of the bed. "You can't do that."

Mellssa walked over to Laxus and took his hands in hers. "I can't keep you safe here."

"Where else am I meant to go?" The boys bottom lip quivered as he looked up into Mellissa's eyes. "I can't go back to the pixies."

"I have a plan." She knelt so her face was level with the boys. "The idea is to keep you moving around. If you don't stay in one place, you'll be hard to find."

Laxus frowned as he rubbed his chin. "That makes sense, but I don't know if I could do that by myself."

"I don't intend for you to go alone."

Victoria grabbed Mellissa's shoulder. Tugging at her forcing her to stand and face her. She wagged her finger in the girl's face. "You are not sending me away with him. I refuse to leave you."

Mellissa gently placed her hand over hers. "I know and I don't want you too. This needs to end and I don't know if I can do that." Stomping her foot Mellissa groaned and looked up at the ceiling. "My hesitation is what lead to this. Even after everything Humarya had took from me I couldn't kill her. It was my failure to stop her that allowed Kadon to take her out and steal the dark stones for himself."

Victoria gave her friends hand a squeeze. "Mellissa, none of this is your fault."

"I don't know who's fault this all is but what I do know is that I need you and Harkura by my side. When it comes down to it I know you both won't hesitate if I do waiver."

"You've got that right," said Harkura. "I will not hesitate to destroy anyone who threatens my Queen." He flipped both daggers round grasping both their hilts and slashing down at the air.

Victoria's forehead creased as she peered at Mellissa. "If not either of us, then who?"

Mellissa turned to her and opened her mouth to talk when Matt burst into the room. "Hey," he said panting, "That Samson guy said you needed me."

Victoria narrowed her eye at her brother and curled her top lip. "Why are you panting like that?"

"He also told me what happened last night, and I wanted to check on you." He pointed at Victoria and clicked his tongue. "But you are obviously doing fine, so no need to worry. Can't believe I slept through all that." Victoria cringed as he wiped the sweat dripping from his forehead with the back of his hand. Matt pointed to the bed. "Can I sit there?"

Victoria marched over to the bed and sat next to Harkura blocking her brother. She crossed her arms. "No, you can't. Now shut the door." She pointed at the open door. "I know our mother raised you better."

Matt huffed as he shut the door, he had left open. He turned back to his sister. "Happy."

"No but it's an improvement. What did you want Matt?"

"I'm so glad you were uninjured last night." Matt pulled a face at her, and she responded with her own rude gesture. "Hey, I was called for by the Queen." He bowed dramatically in front of Mellissa. "At least that's what Samson said. He wasn't having me on, was he?"

"Samson is not that sort of guy," said Victoria, "If he said Mellissa asked for you then she did." With one eyebrow raised she peered at Mellissa. "Why did you want him?"

Mellissa stood, interlacing her fingers as she did. "I was actually just explaining that to you."

Harkura's daggers fell onto the mattress. "You're sending him?"

"More like asking," replied Mellissa.

"Asking me what?" Matt winked as he gave Mellissa a crooked grin. "What does the Queen want with little old me?"

Rolling her shoulders back Mellissa took a deep breath. "The tree of time and you are now one and this has given you new abilities." Mellissa peered at Matt, and he nodded. She stepped closer to him so that she was in front of him. "Last night we were betrayed, and they tried to take Laxus with them." Mellissa's gaze turned to the pixie boy. "It is no longer safe for him here." She looked up at Matt her brown eyes wide. She took his hand in hers. "I know I have no right to ask this."

Matt reached forward brushing a stray hair form Mellissa's face. He smiled as he made a goofy face. "Mellissa you are my best friend you can ask me anything."

"Excuse you, who is her best friend?" protested Victoria.

"Hey, the girl can have more than one best friend."

Victoria crossed her arms and smirked. "But I'm number one."

Matt made a rude gesture at his sister, and she made one back. He rolled his eyes. "Fine you can be number one and I'm number two best friend."

"That's right." Victoria huffed.

Matt rolled his eyes at her and turned his attention back to Mellissa. "As I was saying, you can ask me anything, so go ahead and ask."

Mellissa stood tall, holding her head high. "Would you be willing to take Laxus on a journey. Protect him and keep him safe. Would you do this for me?"

The room had suddenly become too hot. Victorias head was spinning. Grabbing Harkura's arm, Victoria took in a sharp breath. All she could hear was her heart pounding in her chest, and Matt's voice. "Yes. I'll do it."

Harkura wrapped his arm round her shoulders. "It's okay, just take slow breaths."

Victoria's grip on Harkura's arm tightened. Her chest felt tight. Harkura shifted his position, so they were face to face. When his indigo eyes met hers, the fog in her mind cleared. It was like his stare had grounded her back in reality.

"Victoria are you okay?" asked Mellissa.

Letting go of Harkura, Victoria turned round and stood. "You can't go Matt. I'll do it instead."

"Victoria," Mellissa started.

Victoria jabbed her finger at Mellissa. "Don't Victoria me," she said imitating Mellissa's voice. "How could you not run this by me first?"

"I tried to, but we got side tracked by all the ways you are Harkura were going to get your revenge on Beatrice and co." Mellissa's bottom lip quivered. "I'm sorry but I need you here."

"I am not your subject," yelled Victoria, "You can't order me around and the same goes for my brother."

"She isn't ordering me to do anything," interjected Matt, "She asked a favour, and I said yes."

Victoria snickered. "Well, I'm not letting you. I'll do it instead."

"Vicky why do you think it's better for you to go in my place?" Matt's jaw tensed and he clenched his fists. "You think I can't keep the boy safe. Is that it? I'm the ex-guardian that messed up on our first proper mission. You think you're better at this than me."

"That's not it." Victoria turned her back on her brother, as she felt her eyes filling with tears. Clenching and unclenching her fists to try stop her feelings overwhelming her.

"Then what is it?" Matt asked, "Vicky look at me."

"I just got you back." She shouted as she whirled round to face him. "You haven't even seen mum and dad yet. There is no way you are going off all alone on some dangerous mission." Victoria clutched her hands to her chest. "I just got you back," she repeated her voice lowering to a whisper.

Matt pulled her into a hug squeezing her tight. "I'm sorry sis."

Victoria snorted and wiped her face on his t-shirt. "I don't think I'm better than you."

"You know I think you staying by Mellissa's side is actually the more dangerous job." Victoria scowled at him. He put his hands up in front of her. "Hey, you guys are actively going after Kadon, while Laxus and I will be hiding from him."

"I guess you have a point."

"Also, I don't plan for it just to be Matt and Laxus," said Mellissa, "There is someone else I need to talk to."

"Who?"

"I need to ask him first because I don't like just ordering people around."

"Sorry about that."

"It's fine you were just worried about your brother." Mellissa smiled but it didn't meet her eyes. Something else was on her mind. "Like Matt said, this is actually the safer mission."

Matt walked over to Laxus and held his fist out to the boy. "We'll be an awesome little team right." Laxus nodded as he pressed his fist to Matts.

Victoria's heart panged with guilt. She was so self-centred. She had just rejected the job and then caused a scene because she didn't want her brother doing it. Laxus safety was more important than her petty feelings. No wonder Matt had thought it's because she saw herself as more capable. With out stopping to think she would run into dangerous situations all the time. Hiding behind the fact it was her duty as a guardian, never thinking about how these things worried the people who cared about her. All those times she had gotten annoyed with Mellissa for doing the same thing she did. She knew what it was to be the person worrying but had never connected the dots, that there were people who worried about her.

Matt was more than capable, and his powers had grown since being trapped in the tree. She should have faith in Mellissa's plan. Even when they didn't always make sense, she usually knew what she was doing. And Matt was right this was the safer task. She looked at the other four people in the room. They were probably the most important people in her life. Her brother would return from this mission, but she wasn't as sure about the rest of their fates.

# 23

# Doubts

## *Gregory*

Greg paced in front of the cottage. His head was a mess. Thoughts of Beatrice's betrayal had plagued him late into the night. Why had she turned her back on her duties? She had left and abandon the very people they were meant to serve and protect? He wanted answers. Answers that he knew, even if he found her, Beatrice would never give him. But maybe Emerson would. Greg had made his way to the cottage that was now Emerson new prison. It was away from all the others and surrounded by guards. But he hadn't gone in. Instead, he had been walking up and down the length of the front of this house for almost half an hour. Greg stopped walking and stared at the red door. He glanced at the guard by the entrance. The guard nodded at him as if giving him permission to enter. Taking a deep breath, Greg opened the door. He stepped through the door into a cosy living room.

Emerson was sat in an armchair by the fire sipping tea. "I was starting to think you were never going to come in. Come sit I made tea." Emerson gestured to an arm chair across from him. In between the chairs was a wooden table with a pot of tea, milk, sugar, and a cup.

Greg sat down. Emerson placed his cup down and poured tea into the empty one. "Milk and sugar? Sorry I can't remember how you take it."

"Just milk no sugar."

Emerson poured some milk into the cup and stirred in until the liquid was a golden colour. Smiling he handed the cup to Greg. Taking the cup, Greg peered at the contents. "Don't worry it's not poison." Emerson held his hand out. "If you want, I'll take the first sip."

"No, I believe you." Greg sipped his tea. It tasted exactly as it should, strong and earthy but creamy. "This is much cosier than your last cell."

Emerson chuckled. "That it is. Queen Mellissa makes much nicer prisons than the warlocks." Interlacing his fingers he leaned back in his chair. "What can I do for you Gregory? We both know you didn't come here for tea and to admire my new cage."

Greg stared at the fire. Flames danced along the log in the hearth, warming the room. "Beatrice has betrayed us. She tried to kidnap Laxus and give him to Kadon."

"I assume Mellissa saved the pixie boy." Greg nodded without daring to look away from the flames. Emerson tutted. "Then what do you need from me?"

Placing his cup down, Greg leaned forward resting his elbows on his knees and letting his head hang. His mind was a mess. Why had he come to Emerson? He couldn't tell him why Beatrice did what she had. The why wasn't the problem. Greg swallowed the lump in his throat. "Is this the legacy of the changeling elders?" His heart hammered in his chest as he looked up at Emerson. "Are we all just destined to betray those who trust us? Who rely on us?"

"I see," Emerson pressed his lips together as he stroked his beard. "You're worried you will end up like me and Beatrice."

Greg snickered as he leaned back in his chair and looked up at the ceiling. "Or worse my mother."

"You could never be like her." Emerson growled as his top lip curled. "Gwendolyn is the most selfish person I've ever met with Beatrice being runner up." He sighed as he rubbed the bridge of his nose. "I was selfish. One thing you are not Gregory is selfish."

"You think?"

Emerson leaned forward and looked at Greg. His gaze and features sharp. "Us changelings like to think we are superior to everyone. We are the hubs of knowledge in the magic world. We are smarter than everyone else. And us that lead are the worst. Just because we don't call ourselves kings or Queens, we are a monarchy. We were brought up to rule over our people. I mean my whole deal with Humarya was so I could rule alone without you and Beatrice, and I bet she wants exactly the same now from Kadon."

"Was it really that bad working with us?"

"With you not so much. Beatrice yes." Emerson put his hands out to the fire and rubbed them together. "I was entitled Gregory and so is she. These humans have not welcomed us since the veil was destroyed. Beatrice wants to be adored again. It's why she never liked Mellissa. She was never in awe of her or any of us for that matter."

Greg's heart ached. Part of what made Greg love Mellissa is what made Beatrice hate her. He pressed his fingers to the sides of his temple, trying to process Emerson's words. "You say I'm not like you guys, but I was brought up to become an elder just as you were."

"Not quite the same." Emerson shook his head. "I actually think your mother faking her death is the best thing she ever did for you."

"Yes, because growing up motherless was such fun."

"It may have broken your father's heart, but it stopped you being brought up as a spoiled pampered prince. Your father didn't have enough time to raise you. Instead, you ended up with his assistant or your aunt Tilly. You actually spent time amongst the very people we are meant to be leading."

Greg thought back to his childhood. Growing up thinking his mum was dead and trying to live up to his father's impossible expectations had been hard but there had been good things as well. All the time he spent with Samson and his older cousin Cynthia had made his life less lonely. They were together so much they felt more like siblings. He had hated the days his dad had dragged him to the office with him. His assistant Anna would take him out with her on errands and he got to meet all sorts of people. The hard things had made him appreciate the good so much more.

"You're right Emerson." Standing up Greg stretched his arms out. "Thanks for the tea and the chat."

"Anytime Gregory, I'm not going anywhere."

"Prison has really changed you."

"It's given me perspective." Emerson interlocked his fingers and peered up at Greg. "Tell Mellissa if she ever needs a master illusionist, I'm her guy."

Greg nodded. "Bye Emerson." He walked out the cottage, closing the door behind him. As he strolled through the elf village towards the castle Greg could feel the tension in his body easing. He had thought he needed to know why Beatrice had betrayed them. Why Emerson and his mother had done what they did but that wasn't the case. His true goal was to make sure betrayal wasn't something all Elders were destined for. All this talk of prophecy had him starting to think all their fates were already written. But the future was still unknown. It's why the original vision had changed over time. The future was something they were creating right now. With every choice and action, they made. His talk with Emerson had given him perspective.

Greg walked into Mellissa's room and was greeted by her throwing her arms round him. He caught her and staggered into the room, closing the door as he did. "Hey what's wrong?"

She stepped back and smiled. "Nothing I was just a little worried when I came back and you weren't here."

Greg pulled his coat off and draped it over the back of the armchair. "I woke up and you were gone."

She scrunched her nose as she pouted. "Sorry about that. I was just worried about Harkura and Victoria."

"I know," He kissed her forehead as he walked past her, then sat in the sofa. "You were with them, right?"

"Yeah, but where did you go?" She came and sat next to him.

"I had tea with Emerson."

Her eyes went wide as her jaw dropped. "You what?"

"Beatrice betraying us was really bothering me. I'm now the only changeling elder left."

"So, you went to speak with Emerson about it and he helped."

"Yeah, he did." He leaned towards her and whispered. "Being locked up has given him perspective."

"Okay and he didn't try convince you to set him free?"

"Nope but he did say if you are in any need of an illusion, he is your guy."

"Wow he really has changed. Even before the whole betrayal thing he never wanted to help me." Mellissa took a deep breath as she took his hand. Greg stomach churned as she sucked her bottom lip in, her eyes darting around the room.

"What's wrong?" he asked.

"Nothing I just need to talk to you about something." She pushed her hair behind her ears. "About Laxus actually."

Greg shoulders sagged and he leaned back into the sofa. "Next time lead with that."

Her eyebrows raised as she waved her hands at him. "Sorry I didn't mean for it to sound like that but it is important."

He interlaced his fingers with hers. "I'm listening."

"I've already spoken to him about this and Harkura, Victoria and Matt."

Greg gritted his teeth as a wave of anger shot through him at the list of people, she had spoken to first. "And now me."

"To be honest I've been avoiding talking to you about it." She looked down at their fingers intertwined avoiding his gaze. "I know this is the right thing to do but at the same time I don't want it. I don't want any of this."

Greg stroked her cheek with his thumb, slowly running his fingers along her jaw he hooked his hand under her chin. Gently he tilted her head upwards, so she was looking at him. "Just tell me what the problem is."

"Laxus can't stay here anymore. He and Matt have agreed to go in to hiding together."

"You asked Matt to protect Laxus?" Mellissa nodded. Greg shrugged. "Then what's the problem?"

"I want," She took a deep breath as her grip on his hand tightened. "No, I need a healer to accompany them. One that I know can handle both Matt and Laxus."

"You want me to go." Letting go of her hand, Greg stood. He ran his fingers through his hair. "Are you sure about this?"

"Beatrice had Laxus. Kai and Akito, they all know too much. Laxus isn't safe near me."

"Thats not what I mean." Greg shook his head; his stomach was in knots. "Are you sure you want me to go? The last mission I went on, I screwed up big time."

"That wasn't your fault."

"Yes, it was. You told me not to go but I didn't listen. I was arrogant and now I have this permanent reminder of my failure." He jabbed his finger at the burn scar on his cheek. "You don't want me protecting Laxus. I couldn't even protect myself."

Mellissa stood and grasped his hands in hers. "None of what happened is your fault. You scar isn't a reminded of your failure." Her eyes filled with tears. "It's mine," she yelled. Greg was stunned into silence. She clutched her hand to her chest. "All of this is because I failed to kill Kadon properly the first time. Because I didn't end Humarya when I had the chance. My dad had just died I was so angry I had her beat, but I hesitated giving her the chance to get away."

Greg cupped her face in his hands. "No, none of that is true. You can't talk like that."

Tears rolled down her cheeks wetting his hands. She sniffled. "Then neither can you."

He rested his forehead on hers. "Deal." They stood like that in silence for a moment. He breathed in her cherry blossom scent and sighed. "But are you sure you want me to go?"

"I don't want you to but yes." She stepped back away from his touch. Brushing her hands over her face she dried her tears. "With Matt's new tree of time powers it should allow you all to stay hidden and escape if found. In a fight Matts fire is great for offense and you're skilled in defence. If one of you gets injured, you can heal them." She shrugged as she wriggled her nose. "You two will make a great team."

Greg chuckled. "When you put it like that Matt, and I sound like the perfect duo."

"I don't want you to go, when you're not here I feel like a part of me is missing. Like my heart can't be whole until you return." Her bottom lip quivered as she forced a smiled. "But I know this is the right thing to do."

Greg's heart felt like it was about to burst. He wanted to scoop her up and take her away from all of this, but he couldn't. That would be selfish and that was something he didn't want to be.  "I'll do it. Matt and I will be a fearsome duo and keep him safe. Just promise me you will beat Kadon and be here for me to return to."

Her eyes glistened. "You once said you'll always find your way back to me."

"I did."

"Well, I promise the same and it will actually be easier for me with my teleporting." In one large step Greg closed the gap between them, pulling her close and wrapping his arm round her waist. She tilted her head upwards staring into his eyes. He leaned in and kissed her. Her body pressed into his as her lips parted.  His finger ran through her hair getting tangled in her curls. She pressed her hands between their bodies and pulled away. Greg grumbled as their kiss ended too soon.

"We have a council meeting to prepare for." She bobbed his nose with her finger. "You are attending this time."

He pressed his lips to her cheek and trailed kisses along her neck. "We only have half a council, and this is more fun," he said between kisses. She tilted her head meeting his mouth with hers. She ran her fingers through his hair interlocking her fingers at the back of his neck. He ran his hands along the curves of her body pulling her closer to him.

She sighed as she placed her hands on his chest and gently pushed him back. "Stop tempting me we have a meeting. Victoria and Harkura will be here soon to go down with us."

He placed his hands on her hips tugging her closer. "That is what locks are for."

She pressed her fingers to his lips as he leaned in for a kiss. "Stop it, if you keep this up, I won't be able to resist."

He smirked and raised one brow. "That was my whole plan."

She gently pushed him back creating space between them. Fanning herself with her hands she walked towards the exit. "Let's go find my guardians before they barge in."

She opened the door and turned holding her hand out to him. He slid his hand into hers interlocking their fingers. Together they walked out the room. Greg looked down at his girlfriend as they walked. He could do this. This mission to hide Laxus would work out because this time they were on the same page. She had faith in him and he believed in her. They could do this. She was his light in the darkness.

# 24

# Those Who Remain

## *Mellissa*

I stood at the top end of the table in the second dining room. Harkura and Victoria either side of me.  All the members of the council had gathered here.  I looked around, recalling when I first met the council. So much had happened since then. Back then I had been a scared girl, unsure of her place amongst them. But now all of them were looking to me for answers.

The council members had also dwindled since then. Before everyone cared about who had the most representation and trying to dominate the meetings. With the destruction of the veil, and the latest set of betrayals, those things were no longer deemed important.  Greg was now the only Changeling left on the council. Both of his co-leaders had betrayed us. First Emerson to Humarya and now Beatrice to Kadon. Lord Ping had never replaced his old partner after his betrayal and the leprechauns only ever had Brandon on the council. Sir Cole had taken sole responsibility of the warlocks after Lady Gabrielle's death.  With Kai and Akito's betrayal, Yuko had become the sole representatives of the water nymphs. The only groups still with multiple council officials were the dwarfs, with Caleb and Hogan and the witches, represented by Kate and Lee.

The other two crystal keepers had joined us for the meeting. The second dining room had a large double window that opened out towards the gardens. This was where Ignis rested his head. Rowan stood beside him with his arms crossed. Radius was sat to my right. Everyone was quiet as they stared at me.  I pulled my chair out and gulped. This was where Lady Gabrielle should be sitting. Taking a deep breath a slid into my seat.

"I know everyone is still in shock with what has happened, but we need to push ahead with our plans."

"You mean the one where you persuade the humans that we are nice people," said Lee.

"Yes." I replied ignoring his condescending tone, "If we can get the humans to stand down then we can focus on the Kadon issue."

Lee groaned as he rolled his eyes. "Right because you did so well persuading our own people not to betray us."

"That is low even for you," snapped Greg glaring at the man.

"You seriously think you can just talk things out with them?" asked Lee.

"I think it's worth a try," replied Greg.

"So do I," said Radius. "I shall go with Queen Mellissa."

"Great," I said, "and you can do the talking."

Radius frowned as he rubbed his chin. "I do not think I am best suited for the job. I don't understand the humans like you do."

"I agree with the sea king," said Kate. My eyes widened as I looked at her. She placed her hands together on the table straightening her back and pressing his lips tightly pressed together. "You will have to be the one to convince them."

"I can't believe I'm about to say this," Yuko said, "but Kate is right. Queen Mellissa you are half human, half elf. A child of both worlds."

Lee groaned. "This is ridiculous."

"Will you pipe down?" Snapped Yuko, "I don't hear you coming up with any good ideas."

"Talking didn't stop Beatrice from walking out on me," yelled Lee, "I mean us. She walked out on us." Lees shoulders sagged as he hung his head. "I can't believe she betrayed me."

Kate placed one hand over his and rubbed his back with her other. Hogan slipped a metal flask out the inside pocket of his jacket. "Have some whiskey, it'll help." Lee took the bottle and took a large gulp. His face screwed up from the taste, but he took another swig.

Kate looked at me her eyes pleading with me. "I tried to warn you that having faith in everyone wasn't a good idea."

"I know," I said, "I just didn't want to believe it."

"I could have been clearer in my meaning. I could sense something was off with Bea." Kate lowered her glance staring at the table. "She was so angry about everything since the veil fell." Lee let out a quiet sob beside her. She gently rubbed his back. "I know how Lee can come across during meetings but deep down he does care. Bea on the other hand is exactly the same, actually worse in private. I'm the quiet one so she never took notice or tried to pretend to be nice in front of me." Her forehead creased as she frowned. "I should have come to you in private with my concerns. Made it clear what I suspected."

"I should have done more to prevent this," interjected Yuko, "I should have sensed how Akito and Kai were feeling." Yuko was hunched over placing her head in her hands.

"You are not to blame," I said, "No one here is."

"Mellissa's right," said Greg, "The only thing we can do now is push forward with a plan."

"What exactly is the plan?" asked Hogan.

"Radius and I go talk to the human leaders." I replied.

"I think all three crystal keepers should go," said Brandon, "To show a united front."

"I will not go," said Ignis in his gruff voice. "The humans fear me most, but I shall send Rowan in my place."

"So, its decided." Radius clapped his hands together. "Mellissa shall teleport the three of us to this UN place."

"The five of us," said Harkura.

"Mellissa is not going anywhere without us," said Victoria.

Harkura pounded his chest. "We are duty bound to protect her."

"Fine," I said, "The five of us."

Rowan stepped forward and clasped his hand over his chest. "It will be my honour to accompany you."

"And what of Laxus?" asked Caleb, "Beatrice tried to take him, and Gwendolyn attacked the castle to try kidnap the boy."

Greg reached for my hand under the table. He interlaced his fingers with mine and gave my hand a squeeze. My heart ached but it had to be done. "Laxus will be going into hiding with the protection of Greg and Matt. The plan is for them to stay on the move never staying in one place too long."

The group gasped. "Are you sure about this?" asked Yuko.

I held tight to Greg's hand. "Yes. Their combined powers are well suited for the job. Laxus will be safe with them."

Yukos mouth turned down and her eyes were full of worry. "That's not what I mean."

"I know but this is what makes sense." I took slow breaths trying to keep the appearance of control. "Kai especially knows how much Greg getting kidnapped by Humarya affected me. They won't expect me to be okay with sending him on another mission."

"I see your point." She rubbed her chin. "Well, if you are sure."

"I am." Interlacing my fingers I looked across the table. "Now all that's left is to go over what exactly we should say to the humans."

We spent the next few hours going over the plan and what I should say. My chest felt tight and my body tense, but I pushed my feelings down. I would not crumble. I would see this through.

I was sat on the end of my bed watching Greg pack. He was filling a large rucksack with supplies. With every item he packed the more real this all became. He was leaving in the morning, and I was crashing a UN security meeting.

"Is it really selfish that I don't want you to go?" I asked.

"No, it's not." He stopped packing and walked over to the bed standing in front of me. Leaning forward he pressed a kiss to my forehead. "I think it's a perfectly normal way to feel."

"The problem is that there is no end date to this." I crossed my arms and pouted. "I think this would be easier if I knew when you were coming back."

"I won't be gone long because you're going to defeat Kadon."

"You don't know that."

"Yes, I do because I believe in you." Leaning on the end of the bed he looked at me his emerald eyes sparkling with mischief and smirked. "Just say the word and I'll stay."

Heat flooded my body as my heart pounded in my chest. "Don't look at me like that." I covered my face with my hands so I couldn't see him. "You make it hard to do the right thing."

He tugged at my hands pulling them away from my face. I squeezed my eyes shut. "If I look at you, I'll get lost in your stare."

"Stop ruining my plans." His breath was warm on my cheek as he spoke. A shiver ran through me as he pressed kisses along my jaw. His fingers slid round my waist, and he tickled me. I jerked sideways giggling. I tried to roll away, but he had me pinned. "Fine you win." I said as I swatted his hands away.

He prodded my side. "I still don't see your beautiful brown eyes."

"Move away first." I felt him shift away, leaving me with a chill. Opening my eyes I sat up and turned to him. His stare turned my heart mush. "That's not fair."

He held his hands up. "I'm not doing anything." A smile crept along his face as he shuffled closer. "Do you remember when we first met?"

"How can I forget? You were a talking rabbit."

Greg laughed. "Yeah, you were pretty freaked. But after that when you met me as me. What you said about how you knew I was the rabbit."

"I said your eyes were the same."

"You've been getting lost in my eyes since day one." His green eyes glossed over as he glanced down at my lips.

My face heated. "Oh shush." Brushing my fingers along his right cheek I sighed. "I wish we had more time before you had to go."

"Unfortunately, time isn't on our side but hopefully one day it will be."

"I don't think time is ever on anyone's side. We just got to make the most of what we have." I tugged at his shirt pulling him closer. "And I think I know what I would like to do with my time."

"Hold that thought." He took my hand in his and pressed a kiss on my palm. "Don't move I need to get something."

He got up and walked into the dressing room. "What are you doing?" I called after him. He didn't respond. As I got up, he walked back in the room with his hands behind his back. "What are you hiding?"

"Just come out onto the balcony with me and I'll show you."

I narrowed my eyes at him. "Okay."

He bobbed his head towards the balcony doors. "You go first." I walked over to the doors and opened them wide. As I stepped outside all I could hear was my heart hammering away. Things had suddenly got weird. The cold night air made me shiver as I looked out at the forest. Greg stepped out beside me but he angled himself so I couldn't see behind him. I placed my hands on my hips. "What is going on?"

A grin spread across his face. "I thought you were cute when we first met but infuriating."

"I thought you were a know it all."

He chuckled. "And you were not shy about telling me so. But that was when we first met." He stepped forward stroking my cheek with one hand. "Now I couldn't imagine my life without you." I groaned as he removed his hand from my face, missing the warmth of his touch. "Mellissa, I'm not asking you this because we are in the middle of a war, and I think one of us won't make it. I'm asking because I know we will get through this. One day things will slow down. We will live a boring life together where we will forget what it is to fight."

"Asking what?"

He pressed his finger to my lips cutting me off. "This is not how imagined doing this. I thought I was going to wait plan some big event, but this moment now just feels right." Taking my hand in his he revealed what he was holding in his other hand. It was a small box. I looked down at it my forehead creased.  "You just said we got to make the most of the time we have, and I know I want to spend all of mine with you." He dropped to one knee, and I gasped. The world seemed to vanish, and I couldn't look away from him.

He clicked the box open revealing a gold ring with an opal at its centre. "Mellissa Hail will you marry me?" It felt like the world stood still. My heart felt like it was about to burst. "Yes," was all I managed to say. Greg took out the ring and slid it onto my finger. Holding my hand up to the light the opal sparkled along with the cluster of sapphires surrounding it. "It's beautiful."

"It's family heirloom. That ring has been in the Ainsworth family for years." He stood taking my ring hand in his. "And it's a perfect fit."

Pressing a kiss to my knuckles, his eyes glistened in the moon light. I melted under his stare as he tugged me into his arms. Pushing up onto my tiptoes our lips met. I wrapped my arms round his neck pulling him closer. My heart felt like it was about to burst. I giggled a I ran my fingers along his jaw. "You're my fiancée now."

"Yes I am." He wrapped his arms round my body and as he stood to his full height, I was swept off my feet. Wrapping my legs round him I smothered him with kisses. Heat radiated between us, and I could feel his heart hammering under my touch as he carried me back into the bedroom.

# Parting Ways

## *Mellissa*

"So that's what all the loud sex was about last night," said Victoria wriggling her eyebrows at me.

I covered my cheeks with my hands as I felt them heat. "We were not that loud."

I had pulled Victoria into the second dining room away from everyone else, sat her down at the table and spilled the beans on last night's spontaneous proposal. I hadn't expected her to jump for joy like you see girl-friends do in the movies, but I hadn't seen that response coming.

Victoria rested her elbow on the dining table. "I went to knock on your door but walked away."

I folded my arms and pouted. "You never knock."

"Harkura and I got halfway down the corridor and decided to turn around."

"Harkura too."

Victoria smirked. "And Laxus."

My face felt like it was on fire as my eyes went wide. "Oh my god that is mortifying."

"Worse than when Mary caught you two in his office." The smile on Victoria's face widened. "Or when we walked in on you guys with your dad in tow."

Mellissa groaned as she laid her head on the table. "Don't remind me."

"You know they invented locks for a reason." She was laughing so hard tears formed at the creases of her eyes.

"As if you and Harkura would be discouraged by a locked door." Glaring at her, I flicked her elbow.

She dabbed the sides of her eyes with the pads of her fingertips. "Go on then show me the ring." Victoria waved her hand at me. My heart fluttered with excitement as I sat up in my seat and thrust my hand in her face. She grasped my hand lowering it. Peering at the gold ring Victoria nodded approvingly. "It's actually very nice. An opal is a nice change from a diamond. Are those sapphires?"

"Yes. It's a family heirloom."

Victoria cringed. "It wasn't his mums was it."

I pulled my hand away and held it to my chest like she had just electrocuted me. "No. It was his grandmothers. Apparently, his father passed it onto his aunt Tilly when he thought he wasn't going to be able to have kids."

"Huh but she gave it to Greg instead of her own kids." Victoria wriggled her nose. "She must like you." I looked at the ring on my finger and smiled. Victoria draped her arm over my shoulders. "If you're happy then I'm happy for you."

My face was flushed, and I was warm. "I am happy. Very happy."

We both turned towards the room entrance as we heard the door open. Harkura walked into the room holding a clipboard. "There you two are. Laxus and Matt are in the foyer ready to leave. Where's Greg?"

"He's talking to Samson he'll be down soon," I replied.

Harkura looked down at the clipboard his finger scanning over what was written. "We need to go over what you plan to say to the human leaders again. I assume you'll want to say more goodbyes with Gregory first."

Victoria put her hand up like a child in class trying to get the teachers attention. Harkura raised an eyebrow. "What is it, Victoria?"

She coughed clearing her throat. "That was not *I'm gonna miss you while you're gone* sex, we overheard last night but celebratory sex."

My pulse raced as my cheeks burned. Harkura glanced at Victoria like this was just common chit- chat. "Oh what were they celebrating."

Victoria grabbed my left hand and held it up in the air pointing at the ring. "They're engaged."

Harkura dropped the clipboard and clapped his hands together. "Oh, this is wonderful news." He wrapped his arms round me forcing me to stand up. He hugged me so tight I could hardly breathe. "I cannot wait to start wedding planning."

I stepped back holding my hands up in front of me. "Slow down. We only got engaged last night. Let's get through our current crisis and then we can talk about wedding plans."

Harkura grinned and his eyes sparkled. "It will be magnificent. I'm thinking emerald and gold as a colour scheme." He picked up his clipboard and turned the paper on it over. Scribbling away on the page he listed off all the wedding things we needed to think about.

"Harkura, we need to focus." I waved my hand at him. "We need to not be at war before wedding planning."

He glanced up at me as he tapped his pen on the clipboard. "I assume Victoria will be your maid of honour."

"Probably." He looked back at his list and continued writing.

"He is not listening." Victoria stood and nudged her shoulder against mine. "What do you mean I'll probably be your maid of honour. Who else is in the running?"

I massaged my temple with my fingers as I sighed. "Victoria will you be my maid of honour?"

"Of course I will." She squealed and hugged me. All tension in my body eased as I relaxed into her embrace. This was nice having something to look forward to and not just all the doom of our current situation. It was hope for a more peaceful time.

"What's going on in here?" asked Matt. He and Laxus had just walked in. They both had on big winter coats and rucksacks.

Victoria let go of me. Turning to Matt her smile beamed with excitement. "Mellissa and Greg are engaged and I'm her maid of honour."

Matt dropped his bag on the floor and marched over to us. Scooping me up in a hug he spun me round. "Thats awesome."

"Thanks." I laughed.

"Hey what's all the commotion about?" asked Greg. He was stood in the doorway holding a coat in one hand and his bag in another. Matt put me down. I grabbed on to Victoria to steady myself.

"Dude." Matt launched himself at Greg, hugging him. Greg glanced at me eyes wide, one brow risen as Matt patted his back enthusiastically.

Laxus cleared his throat as he tugged at Greg's sleeve. "I hear congratulations are in order."

Greg's forehead creased and then his eyes went wide in realisation. "Oh yeah thanks guys." He looked at me and smiled. "You told them."

My heart melted under his gaze. I wanted to be the one hugging him instead of him having Matt hanging off him. I rolled back and forth on the balls of my heels stopping myself for running into his arms and kissing him. "Yes but isn't that what you were talking to Samson about for so long."

"He's my cousin and he is very happy for us."

"Well Victoria is… she is my person and good news spreads." I pointed to the girl who was now the closest thing I now had to family and then gestured to the rest of the group. Biting my bottom lip I looked him over. Butterflies filled my stomach. "Are you all ready to go then?"

He looked down at what he was holding. "Yeah." It was like the joy from the room had been sucked out as everyone went quiet.

Victoria squeezed my shoulder. "We'll give you guys a moment." She ushered the group out leaving me standing across from Greg.

"Is it weird that I miss you already?" I asked.

Greg shook his head. "No because I feel the same way."

"Good because I thought I was going crazy." My stomach was in knots as I ran my fingers through my hair.

He placed his bag on the floor and laid his coat over it. He stepped forwards and I met him halfway.  Gripping the front of his sweater I pulled him close. His lips met mine and it felt like my body soared. My heart hammered in my chest as heat radiated between us. His hands wonder along my body as I interlocked my finger in his hair. There was an urgency in his kisses. Like it wasn't enough. I would never have enough of his kisses. I was left lightheaded as we finally parted. His fingers caressed my cheek. "I love you."

I leaned into his touch his hand warm against my cheek. "I love you too." He interlaced his fingers with mine. We walked towards the exit. Picking his stuff up on the way out, we joined the others in the foyer. With every step it felt like someone was tightening a vice around my chest.

Matt was hugging Victoria and Laxus was saying his goodbyes to Harkura. Samson stood to the side of them, his eyes lit up as he saw us. He walked over to us with a smile, but his eyes were sad. I imagined that's also what I looked like. "I hear you are soon to be my cousin in law."

"You hear correctly," I replied, "Now I need to say bye to the others." I slipped my hand from Gregs, and a coldness swept over me. He put his coat on as he spoke to Samson. Plastering a smile on my face I approached Laxus. "You'll keep an eye on both of them for me, right?"

Laxus pink eyes glistened as he wriggled his nose. "Of course I will. They don't call me the great pixie protector for nothing."

"I don't think I've ever heard that."

"Well, they will from now on." He frowned as his chin quivered. "I'm the only protector of a dark stone still standing."

My heart felt like it was about to implode. I knelt and hugged him. "Promise me you'll stay standing oh great pixie protector."

Wrapping his arms round my neck he squeezed me tightly. "I'm sorry I caused you so much trouble."

Pulling back so I could look him in the eye, I gripped his shoulders. "I'm glad that when you were in trouble it was my doorstep you ended up on." He nodded as he snorted holding back the tears that had been forming.

Matt patted Laxus' on his back. "Don't worry I'll keep him safe." His gaze wondered over to Greg. "I'll look out for them both."

Standing up I smiled. "I know you will." I placed my hand on his heart. "You may no longer be my guardian, but you still have the traits of one. I know you will protect them but remember you are a team."

"But I'm totally team leader." He winked at me making me smile.

"It's weird saying goodbye when you only just returned. I've barely been able to spend any time with you."

Matt shrugged. "We'll have plenty of time to catch up after." He wrapped me up in a bear hug. "You know I'm jealous of your relationship with my sister."

"You are?" I tried to look at him but he held me tight so I couldn't see his face.

"I used to be your person but I'm glad that you had each other in my absence." He let go of me and grinned. "You've grown and matured so much."

"So have you. In essence you are still our Matt but you're different." I brushed my fingers along the side of his eyes. "You've seen more than any of us. More than you should have. More than you've told us about."

He wriggled his eyebrows as he leaned towards me. "I'm wise beyond my years."

I giggled as I swatted him away playfully. "You could say that."

"It's time," said Greg from behind me.

"Okay cool bro." Matt shifted his bag on his shoulder and placed his hand on Laxus' shoulder. His eyebrows rose as he looked at me. "We'll see you soon."

I swallowed the lump that had formed in my throat. "Yeah." Matt guided Laxus to the castle doors.

"Mellissa," said Greg. I felt his hand on my back. My throat was sore and my chest tight as I turned around. Before I could say anything, he kissed me. It was a slow soft kiss that left me longing for more as we parted. "You are my light of hope."

I went to talk but no words came. There wasn't anything I could say that could communicate what I was feeling. His gaze didn't leave mine as he joined Matt and Laxus. My eyes stung as I forced back the tears that threatened to fall. I waved him off with a smile. They walked through the doors and as they shut behind them it felt like a part of my heart had walked out the door. Harkura squeezed my shoulder. "This is the safer mission. The plan is to keep Kadon's attention on us."

Rubbing my eyes I nodded. "You're right everything will work out. We just need to stick to the plan."

"We should get ready for this UN meeting then," said Victoria. I followed my guardians down the corridor and up the stairs. My limbs felt heavy as we walked. It was like something was weighing me down. I swallowed the lump in my throat. Focusing on the task at hand I forced myself onwards pushing this feeling of dread away.

# 26

# UN Security Council

## *Mellissa*

My hands were clammy as I placed a golden tiara on my head. I turned round to face Harkura and Victoria. "How do I look?"

Victoria reached out and repositioned the tiara on my head. "Very Queenly."

I scrunched my nose. "Really? Are we sure about the dress maybe I should wear a suit or armour." I lifted the skirt of my jade green dress swaying it side to side.

"Armour would make us seem like a threat," said Harkura. He looked me up and down. "The dress is formal but very regal."

Victoria swatted my hands away from my dress and smoothed the creases out of my skirt. "You look like the Queen you are, which is exactly the message we want to send."

Harkura nodded. "We want them to recognise you as someone important. As someone to be respected."

I chewed my thumbnail. Victoria pulled my hand away from my mouth. "Stop that."

"This needs to go well." I said, "I can't afford to mess it up".

Victoria looked me straight in the eye. "We've practiced what to say. Gone over multiple scenarios on how they could react. You have got this."

Harkura took my hand in his. "And we will be there to support you."

There was a knock on the door. Radius stood in the doorway with Rowan behind him. They entered the room. Radius tugged at his shirt collar; it was the first time I had seen him in a tie. "It's time," he said in a gruff voice.

I nodded. "Okay."

"Everyone remember the plan?" asked Radius.

Rowan nodded as he puffed his chest out. "Queen Mellissa teleports us directly to the chamber the meeting is in. The three of us" He pointed to himself and then Victoria and Harkura. "Immediately take up a defensive position. We leave all the talking to the Queen."

"That is the condensed version." Radius held his hands out to the group. "Let's get this done." Standing in a circle we all took the hand of the person next us.

"Ready?" I asked. They all nodded affirmatively. All I could hear was my heart hammering in my chest. Swallowing down my rising panic I teleported.

We materialized in a large room. Radius swiftly surrounded our group with a light barrier, almost invisible to the eye. Bright spotlights shone down on a curved table that didn't quite make a complete circle. A mural of a phoenix rising from ashes was depicted on the back wall. Victoria and Harkura flanked me on both sides and Rowan took up the rear. Our little group walked down the stairs towards the table of delegates as the room filled with screams and cries of rage. Within seconds of reaching the bottom step, we were surrounded by guards with guns pointed at us. I took a deep breath pushing down my feelings of dread. Putting my hands up I stepped forward. "We mean you no harm. We just want to talk."

"Who are you?" Asked a man with a strong Russian accent. Looking around the room at the world leaders, I recognised not one of them. I really wished I had paid more attention to the politics of the world growing up.

"I'm Mellissa Hail, Queen of the elves."

"You are no queen." Someone shouted with a French accent. "Guards seize them."

Victoria stepped in front of me, hands glowing with magic. "No one will touch her." Heat radiated beside me from Harkura. This was not part of the plan. Their instinct to protect me was outweighing their diplomacy skills.

The guards shakily pointed their guns at her. "Stop that now." One of them shouted.

A gun went off. Radius clenched his fist pushing more power into the barrier surrounding us. The bullets hit the barrier and fell to the floor. More screams echoed off the high ceiling. The delegates looked at us in horror.

I stepped round Victoria. "Like I said, we just want to talk."

"You broke in here and threatened us with these weird abilities," snapped a man.

"That was not my intention." I interlaced my fingers and stood tall trying to give off the authority I had seen Lady Gabrielle do so many times. "The same way your guards jumped to protect you all, mine do the same but," I put my hands out to Harkura and Victoria. They both pulled back their magic. "We do not wish to fight but only talk."

"I think we should hear them out." Said a woman. This person I recognised as the British prime minister.

"I agree." Said the Russian man. "If they wanted to harm us, they could have by now."

The man who had been speaking when we entered, gestured to the centre spot in front of the curved table. "Very well elf girl," he said in an American accent. "What have you got to say?"

I walked forward past the guns pointed at me, King Radius and Rowan stood either side of me. Victoria and Harkura took a wide stance, glaring at the guards. I looked at the room. The decision these people made would be communicated to all UN members. My mouth was dry and sweat prickled the nape of my neck. I let out a long breath and cleared my throat. "I'm Queen Mellissa, ruler of the elves. This is King Radius ruler of the merfolk and this Rowan; he has come on behalf of the king of the sky people."

"Why does this sky king not grace us with his presence?" asked the American man.

"Because he is a dragon, and his presence tends to scare people." The leaders whispered amongst themselves. I stood tall and brushed out the crease in my skirt. "We have come here to show you that we are not a threat, and to ask you stop attacking us. Please."

"You appear out of nowhere with these new land masses and expect us to believe you are not a threat?" said the prime minister.

"I understand it's scary. It was frightening for us too. Our world has been turned upside down. We never meant for any of this, but we can't undo what's happened."

"And what exactly has happened?"

"There was a veil that separated our worlds into one of magic and one without. That was destroyed and now our worlds have reconnected. We don't want to fight you. We want to live in peace alongside you.

"If what you say is true, why did you attack London, then Beijing and Moscow?" asked the Russian lady.

"You people swooped in casting shadow over everything," yelled the American.

My mind spun. I hadn't known about those attacks. Swallowing the lump in my throat I continued talking. "That wasn't us. That was Kadon." I tried to look stern the way Lady Gabrielle used to when talking about serious matters to the council. "He is an enemy to us all. He is the one who brought down the veil. He wants to rule over all of us and doesn't care how many people die for him to get his way."

"Why should we believe you?" asked the American man. "You're just a child. Shouldn't the king there be the one talking."

I tighten my fists digging my nails into my palm. Radius placed his hand on mine. "This child as you call her." He stared down at the man. "Is one of the few people with the power to stop the mad man attacking your city's." He rolled his shoulders back and stood tall puffing out his chest. "I may be older than Queen Mellissa, but I would follow her lead anywhere. She is the bravest person I know and our only hope to win this war."

"Then this is a war," said the man.

"Yes," I replied, "but not between us. It is a war against Kadon."

"What do you want from us?" asked the Russian.

"Only to stand down and keep your people away from the upcoming fight." I stared out at the room hoping I looked confidant. "Kadon is too powerful for you to face. I promise you we will stop him and end all the bloodshed.

"How can we trust that you can stop him?" asked the French minister. "You let him destroy this veil and destroy so much already."

"We need to discuss what you have said." The American narrowed his eyes at us. "In private."

I nodded. "Very well we will be in the foyer." I stepped back with my head held high and walked back towards the stairs. Victoria and Harkura fell in line beside me, and Radius and Rowan followed behind.

"That went better than expected," whispered Victoria.

My legs felt like jelly. I focused my sight on the door, just a few more steps and we would be out. There was no way I was letting them see any weakness in my armour. As I placed my hand on the door handle a wave of dread shot through me making the hair on the back of my neck stand up. I spun round. "He's here." I ran back down the stairs. "He is here." I shouted.

"What are you on about?" yelled the French minister. "You agreed to let us discuss this in private." I looked around the room trying to figure out where Kadon would attack from. My head was spinning. The UN members stood and were shouting and my people saying something back. Radius was looking up at the ceiling he must sense Kadon's presence too, so I wasn't imagining it. I tuned out what they were all saying as I tried to think. All I could hear were my own rapid breaths. It felt like time slowed as realisation dawned on me. "He isn't here for us but them." I looked at the security council. A loud bang shook the room. Flashing lights around the room lit up and a siren blared. A chorus of screams echoed around me as the ceiling caved in. Running forward with hands outstretched I summoned a massive amount of light. Twirling my arms round I spread the light around the room deflecting the falling debris.

"What are you doing?" screamed the Russian man. Guns were aimed in my direction again.

"Are you stupid?" shouted Victoria, "She just saved you."

The French minister pointed up at the ceiling eyes wide. "I don't think that was them. It came from outside."

Security burst into the room from a door at the side. They surrounded the security council members. As they went back towards the door they came in from, shadows stormed into the room. They came from all directions surrounding us. Radius and I ran in opposite directions radiating light. We pushed back the shadows. "Theres no way out." I heard an unfamiliar voice shout.

Sweat dripped down my brow. Lifting my right hand up I summoned the heart crystal to staff form. Gripping it tight, I channelled all my energy into the heart. Light burst forth dissipating the shadows. "There is a way out," I shouted. "The way we came in." I held my hand out. "But we have to be touching."

They all stared at me in silence. Another bang had them moving. They all ran over grabbing at me. I stepped back. "Slow down. I can't take everyone at once."

"Take the human leaders first," shouted Radius. He had his trident held up above his head, light seeping out of it and round the room. The security team pushed the delegates forward. They all laid a hand on my arm or shoulders. The building shook again and more of the ceiling came in. Shadow danced around the edge of the light Radius was making. I looked at the security team and guards. They all looked fraught, eyes wide and shaking. "All of you hold onto someone who is making contact with me." No one moved. "Now," I shouted. They all huddled together. This was the largest amount of people I had ever teleported, but I wasn't leaving any of them behind. We had a low chance of surviving Kadon, but they had none. Pushing my magic outwards around all the bodies surrounding me, I teleported.

We materialised in the middle of a crowd. Shouts of shock sounded around us. The delegates gasped. "How?" asked the French man

"Where are we?" asked the American

"The houses of parliament," responded the British prime minister.

"Yeah, London was the first place that popped into my head when I thought about government type places." I stepped back pulling myself from their grip. "I have to get back."

The Russian man grabbed my arm. "Wait, where are you going?"

"I must go back. You're safe but so many others aren't".

He peered at me like I was some peculiar object. "You really care."

I yanked my hand free. "Yes." The prime minster clasped my wrist. I spun round. "Now what?"

She pressed her lips together and her brows drew together. "You saved us. Just know that I believe you when you say you're different to that shadow monster." I nodded. She let go of me. Once I was free, focusing on my guardian's energy I teleported.

# 27

# **Black Sun**

## *Victoria*

Victoria's heart raced. Shadows slithered around the edges of the light Radius was emitting. Mellissa had just teleported away with all the humans that had been in the room, leaving them behind. Victoria shuddered as the hairs on the back of her neck stood up. The shadows grew darker. Radius let out an almighty howl as he dropped to his knees. The darkness sliced into the light. As Victoria breathed out the air turned icy. Whipping round, she shot ice from her hands, freezing parts of the shadow. Explosions above shook the building. Black water smashed through the ceiling. Swirling her hands around, the tidal wave of water turned to ice. Bending over and gripping her knees Victoria panted.

Harkura ran to her side. "Nicely done." He placed a hand on her shoulder. "Are you okay?"

Victoria placed her hand over his. "Just catching my breath." The ice exploded and black sludge shot at them. Harkura dove into Victoria's side, and they crashed onto the hard tiled floor. Victoria's ears were ringing as she sat up.

Kadon stood on top of the security council table. His eyes were pure black, and his grey skin cracked by shadow. "Where are they?" he yelled.

Harkura jumped to his feet. As he threw his hands out beside him flames appeared in them. "If you're looking for the human leaders, Mellissa already took them to safety."

Kadon's jaw tensed as the vein on his forehead bulged. "That meddlesome bitch." Kadon pressed his arms together in front of him palms open. Water swirled around in his grip. "I'll kill all of you instead. Should teach her a lesson." A funnel of water blasted at them. Radius swung his trident high, deflecting the attack. At the same time Rowan flapped his wings creating a whirlwind. He directed it at Kadon, sweeping him off his feet. Harkura rushed in throwing fire balls as he did. The flames caught on the whirlwind and Kadon was ablaze. The room shuddered as Kadon yelled out in frustration. Water seeped through cracks in the wall.

Suddenly the flames were flying at them on a gust created by Kadon. Victoria pushed her hands forward magic surging creating a wall of ice. The four of them took cover behind it just as the building walls imploded. Water surged into the room flooding it. Radius swirled his trident round taking control of the current. Holding his trident high, he stepped out from behind the ice and pointed it at Kadon. All the water flew towards him. Kadon held his hand up stopping the attack before it hit. The water flowed between the two men both pushing their own will into it. Kadon pushed his other hand out pushing harder on the water.

Radius gripped his trident tighter as sweat dripped from his brow. "We need to get out of here." He gritted his teeth as his feet slid backwards on the tiled floor. "Rowan take Harkura. Victoria with me." He held his hand out to her without taking his eyes off Kadon. Victoria launched herself towards him, grabbing his hand. He pulled her into his arms and shot up into the air. Rowan followed behind carrying Harkura. Victoria held tight to the king as they flew up through the collapsed ceiling, past the other floors of the building. Blasting light in front of them they smashed through what remained of the roof.

Victoria took a sharp inhale of breath as she took in the sight below on the streets. "What have they done?"

Radius looked below. "It's worse than we feared."

Kadon hadn't come alone. Below was a group of water nymphs and changelings standing guard round the building. They had humans bound and on their knees.

Kadon burst out of the building. He hovered in front of them and glanced at the ground. He looked at Radius and smirked. "I delivered the justice you are incapable of."

Radius growled. "This is not justice. They are innocent civilians."

"You're pathetic Radius." Kadon grinned so wide his fangs showed. "You're the worst crystal keeper of all. The weak link bringing them down."

Radius let out of cry of rage. Magic surged from the king. Victoria wrapped her arms round his neck holding tight. Light exploded from Radius. He shone like a star. Victoria shut her eyes channelling her ice magic, cooling herself against the heat of Radius's power. Victoria's eyes shot open a something slammed into her back, and they were falling. An icy wind sliced at her limbs. Her grip on Radius loosened and the wind blew them apart. Yelling Victoria pushed her arms out. Ice shot out and crashed onto the ground. It grew upward. Victoria slammed into her creation and slid to the floor. She winced as pain shot threw her. Radius landed beside her his brow furrowed. "Are you okay? I'm so sorry I dropped you."

Rowan landed a few paces away. Harkura jumped out of his arms and ran to Victoria. He knelt beside her. "Are you alright?"

Victoria clasped the side of her abdomen her lungs burned with every breath she took. "I'll survive." Harkura pulled her up, placing his arms round her body and supported her.

The earth shuddered as Kadon landed with a boom. "You won't be surviving for much longer." He tilted his head to the side and gestured to the crowd behind him. Kai and

Akito came running. He pointed at Victoria and Harkura. "You can prove your loyalty to me by killing those two." The two water nymphs nodded, and their stares landed on the two guardians.

"Kai, Akito don't do this." Victoria said her eyes pleading with the pair. "It isn't too late; Mellissa will forgive you."

Flicking his wrists Kai created a pair of water whips. "We gave your Queen a chance."

Akito lifted her hand hovering a ball of water above it. "She isn't strong enough for what is needed but King Kadon is."

Harkura growled, his face tight with rage. "Kadon is no king."

Kadon clicked his fingers. "Deal with them. I'll take care of the king and bird."

Harkura and Victoria dove in opposite directions as Kai and Akito charged them.

Darkness encased Kadon and he shot past Victoria like he was a shadow himself. Her hair whipped up and she felt a graze against her cheek as he did. Just before he made contact with Radius a bolt of lightning slammed into him. Mellissa dropped down out of nowhere. As she hit the ground it rumbled. The pavement cracked and vines shot up slamming into Kai and Akito. They snaked round the others holding the captive humans, who took the opportunity to run. Kadon came up behind her a shadow sword in hand. Victoria screamed her name as he swung it down towards her best friend's head. In the blink of an eye Mellissa had disappeared and reappeared to the side of him. Lightning crackled out of Mellissa's hands and jolted into Kadon. At the same time Radius released a pulse of light and Rowan swirled the air around throwing Kadon into the air.

Kadon roared and darkness burst out of him. Waves of shadow shot into the sky and circled all around. Everyone went down and they all hit the pavement with a thud. Victoria's head was spinning as she sat up. She rubbed her eyes trying to clear her vision. Blinking she tried to refocus herself, but it didn't work. Everything was dark. It was as if the sun had suddenly gone down.

"What have you done?" shouted Mellissa. Victoria's mouth dropped open and her heart froze. The sun was covered in shadow.

Kadon laughed frantically as he pranced around manically. "I've become a god." His gaze landed on Mellissa, and he licked his lips. "I'll give you back the sun if you kneel before me and become mine.

Rage surged through Victoria. The way he looked at Mellissa made her nauseas. "Never," shouted Mellissa.

An almighty bang rang through the air as Mellissa and Kadon collided. They were both moving so fast they were blurs. It was like watching a shadow battling lightening.

"Victoria," yelled Harkura. Victoria spun round to see a hydro-blast heading straight for her. Fire collided with it creating water vapour. A warm mist splattered on her face. Harkura ran it front of her his arm stretched out in a protective way. He glared at Kai. A ray of light shot over Victoria's head and slammed into Kai. He was thrown back crashing onto the pavement. Radius pulled at Harkura's arm. He turned to Victoria his eyes wide and wild. "We need to get out of here."

"We need Mellissa." Victoria looked up at the clashing light and shadow. "If we stay huddled together then she only needs to make contact with one of us."

Harkura frowned as he looked up at the battle in the sky. "She can't break free from him."

"Then we give her an opening," said Rowan. He rolled his shoulders spreading his golden wings wide. "We strike together."

Radius nodded while taking a wide stance and aiming his trident at the shadowy figure of Kadon. "On three." Victoria and Harkura took up position beside the other two. As Radius counted Victoria let her power grow. When Radius yelled three all four of them fired their attacks. Fire, ice, light and air all slammed into Kadon blasting him out the sky. Mellissa floated in the air mouth ajar.

The group of four stood in a line holding hands. "Mellissa," screamed Victoria her heart pounded so hard she thought it might beat out her chest.

In a flurry of light Mellissa appeared by her side. "What is it?"

Victoria grabbed the girl's wrist. "Teleport now." Warmth spread from Mellissa's arm into Victoria's hand and through her body towards the other. A force tugged them forward as Mellissa teleported.

# 28

# Dark Night

## *Mellissa*

We materialised in the middle of the main hall of the castle. A group of people let out startled yells.  This was where we had made up a makeshift medical centre during the evacuations, so I had thought to come here after escaping. But of course, this wasn't one of our planned evacuations, so the hall wasn't littered with healers and the council members waiting to greet people. There were just a few random staff members wondering about.

"Someone get a healer," said Radius to no one in particular. His voice rung with authority. Two people scurried out the room. My chest heaved as I sucked in air, my body shaking uncontrollably. While I had been fighting, I had been running on adrenaline. Just going where I was needed but now that we were safe everything that had happened was hitting me all it once. My legs buckled from under me as they turned to jelly. Spreading my fingers across the cold tiled floor, I examined their smoothness and slate colour trying to ground myself.

Victoria tugged at my hands, but I pulled away. She grabbed my shoulders firmly, pushing on me, forcing me to look at her. "We're safe. We are back."

I shook my head. "He blocked out the sun." Victoria wrapped her arms round me squeezing tight. I rested my head on her shoulder any remains of adrenalin washing out of my body. Tears filled my eyes. "The humans will never back down after that."

Victoria stroked my hair while making shushing noises. Harkura came over. He looked us both over. "Are either of you hurt?"

"Nothing major," replied Victoria.

"How did he know about the meeting?" Harkura rubbed his chin as his brow drew together. "He came looking for the security council not us."

"Beatrice." I clenched my fists as anger bubbled up in me. "She was there when I was making plans with Ignis. We had argued because she wanted me to kill them all."

Victoria's top lip curled. "That bitch."

I ran my fingers through my hair. "At the time I thought she was just angry. I never thought she actually meant it. I'm such an idiot." My voice caught as my mouth went dry.  My heart ached. I had been so stupid not to see it. Beatrice had meant every word she had said that day. She had shown me her true colours long ago, yet I turned a blind eye because I didn't want to believe it was true. Rowan coughed drawing our attention. I rubbed my eyes and swallowed the lump in my throat. "Is something wrong Rowan?"

He stood with his hands behind his back puffing his chest out. "No, I just wanted to say, I think that went better than you think."

"How so?" I asked.

"Kadon's attack was awful, but you saved those people. You proved to them with your actions that you are not the bad guy."

I bit my bottom lip as I thought about what had just happened. The British prime ministers voice echoed in my mind. *'Just know that I believe you when you say you're different to that shadow monster.'* And the Russian minister seemed to not want me to leave them. My heart skipped a beat as a little bit of hope shone in the gloom that this day had been. "You might be right."

Rowan bowed his head. "As always it was an honour to fight by your side."

The doors swung open, and a group of healers filtered in. They rushed over to us all. They split into teams of two or three checking us all over separately. I sat down letting the healers do their job. My arms were scratched to shreds, and I had a large bruise on my left side but nothing major.

A bang echoed through the hall as Josh stumbled into the room. He quickly crouched picking up the tablet he had dropped. Holding the device up he grinned. "Not broken." I laughed. Joshed jogged over to me. "I guess the mission was a success."

I arched a brow as I peered up at him. "All five of us are injured not exactly what I would call a success."

He turned round looking at the others all being seen to by healers. His gaze returned to me. He pressed his lips together and his brows looked like they were about to fly off his forehead. "I'm not good at reading the room."

"I know but it's okay. I assume you have some news by the way you ran in here." I held my hand out gesturing for him to hand me the tablet. "Please tell me you have some good news." I emphasised the word good, hoping that putting extra energy behind the word would make it real.

He swiped his finger across the tabular screen and pressed some buttons. "I intercepted this message between the UN members." He turned the screen round and handed me the device.

I read it and reread it. "Does that mean what I think it does?"

"They are standing down until they can figure out who is the real enemy." He rolled back and forth on the balls of his feet. "While one unknown entity attacked them another saved them. You did it Queen Mellissa."

A warm glow filled my stomach. I jumped up and hugged Josh, startling the healer who had been working on my arm and him.  We both jumped up and down on the spot squealing.

"What are you two so happy about?" asked Victoria.

"Rowan was right," I said. "The humans are temporarily stopping their attacks because I saved them."

"Thats wonderful news," interjected Radius. "It's given us the time we need to figure this out."

This mission had gone better than I originally thought. I had gone toe to toe with Kadon but somehow come out with only minor injuries. Most importantly the humans would not be attacking anymore. We now had a fighting chance.

Radius and I stood outside the large cave in the forest. Ignis sat in the entrance, bobbing his head occasionally as Rowan spoke. The hawkling man had volunteered to debrief his master. I had been more than happy to let him. Trying to put everything that had just happened into words made my head spin. On one hand our mission had been a success, the humans were standing down but on the other side of things, the sun was gone. It did not seem possible for something of this magnitude to happen. I had not really comprehended how powerful Kadon was until now. All the encounters I had had with him had me questioning if he had even been trying. Had he just been toying with me all this time?

"I should have seen this coming." Ignis huffed as he sat up on his back legs. "I have the power of foresight, but it never shows me anything useful."

Rowan placed his hand on his master's side. "We all know that you cannot choose what you see."

"This is my fault," I said, "The moment Beatrice betrayed us I should have known she would spill everything she knew to Kadon. I should have seen this betrayal coming."

"I was in that meeting too." Ignis shook his head as his features creased. "I heard what Beatrice had wanted to do. When we would not act as she wanted, I should have known she would take her ideas to the enemy. I have much more lived experience than you, but it has not made be wiser."

Radius gripped my shoulder, his brow furrowed. "Don't beat yourself up, hindsight is a marvellous thing." He sighed as he looked up at the sky. "The more important issue is the sun. What are we going to do?"

Ignis's gaze turned upwards. "I don't understand how Kadon has accomplished this?"

Rowan crossed his arms and frowned. "This black ooze spilled out of him and then shot up out into the atmosphere. It was like it then latched onto any light sources snuffing them out."

I rubbed my chin. "What if the three of us each release a massive jolt of light up into the atmosphere?" You know try counter what Kadon did."

"It's worth a try," said Ignis.

Radius stepped forward gripping his trident tight. "Then let's get to it." The moon crystal in the centre of his fork glowed brightly.

Ignis pressed a claw to his chest. Light burst from a crystal embedded in his body. I'd never noticed the sun crystal so openly on display before. They both looked to me. Calling to the heart I transformed it into its staff form. Holding it tight I pointed it up at the sky. Light illuminated from the crystal at the top. The area grew brighter and brighter. Rowan covered his face with his wings. Three separate beams of light shot up into the sky and into the outer atmosphere. Gritting my teeth I pushed more magic into my beam. The whole island of Urbem Folium was filled by light.

Radius dropped to his knees panting. My arms sagged as my magic cut out. Sweat dripped from my brow stinging my eyes. Ignis slouched to the ground beside us. Rowan patted the dragons head, his features tight. As our light dimmed from the area, the darkness returned. My shoulders sagged as I flopped down on the grass. "Nothing."
My heart sunk. Kadon's spell was stronger than the power of the three life crystal combined.

I burst into Joshes office, making him jump. He stood from his seat, his eyes wide. "What's wrong?"

I slammed my hand on his desk. "The sun is gone Josh."

"Yes I noticed." He rubbed the back of his neck as he wrinkled his nose. "I assume that's why three light beams shot into the sky a few moments ago" I glanced round the room. There were no windows in here. It was how Josh liked it. While most of the other elves liked being out in nature my adviser was more of the inside sort. "My program monitoring the worlds satellites picked it up." He said answering the question I hadn't yet formed.

I waved my hands around at all his equipment. "Yes, that's what I came here for. Can your computers tell us what actually happened to the sun?"

Josh sat back down in his chair and spun it round so he was facing his main computer monitor. "Sort of. The burst of magic Kadon shot into space was also picked up by the satellites, but then they stopped recording for a few minutes after the event."

I pulled the other chair in his office over and sat beside him. "So, the initial wave was recorded but what it actually did was not."

"Precisely."

I groaned. "Great. How am I meant to break this spell when I don't even know what exactly it has done."

Josh tapped on his key broad and clicked his mouse a few times. "From the data I have access to it shows that the sun is still there."

I leaned forward peering over his shoulder at his screen. "That's good. We have a chance at fixing it then."

"Yes, but it's like something is blocking it. Like a black layer has been wrapped around the whole thing."

"But why didn't the light from the life crystals destroy it? That is usually the best way to break through these shadow attacks."

Joshes forehead creased as he tapped his chin. "I don't know." He began typing on his keyboard again. Leaning in close to his screen he looked through different documents on the screen. I peered over his shoulder, but he flicked between his different tabs too quickly for me to take in what any of it said. I leaned back in my chair and folded my arms. Swinging my chair side to side I played with some paper clips on his desk, resolved to the fact I could not read and absorb data anywhere near as fast as Josh. His fingers froze over his keyboard as he frowned. He turned to me, and his forehead creased. "I don't think the sun is the only star affected. They all are."

I gripped the arm of my chair. "What?"

"That's why the life crystals light didn't break the spell. You need to release all the stars at once. If you miss even one it won't work."

The room span as I processed what Josh had just said. "How did Kadon manage to spread his magic so far."

"I don't know." Joshes fingers pressed into the side of his chair as his eyes darted side to side as he looked round the room. "Maybe it's the concentration of power."

"I'm gonna need you to explain further."

He looked up at me, his gaze intense. "We are all here thinking that the three life crystals trump Kadon's two dark stones, but the way the magic is distributed is affecting it's power level."

I stared at him my mouth a jar. "Huh?"

Josh pulled a piece of paper from his printer and drew three circles on it. "So, these are the three life crystals. The beams you shot into the atmosphere were three separate ones." He drew a line from each circle. "Now we have the dark stones. Each stones power is equal to a crystal." He drew three more circles but two where on top of each other. "But Kadon has taken two of these and stacked their power.

Giving his wave of magic a much greater reach." He drew a line from the two stones to the end of the page.

I traced my fingers along the lines drawn on the paper. "What if I borrowed one of the other crystals and replicated what Kadon did but with light instead?"

Josh gripped my hand tight. "Mellissa that is dangerous. You've seen the effects wielding two stones has had on Kadon. The shadows are cracking his body."

I gasped. "That's what those black marks are on his face?"

Josh tilted his head to the side. "You didn't know."

My face heated as I squirmed in my seat. "I thought he was just oozing power."

"That is sort of true." He bobbed his head side to side as if he was weighing his words carefully. "Those cracks are the magic trying to break free. It's all too much for him to contain eventually it will burn him up."

"It's killing him." My jaw dropped as Josh nodded. I had been so blind to what was right in front of me on many fronts. I chewed on my bottom lip as I thought about what this meant. "If his stolen power is killing him, then all we have to do is wait him out. The spell he cast over the sun will disappear when he dies."

Josh tugged at my hand, making me look at him. "But what sort of damage will occur in the meantime."

I pulled my hand away as I leaned back in my chair. My mind swam with all this new information, trying to envision the different possibilities. We could not wait for the stones to run their course. By the time they had done enough damage to him, there may no longer be a world to save. "Then what do we do? He keeps beating us."

"Find a way to stack your powers on top of each other's rather than attacking separately".

"And how do we do that?"

Josh held his hands up in front of his chest. "That is not my area of expertise. I am the tech guy. You now need the fighter guy."

I massaged the side of my head. "You mean I need Harkura."

"Yeah." Josh smiled as he placed his hand over mine. "I know you'll figure something out."

"Thanks, Josh." My shoulders were heavy as I left his office. It felt like the pressure of everything was pushing down on me. There was a way through this I just had to find it.

I sat on the cold floor of my balcony, gazing at the forest. The wind rustled my hair, the cold air prickling my cheeks. The trees swayed in the breeze. Everything almost looked exactly as before. Except there was no light. It was hours past the time the sun should have set, yet no moon or stars came. Josh had been right. It wasn't just the sun that had been affected. A part of me had hoped he was mistaken but here I was looking up at the night sky not a single star in sight. Before this war, before the veil came down. The quiet of the forest almost made me forget what we were up against. Not that long ago we had celebrated Christmas, had a New Years eve party. My dad had been alive, and he was going to move to Urbem Folium. It felt like a lifetime ago. A tear rolled down my cheek. My heart longed for a different reality. One where my dad was still here. Greg and I would get married. My dad would walk me down the aisle. He would make an embarrassing but sweet speech. But instead, I got this. The version where my dad died, and the world was being plunged into chaos.

"Hey." I jumped at the sound of Victoria's voice. She sat down beside me on the floor of the balcony. "You okay?"

I pulled my legs up to my chest wrapping my arms round myself. "Yeah."

"Then why are you out here all alone in the cold?"

Looking out at the horizon I sighed. "I just needed space to think. Everything is such a mess."

Victoria brushed her hair from her face. "I know everything seems hopeless. I mean the sun was bad enough." She pointed up at the sky. "But now there are no stars. This all feels very end of days."

I nudged her shoulder with mine. "If you came here to try cheer me up, you're doing a terrible job of it."

"Don't interrupt me." She flicked my arm. "Now where was I?" She wriggled her nose and looked up at the sky. "Oh yeah no stars and end of days." A smile crept onto her face. "But there is still light." She glanced at me her eyes shining. "You're that light Mellissa. I watched you fight Kadon today. You kept up with him."

I shook my head. "He had me on the defence the whole time."

"He has two dark stones. You only have one life crystal. He was like this monstrous shadow but you." She took my hand in hers and squeezed it. "You were like a bolt of lightning. This force of nature cracking through the darkness."

"I don't know about that."

"Each time you have fought him you have grown and then when you face him again you are able to respond to his attacks better." Victoria interlaced her fingers and stretched her arms out in front of her. "All you need is something to boost your power. Thats where Radius and Ignis come in. I believe with them backing you up you can do this."

I rested my head on her shoulder and looked out at the scenery. Even with no light the forest was beautiful. "I really hope you are right."

"I am right and this training session that Harkura has planned for the morning is gonna whip you three into fighting shape."

I grimaced. "What sort of plan has he got?"

"I'm not completely sure on the details but he was still drawing up his ideas when I left his room."

"He is really taking this seriously."

"You knew he would, it's why you gave him the task." Victoria nudged my shoulder. "Come on let's go inside where it's warm."

My chest tightened as I glanced back at the balcony doors. "It's too quiet in there."

"You can say that you miss him. I will not gag at your lovey-dovey crap."

"It feels silly. I am a grown adult; I don't need my boyfriend around all the time."

Victoria pulled her legs up, resting her arms on her knees. "We are in a very strange and dangerous situation it makes sense to want to have your home comforts around."

"Did you just call Greg a home comfort?"

"You know there are solo methods you can use to help relieve those urges."

I flicked her arm. "This isn't about sex."

"I know. You're just missing his warm embraces." She drastically spread her fingers across her chest and flicked her head back making her hair swoosh.

I slapped her arm playfully. "Stop." Sighing I looked up at the sky. "It's not just that. With out the distraction. All the quiet has made the absence of another even louder, that I cannot ignore like I have been." Spreading my fingers wide in front of me, I starred at my shiny engagement ring. "My dad missed me getting engaged and there are going to be so many more moments that I don't get to share with him." I chuckled. "That is assuming the world doesn't end in the next few days."

"That is morbid and not funny. The world is not gonna end and your dad would be extremely happy for you." She interlaced her fingers with mine and squeezed my hand. "I also know that wherever he is right now he is cheering us on."

"You really think so?"

"Yeah, I do. He is out there shouting to all the spirits 'that s my daughter kicking butt down there'" A grin spread across her face, and I burst out laughing. Somehow, I felt lighter. All the thoughts that had been plaguing my mind where gone. My dad's spirit lived in my heart. All the guidance and wisdom he had given me growing up was still with me. I bumped my shoulder against Victoria's. "Thanks for cheering me up."

"No problem." She stood holding her hand out to me. "Come on, let's go down to the kitchens and get some food."

I placed my hand in hers and let her help me up. "Now that sounds like a plan."

# 29

# Road Trip

## *Gregory*

Greg huddled close to the glowing embers of the fire. Tugging his hiking boots off he wriggled his toes. His feet throbbed after walking for so long that day. They had set up camp in a small, wooded area off the side of a major road. Matt had led them, here. Josh had given them up to date maps with all the new land masses. It hadn't taken them long to get from their island to the mainland of the UK. According to Matt they were right on the Scottish and English boarder. Something new Greg had learned about Matt today was that his geography skills were great and his map reading skills excellent.

A knot twisted in Greg's stomach as he gazed up at the night sky. There were no stars or moon. The sun had gone down much earlier than it should have that day. It wasn't a proper sunset. More like the sun was there one moment and gone the next.

The sound of the zip on the tent moving made him turn round. Matt walked out the tent and came and sat beside him. Greg glanced at his watch. "I still have twenty minutes left on guard."

Matt shrugged. "I was awake and for someone so little Laxus sure does snore." He prodded at the fire with his bare hands. The flames burned brighter and the heat warmed Greg's face.

Greg looked back up at the sky. "Something's wrong."

Matt nodded. "The natural way of the world has been upset."

"That's a fancy way of saying there are no stars." Greg pointed above them. "Or moon and the sun suddenly went dark earlier." He ruffled his hair as he sighed. "I just hope Mellissa is all right. I wish I knew what had happened at that meeting and to the sky."

"Our only job is to worry about what happens to Laxus and the dark stone he protects."

Greg's forehead creased as he peered at Matt. "How are you so chill about this? Your sister and best friend are off fighting this war while we sit by a fire."

"I will have you know that Mellissa has replaced me as her best friend." Matt pressed his lips together and tutted. "With my sister."

Greg grimaced as he took a sharp inhale of air. "What no. You weren't replaced as her best friend. Mellissa's friendship with Victoria is a different kind."

"Dude, you two got engaged and the first person she told was Vicky." As his brows rose, Matt tilted his head. "They're best friends."

"Yeah, they are but they both still have room for you."

Matt stretched his arms up above his head. "It's fine I get it." A smile spread across his face. "Dude, you asked Mellissa to marry you and she said yes."

"I thought we had already established that."

"That ring was nice."

"Family heirloom."

"So, about the stag do."

Greg laughed as he shook his head. "I should have known that's where this was heading."

"Bro's night out." Matt hammered his fist on his own chest. "No, a weekend of partying. As your best bro I'll make sure you have a good time."

"Um, Samson is going to be the best man."

Matt waved his hand at him dismissively. "Yeah, I know. Samson's the best man in charge of the rings and boring stuff." Matt shuffled closer and hooked his arm round Gregs shoulders. "But I'm your best bro, planner of the most extravagant stag do you'll ever see."

"Umm." Greg rubbed the back of his neck. He wasn't sure if this best bro thing was a weird human custom Matt had picked up living amongst humans or something simply made up by Matt. Greg shrugged giving in. "Fine, you can be my best bro."

"Yes," exclaimed Matt fist pumping the air. Matt grasped his shoulder. "Seriously dude though, the reason I'm so chill about all this is because I have faith in my two best girls." Matt clicked his fingers and made finger gun motions. "They could both beat our butts with their eyes closed.

Greg chuckled. "That is true." The alarm on Greg's watch went off. The ringing sound made them both jump. Pressing the side of his watch he turned the sound off. "That's my shift over." Greg stood and brushed the dirt off his trousers. "I'm gonna try get some sleep."

"Good luck because that boy's snoring…" Matts eyes went wide as he whistled. "Wishing I had ear plugs."

Walking back to the tent Greg's heart felt tight. He did believe in Mellissa's ability, but he also knew how she would risk herself to save others. The knot in his stomach grew. All he wanted was to know that she was still fighting. There was only one reason that she would not be, and Greg couldn't bear to think about that.

Matt stuffed the tent back into the bag with the help of Laxus while Greg cleaned up the area, attempting to remove all evidence of their stay. There was a chill in the air and the trees swayed in the wind.  It was still dark with no signs of the sun coming up. A feeling of dread swirled around inside him. Greg scattered leaves around focusing on his task.

Matt walked up to him rubbing his hands together. "We are all packed up."

"Good, I'm done here." Greg followed Matt over to the pile of packed camping gear. Pushing his hands out and wriggling his fingers, Greg channelled his magic. The area around the bags glowed. With a click of his fingers, it all disappeared.

Matt whistled. "Nicely done. This place looks as abandoned as it did when we arrived."

"Where did you send all that?" asked Laxus.

"Mellissa's closet."

"She won't be happy when her wardrobe doors burst open and all that falls out," said Matt.

Greg chuckled as he picked up his rucksack and hooked it over his shoulders. "You haven't been in her walk-in wardrobe, have you?"

Laxus grinned as he skipped over to Greg's side. "She won't even know it's there."

Matt swung his own bag over his back. "That is one big closet."

"Enough talk of wardrobes." Greg flicked his fringe from his eyes and looked to Matt. "Where are we heading next?"

"I was thinking we should go south." Matt led the way through the trees. "If we head to the port we can hop on a boat."

Gregs brow creased as he frowned. "You want to sail somewhere?"

Matt nodded thoughtfully. "Yeah, I figured sailing around the world would help keep us on the move." He nudged Greg in the side and grinned. "It will also make for an awesome bro trip."

"Bro trip." Laxus echoed Matts words his brows furrowed. "I thought the focus was hiding the last dark stone."

Matt slung his arm over the boy's shoulders. "It is but we may as well enjoy this trip while we are at it."

Laxus pressed his lips together. "So, bro sailing trip?"

"Bro sailing trip." Matt thrust his arms up in the air. "We are gonna have so much fun."

Greg walked along silently while the other two chattered away. They were talking about the different places they could go. This was their chance to see the world. But every suggestion made felt like someone was hammering a spike into Greg's heart. This journey was taking him further away than he had anticipated. The distance between him and Mellissa was growing. There was always distance in their relationship with them living in different cities. They used to go weeks without actually seeing each other in person. But they talked all the time. Even that did not seem like it would be enough. She was where he wanted to return to every night. He rubbed the back of his neck and sighed. He was a grown man he could manage some time away from his girlfriend. No fiancée. Greg smiled as he corrected his own thoughts. She was his fiancée now. They had a future together. Matt was right they were on this trip so they may as well make the best of the situation. Mellissa could teleport. Once this was all over, she would find him wherever they travelled to. Time to get out of his head and enjoy this bros sailing trip.

# 30

# The Calm

## *Mellissa*

The leaves rustled in the wind, as we stood on the outskirts of the city. I huddled beside Harkura trying to warm myself. The sun shining brightly through the castle windows had tricked me into thinking it was warm out, so I had not picked up a jacket. But there was a cold chill in the air pricking at my skin. Radius stood with his arms crossed beside Victoria and Rowan stationed beside Ignis.

"So, what exactly are we all doing out here?" asked Rowan.

"We train together," replied Harkura, "so the next time we face Kadon we are better co-ordinated, and people are not dropped mid-flight." His indigo eyes flashed with magic as his gaze landed on the sea king.

Radius puffed his chest out. "I did not mean for that to happen."

Harkura went to respond but I stepped in front of him before he could talk. Facing the others I tried to make my features neutral. "None of us meant for any of this to happen but Harkura is right we need to learn to fight better as a team if we hope to get the sun back."

Ignis shook his body as he stood. "Mellissa is correct. We seem to do well in pairs but as a trio we are lacking."

Radius crossed his arms. "And how do you suggest we go about improving."

"Harkura has devised a plan." Sliding to the side, I waved my arms gesturing to my fire guardian. "If you would."

Harkura stepped forward, his features sharp and serious. "Defeating Kadon will take all three of you, but Mellissa you will be the one to make the killing blow."

It felt like my stomach had just flipped over inside me. "What?"

"You are the only one with the ability to get close enough."

It felt like everything was moving in slow motion as Harkura continued to explain his plan. "To start with you will all engage him," He pointed to Ignis and Radius. "You two will make sure Mellissa takes no serious hits. Weaken him as much as possible then Mellissa will need to teleport up close and slice him up."

"I can't do that." I spluttered. My mind reeled at the idea of slicing up a person.

Harkura sighed as he massaged his temple. "Fine just run him through or slit his throat whatever is easiest."

I gulped. None of that was easy. The way he spoke so casually about killing someone turned my stomach. Harkura interlaced his fingers, stretching his arms out in front of him. "Shall we practice your team work now?" I nodded my words lodged firmly at the back of my throat.

"Very well," said Radius. He swished his arm to the side and the moon crystal shot from round his neck glowing brightly. As he closed his fist round the crystal it transformed into his trident. "What is the training exercise?"

Harkura pointed to an empty spot on the grass. "Victoria if you would?" Pushing her hands towards the grass, ice formed on the ground. An icy mist formed as she swirled her arms round. When she was done a very life like ice sculpture of a man stood amongst us. "The task is to decapitate this ice sculpture. Us three guardians will act as its magic powers."

Ignis frowned. "This seems rather simplistic. Kadon's power is much greater than this."

"Then this should be a breeze for you three crystal keepers." Harkura walked over to me. He pulled a large dagger from the sheath on his hip. Turning the handle towards me he placed it in my hands. "I recommend covering it with light energy before administering the final blow." He removed the daggers holder from his leg and placed it on mine. I stood frozen to the spot as he tightened it round my thigh.

"Do we start now?" asked Radius.

"No," replied Harkura, "We get thirty seconds head start."

"What?"

Harkura smirked. "I did not say we would just be standing still. Rowan with us."

We split up into a respective teams. The three guardians ran off into the forest taking the ice sculpture with them. Radius began counting down from thirty aloud. I stared at the weapon in my hands. I could do this. This was just practice. I was killing a block of ice. But that ice represented a real person. I shook my head. Those thoughts served no purpose. Kadon was a monster; he did not deserve my mercy. Just as Radius came to the last few numbers, I sheaved the dagger. "3,2,1." Radius muscles bulged as he smirked. "Let's go kick your guardians' butts."

I grasped his bicep, stopping him from running into the forest. "Wait." Sliding my foot across the ground I pushed my magic into the earth. Feeling the vibrations of the forest I located our prey. I pointed to the left. "They are that way, but I only felt Harkura and Victoria on the ground."

Ignis looked up. "Rowan will have taken to the sky."

"Then that's where we'll start." Jumping I took flight. Radius followed suit and Ignis flapped his wings following us. I led us towards where I had felt my guardian's presence on the ground, in the forest. Just before we reached the area ice shot down at us from above and flames burst from within the tree line. Ignis whirled round breathing fire melting the icicles and Radius zoomed in front of me creating a hydro blast as he moved. The flames and water neutralised each other. The air funnelled around me, and I was swept away from the other two. Radius shouted my name. I teleported out of the wind current back to the others.

Rowan darted around us with Victoria on his back. She created ice shards, and he fired them in a wind tunnel. Ignis body ignited, and he acted as a shield of flames. Radius continued to fend of Harkura's attacks from the ground, but I was yet to lay eyes on him. Summoning light I fired at the pair in the sky. But Rowan was quick. He shifted direction dodging my attack.

I narrowed my eyes at them. They had planned this well. Attacking from an unexpected direction. Using distance and speed to make up for the power difference. But I was the faster one here. "Radius," I shouted, holding my hand out to him. As soon as I felt his grip, I teleported. We materialised beside Rowan and dropped Radius on him. Victoria was knocked sidewards as the two men wrestled in the air. Diving at her, I grabbed Victoria and teleported to the ground. Dropping her in the mud I teleported again.

I landed on Ignis's head. "I'm taking us to Harkura." Thinking of the fire nymph I materialised in front of him. And there was the ice sculpture. Simultaneously he and Ignis both blasted flames at each other. While those two pushed more fire at each other I unsheathed the dagger. Jumping from the dragons head I teleported. Encasing the blade in light I swung at the sculptures head. As Harkura had always said, the quickest way to take someone out was with a blow to the head. My body froze just before I made impact. Images of a real person flashed through my mind. Victoria's sculpturing was too realistic. I couldn't do it. I yelped as the sculpture moved. Its arms grabbed me, and I cried out.

Victoria walked out of the trees "And now your dead."

Ignis and Harkura both extinguished their flames. "Looks like this wasn't as simple of a task as I had thought," said Ignis.

My gaze dropped to the grass. I could not bear looking at any of them. With a swish of Victoria's hands, I was freed from the ice sculptures grip. Radius and Rowan landed beside us. Radius marched over to me. "What happened? You had a clear shot."

My grip tightened on the dagger. "I couldn't do it."

"Why not?" He yanked the dagger out my hand. "I'll show you how." He swung the dagger at the sculpture just as I had. Radius eyes went wide as he froze unable to stab the sculpture.

"It's not as easy as you think, is it?"

He lowered his arm, letting the blade hang by his side. "I've never killed anyone before. But this isn't even a person so why?"

Harkura moved in a flash. He pulled a matching dagger from his boot and lodged it the sculptures face. "That's how it's done." Jabbing his finger in both mine and Radius face, Harkura yelled, "How do you expect to defeat Kadon when you can't even take the killing blow on a hunk of ice?"

Victoria tugged him away from us. "They worked as a team and that was the goal right."

"A team of kind-hearted fools." Harkura pinched the bridge of his nose. "Let's try something else. We can work on you layering your attacks on top of each other's."

Swallowing the lump in my throat, I nodded. "Yeah okay." We spent the rest of the day trying to figure out some kind of combination attack the three of us could pull off. Mine and Radius's magic seemed to complement each other's better but whenever we tried adding Ignis's abilities to the mix the magic would blow up in our faces.

Harkura paced back and forth his brow furrowed. "Maybe if we concentrate just on your ability to produce light. It's the same type of magic which should get rid of the incomparability of water, fire and earth."

Radius huffed as he leaned against his trident. "Surely that's what we should have always been doing."

Harkura glared at him. Taking a deep breath, he regained his composure hiding his contempt away under a mask of neutrality. "Mellissa will start by creating a beam of light. Then both of you will add your power to it."

"Okay," I said. Shaking my arms out to the side I let my power flow into my fingers. I pushed my arms up releasing a beam of light up towards the sky. Radius and Ignis both illuminated light and pushed their magic into my beam. I gritted my teeth as the extra power jolted me. This did not feel right. Our magic was not mixing. It was bouncing around each other. A bang echoed through the forest as the beam of light exploded. I face planted the grass and my ears rang.

Cold hands wrapped around me, helping me up. "Are you okay?" asked Victoria as she held me.

"What happened?" snapped Harkura.

Ignis shuddered as he stood. "Our powers will not stockpile."

"You three are not trying hard enough." Harkura pointed at each of us. "Go again."

Radius clenched his fists as he stepped forward. "Who do you think you are to speak to royalty this way."

"There is a reason Mellissa is a better fighter than you." Tilting his head to the side Harkura looked less than impressed. "It's because I trained her, and she doesn't act like a pampered princess."

"How dare you?" yelled Radius his grip tightening on his trident.

I ran in between the arguing pair. "Enough." I didn't yell but I made sure my tone conveyed how serious I was. "We are done for the day. Everyone head back inside."

"But Mellissa we haven't made any progress," said Harkura.

"I said we're done." I turned my back on him and marched through the forest. Once I was away from the others, I let the tears fall. This entire day had been a disaster. We hadn't found a way to combine out powers. Both Radius and I had failed at the task to kill a ice sculpture. Ignis hadn't even attempted it, leading me to believe he wouldn't have been able to do it either. With a running start I took flight. I wasn't going to let anyone see me like this. I landed on my balcony and let myself into my bedroom. Throwing myself on my soft duvet I cried out all my frustration and anger. My heart felt like a lead brick. Because I now knew we could not do this. Out of the three crystal keepers, there was not one of us who could make that killing blow.

Rubbing my eyes with my palms I dried my tears. I sat in the middle of my bed with one of Gregs shirts draped around me. Inhaling. I took in his scent that still lingered on it. This was the closest to a hug from him I was going to get. It had taken every ounce of self-control I had to not teleport straight to him. Victoria was right. He was my comfort. My safe place. And I like an idiot had sent him away. That training session had been awful. It had not made us a better fighting team. All it had done was highlight our weaknesses.

"Mellissa." I jumped at the sound of Victoria's voice. She stood in the archway of my room, with Harkura. She smiled sweetly. "You okay to talk?"

I shrugged. "Not like I have anything better to do."

"Good," She walked in and sat on the end of my bed. I lowered my head hoping she wouldn't see that I had been crying. Victoria nodded her head towards me while muttering something at Harkura. He marched over to my bedside.

He stood with his arms behind his back. "I am sorry for my harsh words earlier. I was frustrated at the situation not you."

I snickered bitterly. "No, you were definitely angry at me and I don't blame you. I was pathetic."

"Have you been crying?" he asked.

Leaning away from him, I shook my head. "No."

"I'm so sorry Mellissa." Harkura sat beside me on the bed and pulled me into a hug. "Please believe me when I say I'm not mad at you."

Tears blurred my vision. "You should be. I was this close," I held my hand up showing them the tiny gap between my fingers. "To ruining my own plan by teleporting to find him."

"I could never be upset with you for missing Greg." Harkura pulled his sleeve up over his hand and brushed away my tears with it. "Today was hard."

"It really was."

"I told you he was your home comfort," interjected Victoria.

"Oh shush you and come hug me." I held one arm out to her while holding into Harkura with the other. Victoria shimmed up the bed until she sat on my other side. Both my guardians embraced me. The rumble of my stomach ruined the moment.

Victoria chuckled. "Are you sure you're not just extra sensitive because you're hungry." I pushed her away, but she only laughed more.

Harkura's forehead creased as he peered at me. "Did you skip dinner?"

"I came straight up here to mope after training."

"That is not good." He stood, placing his hands on his hips. "You can't risk missing meals, when you could be called to fight at any moment. Stay here and I'll go get you something." Harkura strode out the room.

Victoria rolled her eyes. "Always the mother hen, that one."

My stomach grumbled. "You know what I don't mind right now."

"Yeah." She drew out the word. Waving her hand up and down she gestured to my whole body. "When he gets back maybe the pair of us can tackle the rest of this."

I gaped at her. "I do not look that bad. Wait, do I?"

"I mean you've looked worse, but the puffy eyed, ill-fitting shirt isn't a great look."

"Shirt dresses are a thing."

"Only when you wear it properly."

Standing I tugged Gregs shirt, repositioning it on my body.  I grimaced as I realised, I hadn't buttoned it properly. Once I had re-buttoned the shirt I stood with my arms out to the side. "Better."

"One sec." She jumped off the bed and strolled into my closet. A few seconds later she returned with a black belt with a gold clasp. "Arms up." Once my arms were in the air, she wrapped the belt round my middle and fastened it. She stepped back. Rubbing her chin as she looked me over. "Now it's better." Her shoulders sagged as she huffed. "But you're still a mess but I know how to fix it."

Taking my hand, she led me into the living room. Leaving me standing in the middle of the room, she rummaged through the cupboards. When she was done looking through them, she knelt beside the coffee table. She hunched over as she looked under it. "What are you looking for?" I asked.

"Drinks."

"Sorry no drinks in here."

She sat up with a huff. "I should have known." Pouting she tapped her chin with her fingers. "Good thing I have a stash in my room. Back in a flash." She jumped to her feet and swiftly left.

As I went to sit on the sofa a dark chill swept through the room, putting me on high alert. Transforming the heart crystal to staff form I held it out in front of me. My pulse raced.

"My sweet little elf-ling." I jumped at the sound of Kadon's voice. Spinning round, to see a shadow figure. Light shot out the heart. The shadow swirled round and reformed in the shape of Kadon. "That's no way to treat a guest."

"Guests are invited, and you were not." I fired more light at him. The shadow swept around my room. I kept firing but he kept returning. Channelling more power into my staff I illuminated the room. The shadow sizzled away. As my blast dimmed the shadow swirled around the armchair. A wraith like Kadon appeared in the chair, one leg crossed over the other. "Will you stop that; I just came to talk."

I pointed my staff at him. "What have we got to talk about?"

He interlaced his fingers and smiled. "Actually, I've come to make you an offer."

I shuddered. "I'm not interested."

"Don't be like that. We should not be fighting. We should be uniting together, all magical beings against those filthy humans." He held his hand out to me. "Join me and you can rule beside me as my queen."

I glared at him. "Never."

Standing up he stomped his feet. "Are these humans worth dying over?"

"I'm half human. Why would you want me as your queen?"

Kadon stroked my hair. Curling a piece round his shadowy finger. "You remind me of her."

His closeness to me made me feel physically sick. I went to shove him but stumbled through his shadowy figure. Kadon cackled. "I'm a shadow projection, I choose what touches me." A wide grin spread across his face. "But if you become my Queen, I'll let you do all the touching you like."

My stomach rolled and I thought I might hurl. "Never."

"Even with all three life crystals working together, you won't win. Become my bride and I'll bring back the sun."

"No," I shouted, "I will bring back the sun with my own power."

A loud scream filled the room. Ice blasted through the shadow projection of Kadon. His form distorted and reshaped on the other side of the room. "Finally, one of your guardians shows up." He looked at his hand like it was really interesting. "I'm surprised I haven't seen Gregory yet. You know what, I'll let you keep him as a plaything if you must."

Ice pierced Kadon's shadow form again causing him to shoot around my room as she kept firing. None of Victoria's attacks hit and the shadow kept snaking around. "Enough," yelled Kadon taking form. "This is your last chance. Kneel before me or die."

"I will never stop fighting." I shouted.

"You can't say I didn't give you a chance." Shadow Kadon doubled in size towering over us. "My army is coming for you and the pixie boy." His stare bore into me making me shiver. Kadon growled. "When I have all the dark stones, you'll have no choice but to bow down to the god I'll be." His eyes went dark. "Kneel."

With everything I had I slammed my staff down creating a pulse of light. It spread through the castle lighting up the whole building. Shadow Kadon dissipated. Victoria stood on the opposite side of the room eyes wide and jaw slack. My head was spinning as I slumped into the sofa. Kadon was coming for us. I burst into laughter. I could not stop myself.

The room door swung open and Harkura ran in. Sweat glistened on his brow as he panted. "What happened? Why did you light up the whole castle?"

"Kadon sent a projection of himself." Victoria replied. "He threatened to attack us." She jabbed her finger in my direction. "And she is laughing."

Harkura strode across the room and clasped my shoulders. He looked down at me, his indigo eyes full of worry. "Mellissa, what is wrong with you? If Kadon is coming, we have to prepare for battle."

"Oh, he is coming." Sitting up straight I coughed trying to pull myself together. "But you guys aren't getting it. He said he was coming for me and the pixie boy." A giggle escaped; I bit my lip to stop it. "He still thinks Greg and Laxus are here."

"Which means they are safe." Victoria nodded as she pointed at me with both hands. "And the plan to keep Kadon's attention on us is working."

Brushing my hands over myself I stood. My chest felt heavy as the wave of laughter dissipated. Kadon's threat was still real. He was coming for us. "We need to alert everyone." I tensed my body as I looked from Harkura to Victoria. "We need to prepare for battle."

# 31

# Before

## *Mellissa*

The tension in the cave was tight. I had called on Radius and Ignis and we had met in the dragon's cave. I sat by the small fire that Ignis had breathed to life. After informing them of my encounter with Kadon's shadow neither had said a word. Radius stood with one hand against the wall staring blankly at it. Ignis's head was low as he stared at the fire. I tapped my fingers on my knees. The longer they did not talk the worse the fluttering got of the butterflies in my stomach. "What are we going to do?" I asked no longer able to take the silence.

"We must prepare for battle," said Radius his jaw tight, "We have no other choice."

"I know that but how? Do we have a plan?"

"Maybe this is good news," interjected Ignis.

Radius spun round glaring at the dragon. "Kadon just let himself into the castle. Our barrier means nothing to him. I was inside the castle, and I never sensed it." He thrust his hand out in my direction making me flinch. His stare was wide and wild. "He is coming for our Queen, and we must protect her."

"She does not need our protection," Ignis sat up, towering over the two of us. "What she needs is our support."

"Mellissa has done more than either of us have." Radius hammered his fist against his own chest. "We must step up as crystal keepers. We will spearhead this upcoming fight."

Ignis shook his head. "Queen Mellissa will lead us."

Radius' words echoed in my mind. He had said, '*Our Queen.*' The way he spoke - the way both of them were talking, was as if I was everyone's Queen not just the elves. My heart felt warm. They were putting me above themselves. I stood placing myself between them. "Stop arguing. We will deal with this threat as a team." I grasped the crystal around my neck, rubbing my fingers along its smooth surface. "We will work together, three life crystals as one." My heart hammered in my chest as I stared them both down. "Is that clear."

Ignis bowed his head. "Yes, your majesty."

"It is you he wants." Radius brows drew together as he looked at me his eyes wide and pleading. "Let us be your shield."

"I will not hide while others risk their lives for me." I placed my hand on his forearm. "He will come for me no matter what. Let us use this fact to our advantage."

Radius crossed his arms and scowled. "We will not use you as bait."

"Thats not quite what I meant," I said, "I was thinking along the lines of drawing him away from his followers into a fight that's just him and the three of us."

"And what of his army?"

My chest tightened, it felt harder to breathe. The idea of bringing others into this fight made my skin crawl but it had become unavoidable. Digging my nails into my palms I pushed down my anxiety. Standing tall I held my head high. "We call on our own people. Our guardians can lead them."

Radius's muscles bulged as he tensed his body. "Let's get to it then."

I stared at myself in the mirror. The armour I was wearing was light and flexible, but it felt all wrong. I wanted to tear it off and scream. It was okay when it was me putting my life on the line. When it was the three crystal keepers against Kadon, I could make sense of things, but this was different. Now it was a fight between all of the magical world. Those who hated the humans and those who wanted to just live in peace. We had spent the whole day preparing for battle. I looked down at my gloved hands and flexed my fingers. They allowed for good movement, and I had been told they would protect my bones when I punched into stone. When did they have this armour made? How long had my guardians been preparing for this battle? I glared at my reflection. Even with everything Kadon had done, a part of me had hoped to avoid this. To not have to fight a full out war. The Heart Crystal glowed round my neck. I looked down at it, hovering above my chest. The Crystal hummed. "Heart crystal, why did Freya create the veil?"

A projection of Freya appeared and the message to her daughter played again. My heart felt like it was about to burst but for some reason watching that message kept me from completely falling apart. When I first heard it, I almost lost the will to keep fighting but now this message was the tiny glimmer of hope I needed. Tears rolled down Freya's cheeks as she said, "I love you, Marissa."

Reaching forward I hovered my hand just in front of the image wishing I could touch her for real. To comfort her. When I first came to the magic world, all the stories of Freya made her seem like this goddess. Someone so great, I could never compare. But know I was finally opening my eyes to what all the memories of her had been showing me. It hadn't been to expose her relationship with Kadon or bring the prophecy to light. It had been to show me that Freya was just a girl. A girl who had made mistakes, who grew into a woman with a good heart but still flawed. She wasn't perfect but the important thing was that she always tried to do what was right. She had sacrificed herself to give us a fighting chance. Taking a deep breath, I took in my reflection again. I didn't have to be perfect I just had to never give up.

The mirror reflected movement behind me. Turning round I saw Harkura and Victoria walking across the room. They were both dressed in matching armour. Harkura' face was tight and serious. "A large group has been spotted at the edge of the forest, Rowan and the hawks have gone to investigate."

"What about Kadon?"

"He is yet to be spotted."

I tugged at my armour, making sure it was positioned correctly. "Good that means I still have time."

Victoria stepped in front of me putting her hands up between us. "Mellissa wait, we need to talk to you."

"What is it?"

She glanced back at Harkura and then looked to me. Her eyes were glossy as she swallowed. "We need to know that you're ready for this fight."

My brows drew together as I looked between the two of them. "Of course, I am. This is what we have been preparing for this whole time."

Victoria let out an exasperated moan as she looked to Harkura her eyes wide. Harkura stepped round her and placed his hands on my shoulders. "No Mellissa, you have been trying to save people. This is a fight to the death. There can only be one victor."

A lump caught in my throat and my words failed me. Victoria shook her head. "Even now she's still not ready."

I clasped my hands close to my chest. My heart ached. I wanted to tell them I could do it. That I would kill Kadon. A part of me believed I could. He was a monster. But while there was still even that small amount of doubt in my heart I could not commit. My throat was sore and dry, that when I spoke my voice was horse. "I'm weak. I have all this power, yet I can't confirm that when the time comes, I'll be able to take the final strike."

Harkura stroked my cheek. "You wouldn't be you if you could stand here and tell us you were about to kill someone."

Victoria sighed. "When you sent Laxus away you said you needed us to stay by your side for this very reason." She grabbed my hand shaking it. "We are here so use us."

I chewed on my bottom lip. "You are right. Change of plan." I nodded to Harkura. "You'll lead the ground forces and coordinate with Rowan in the sky." I squeezed Victoria's hand. As our eyes met a wave of determination ran through me. "I need you to stay with me in battle. I know you have what it takes if I do not."

Victoria's eyes glazed over. "I won't hesitate to end him." Her grip tightened on my hand. The force of her words hit me like a slap, and I knew I had made the right decision.

I stepped forward and embraced them both. Harkura stroked my hair. "I may not be by your side in this battle, but I will be with you both in spirit."

"Thank you for always protecting me," I said, "I wouldn't be here now without the two of you."

Victoria raised one eyebrow as she placed her hands on her hips. "And we will continue to do so after this battle."

"I'll never escape you two."

"Never." A wide smile spread across her face warming my heart.

"Okay time to join the other crystal keepers. Kadon could attack at any moment." We walked together towards the door. I frowned as my mind churned over what was happening. Kadon's army had already been spotted so why hadn't he? I frowned. "Why didn't Kadon portal his army straight in here? He has already proved he can get through the barrier."

Victoria shrugged. "I don't know, to taunt us. You know how he loves to make a scene."

That wasn't it. I rubbed my chin. He could have marched them in here and taken us by surprise but instead he gave us time to plan.

Harkura grabbed my arm. "To draw our attention away from what's important." He ran to the exit. "I must alert the ground troops and call Rowan back."

My heart sank as I felt a darkness loom over me. "He's here."

Screams and shouts sounded below. I ran through my bedroom straight out to the balcony. Water gushed from all directions. My body felt numb. A cracking sound came from above. The sky boomed as water plummeted into the city. As I went to leap into the air. An explosion shook the castle. Harkura yelled from inside the sitting room and fire exploded through the wall into my bedroom. Victoria cried out. Running back inside I zoomed into the living room. Shadows flew around the room. Victoria and Harkura were blasting like crazy but the shadows kept multiplying and growing in size.

The space in front of me distorted and a portal opened. A gust of wind crashed into me throwing me against the wall. Out stepped Kadon. He was dressed in black armour. His silver hair slicked back, leaving the dark swirls on his face on full display. He rolled his shoulders back and smirked. "I told you, you'd regret this." I screamed as my limbs burned and darkness enveloped me.

# 32

# The Storm

## *Mellissa*

arkness surrounded me. My limbs were heavy and my whole body tingled as if someone was sending small electrical currents through me. It felt like I was sinking, but I could feel the soft carpet beneath my back. My lungs burned as I struggled to breathe. My light was almost gone.

I shot up into a seated position as the weight on me suddenly shifted. My vision was blurred. Sweat dripped from my brow as I coughed. Smoke and ash surrounded me. The wall separating the living room and my bedroom was rubble. My four-poster bed had gone up in flames. A roar sounded from above. I looked up to see the sky. The roof was gone. Kadon flew past followed closely by a giant scaly dragon.

I flinched as someone touched my shoulder. "Mellissa," said Victoria, "We've got to get out of here." She pushed her hands out. The coldness of her magic stung my cheeks. Ice spread across the fire. "My powers won't hold against this much longer." She pulled me to my feet.

My legs wobbled like jelly, as I grasped her hand. "Where's Harkura?"

She pulled me close, digging her nails into my arms. "He can survive this fire. We cannot."

I gritted my teeth and teleported the two of us outside. We landed with a splash. The whole city was flooded. More water was pouring in. Radius and the few water nymphs we had left, were stood in a small circle. They were all moving in sync swishing their arms round redirecting the water funnelling in through portals above the city. Their legs were shaking and faces tight, but they were standing their ground.

I scanned the area. Why was the city filling so quickly? I gasped as I spotted it. A wall of shadow surrounded the city. We would be under water soon if Radius and the others had nowhere to redirect the flow to. "Victoria, stand back." As Victoria backed away from me, I jumped up into the air. Taking a deep breath, I dropped back down with force, water surrounded me. Panic bubbled up inside me, but I pushed it aside. Channelling my power, I punched the ground sending as much magical energy through the earth. My magic pulsed through the underground of the city, cracking the earth. Water began to seep into the cracks. I pulled my arms back and slammed them back down, sending another shock wave. Rocks jutted up slamming into the wall of shadow, but it had no effect. Transforming the heart into staff form, I flew up into the air. I panted as I focused all my power into the heart. The crystal shone brightly atop my staff. Swinging my staff round I fired pulses of light. My light smashed into the shadow wall and it exploded.

Radius and the water nymphs pushed the water out into the forest and over the castle putting out the flames. Victoria quickly ran forward, her hands glowing with magic. She threw her arms up towards the portals freezing the liquid coming through.

An almighty roar pierced my ear drum. I clutched my ears as, the roar turned shrill. The ground shuddered as Ignis fell out the sky. He writhed about as shadows curled round him. Kadon landed beside him and slashed him with a shadow whip. "We need to help him," I shouted to Radius.

The portals around us closed but were quickly replaced by new ones. A large group wearing black armour stepped through. At the front leading the way was Beatrice and

Gwendolyn. They both glared at me. The last to step through were Kai and Akito, leading a group of glass creatures.

Water was launched at us by the group of water nymphs, as the changeling's shifted into large animals. I spun out the way as glass creature slashed at me. Narrowly dodging its next swing, I released a blast of light. It shattered on impact. The glass pieces grew into more creatures. It looked like Kadon's glass creatures could regenerate just like Humarya's could. A blaze of fire blasted its way through the glass creatures. "Harkura" I shouted.

Relief washed over me as watched him charging through the creatures, shattering them with flames. He took a wide stance, bending his knees and putting his arms up. Victoria stood back-to-back with him and smirked. "It's about time you got here."

"You left me in a burning building."

She shrugged. "I knew you'd be fine."

Victoria froze a water blast in progress and Harkura spun round kicking the water nymph responsible in the face. Yuko charged in, bringing with her the rest of our fighters. Spells collide mid-air as battle commenced.

Victoria and Harkura fired in unison, a duo of fire and ice, destroying all the glass creatures around us. Harkura stomped his feet sending a line of flames across the ground burning anything in its path. "Leave this to me and the ground forces. You focus on Kadon." Our eyes meet and his stare filled me with determination. He shoved Victoria towards me. I grabbed her hand and shouted to Radius. He griped my shoulder and I teleported.

We dropped in behind Kadon. I shot straight up into the air leaving the other two on the ground. Radius with his trident and me with my staff, both summoned light. Victoria hurled spikes of ice at him. Our attacks smashed into Kadon's back, hurling him into the forest. I flew over Ignis, covering him in light getting rid of the shadows covering him. "Are you okay?" I asked.

Ignis opened his wings wide and roared. He shook his body, his scales slick with blood. "I'll be fine." His eyes narrowed on Kadon, as he casually strolled out of the trees flicking twigs from his shoulder.

Kadon smirked and floated slowly up into the sky. He lifted his arms and shadows danced between his fingers. I tensed as his eyes locked on me. "My sweet little elf-ling, you know what to do to make this all stop." His smile sent shivers down my spine. Pushing his hands out sparks of shadow rained down from the sky, striking multiple people at once. Screams rung through the forest.

Radius's grip tightened on his trident. "We must end this now." Bending his knees, Radius launched himself into the air, the moon crystal radiating in the centre of his trident. Ignis roared as he flapped his mighty wings, taking flight. As they both took aim at Kadon, I swiped my staff down striking him with lightening, as Radius' light and Ignis' fire smashed into Kadon.

Smoke plumed through the sky. It was a direct hit. I tightened my hold on my staff as a gust of wind blew me backwards. Kadon laughed. "Even the power of all three crystal keepers can't hurt me."  He threw his arms open wide, his eyes turning black. "I am the most powerful being in the world." Shadows oozed from his body. Both Ignis and Radius yelled as the ooze slammed into them, causing them to fall back towards the earth. I turned to fly after them but the air around me turned icy. I covered my cheek with my hand as a sharp pang spread along it. Blood seeped from a fresh cut. I cried out as the air sliced at my body.

With a wave of his arm the air current changed direction, sweeping me up and dragging me towards him. He clutched my face in his hand. "There's still time to change your mind and become my Queen."

"Never," I swung my staff at his head but he caught it in his hand. He swirled me round. When he let go of my staff I was hurled through the air. Shadows slammed into me with such force I was unable to stop my momentum. I hit the grass with a thud. My limbs roared in pain.

Kadon landed beside me. He yanked me up by my hair. "Just give up. You can't beat me."

I gritted my teeth and spun my staff slamming it into the back of his legs. He buckled loosening his grip on me. Twirling away from him I encased myself in a sphere of light. "I will never give up," I yelled, "As long as I'm still breathing, I'll keep fighting." I looked to the other keepers. They came to stand beside me. Their stares locked on Kadon; determination seeped from them. They were not about to give up and neither was I.

Swiping my staff along the ground, I cracked the earth. Twirling it round as I ran, rock and earth pummelled Kadon. Victoria ran along beside me. The air around her turned frosty. She thrust her hands in Kadon's direction and ice rained down on him.

Kadon's eyes bulged as he snarled. He leaped into the air flying up and around our attacks. But Radius and Ignis where already in the air. Ignis breathed fire and Radius blasted light. Standing back-to-back, Victoria and I both fired. Icy rocks flew up into the air. Our four attacks collide causing an almighty bang. Kadon dropped out the sky. Before he could recover the four of us blasted him again. A cavernous hole formed, where Kadon had been.

My chest heaved as sweat dripped from my brow, scanning the area for Kadon. Victoria screamed as she was yanked away from me. As I went to run after her something wrapped around my legs. I cried out as my feet were taken out from under me and was engulfed by shadow.

# 33

# Done With Fate

## *Gregory*

Greg lay awake looking at the tent ceiling. To his left, Laxus was snoring loudly snuggled nicely in his sleeping bag. Matt was outside on watch, Greg needed to rest before it was his turn to take over. Every time he shut his eyes he thought of Mellissa. He would much rather be back at the castle with her. He wished he knew what was going on with the others. Was she laid awake looking at her bedroom ceiling or was she out fighting? Not knowing if she was okay was driving him crazy. Greg huffed as he got out of his sleeping bag. He put on his shoes and coat. Stuffing his hands in his pockets, he walked out the tent. The cold air prickled his cheeks. Greg looked around the leafy trees. They had set up camp in another small wood. They had arrived at the port to find it closed. No ships were going in or out due to the natural disaster of having no sun. Meaning there would be no sailing around the world for them.

Matt had taken it upon himself to lead them to this secluded area instead. It was quiet except for the rustling of the leaves in the wind. Greg's gaze landed on Matt. He stood on the edge of the tree line looking out into the distance. Greg walked over to him. He stood next to him and looked up at the night sky. There was still no moon or stars. The sun had never risen. They had relied on Greg's watch to keep track of the day, only stopping when their legs would take them no further.

With his hands stuffed in his coat pockets Greg meandered through the trees over to Matt. As he approached him, Matt opened his arms wide, up towards the sky. "The final battle has begun."

Greg's heart felt like it had stopped. "What? How can you tell?"

Matt stepped forward sniffing the area in front of them. "I can smell it." Greg frowned. Matt spun around on the spot. "I can feel it in the air." He stopped moving and stared at Greg, his eyes glazed over. "You can feel it too. It is why you can't sleep."

Greg grabbed Matt by the shoulders roughly and shook him. "Your sister and best friend are fighting somewhere out there and you're spinning around in a forest."

Matt tilted his head to the side; his eyes were still unfocused. It was like he was only half present. "There isn't anything we can do; their fate has already been decided." He looked out at the trees, his face blank. Greg's pulse raced as he saw red. He grabbed Matt by the scruff of his shirt and punched him. Matt hit the ground with a thud. "Ow," he yelled rubbing his cheek.

"What happened to the hot-headed warlock that came at me engulfed in flames when he thought Mellissa was in danger." Greg yanked Matt's arm. "Don't tell me their fate is decided. Screw Fate." He jabbed his finger in Matts face. "You have these weird new powers, so use them to help."

"I don't know if I can." Matt's head dropped his blond hair covering his face. Greg let go of him and Matt slunk to the ground. Matt sat on the grass, with his knees to his chest and his arms wrapped round them.

Greg sighed as he rubbed the back of his neck. "Look I'm sorry I hit you."

"It actually helped snap me back to this time window. You don't understand how wild these new powers are."

Greg sat beside Matt and crossed his legs. "Then help me understand."

Matt looked up at the night sky. "The tree of time was named so because it exists at all points of time."

"Yeah, I know."

"Well, that's what I am now. When I first appeared to help Mellissa in the capital, just after the veil had fallen." Matt looked down at his hands, spreading his fingers wide. "It had been maybe an hour at most from when the tree had been destroyed." Matt looked Greg straight in the eye. His stare made Greg stiffen. "I had been out of the tree for a lot longer than that."

Greg's forehead creased as he leaned forward. "How long have you been out of the tree?"

Matt shrugged. "About a hundred years."

Greg gasped. "But you still look the same as before."

"We are a constant." Matt stared out at the horizon. "We exist everywhere at once; it took me years to control my new powers enough to make myself appear where I wanted to be seen. The tree of time was only meant to observe, it never had a role in any of this."

Greg's head was racing with this new information. He ran his fingers through his hair. If what Matt said was true, then the two them shouldn't be interacting now. Matt wouldn't have a voice if all he was meant to do was observe. Greg patted Matt's back. "That's what the tree used to be but when you merged with it, you became something new, something more than when you were separate."

"You're right." Matts eyes went wide, and his brows shot up so fast they looked like they were trying to run off his face. "If I wasn't meant to interact, there wouldn't be multiple versions of the future with me in them."

"You see the future," cried Greg, "Tell me how to win the battle so we can help the others."

Matt ruffled his hair tangling his fingers in it. "It doesn't work like that. It's all a jumbled mess because the future isn't set. I don't know what will happen until it is happening."

Greg held his hand out to Matt. "Do you think you can show me?"

"I can try." Matt took hold of Gregs hand. Matt took a deep breath and his eyes turned white. Greg tensed as magic radiated from Matt and soared into him. His grip tightened on Matt. Flashing images of darkness and light ran through Greg's mind. His teeth chattered as he tried to stop from shaking. Chaos, the sun completely burnt out and darkness falling but that was only one possible outcome. Other visions of the future flooded his mind, those of darkness and chaos but also those of light and peace.  Greg pulled his hand away and fell forward, just getting his hands out in time to stop his face hitting the dirt. He panted, catching his breath. Sweat coated the back of his neck. He looked up and locked eyes with Matt. Matt's eyes were turned down a shadow looming over him. "I told you it's all a mess."

Greg's mind felt like it was on fire. He shut his eyes trying to make sense of all the possible futures he had seen. His heart raced. Greg opened his eyes. Taking slow breaths he calmed his body. He stood and looked into the distance. "I have to go."

Matt jumped up, standing in front of Greg with his hands spread wide. "You saw what I did. There isn't anything either of us can do. Even if I slowed time, it would only prolong what needs to happen."

"I know," Gregs chest tightened as his eyes filled with tears. "But I can't not see her again."

"Even if you transform into the fastest flying creature in existence, you won't get there in time."

Greg clasped Matt's hands. "You exist everywhere at once. Which means a part of you, or the tree is there right now."

"Yeah, I guess."

"Then send me to that part of you."

Matt scratched the side of his head. "I don't know if I can do that."

"Just try," shouted Greg, "Embrace your new existence and take control of your powers."

Matt pressed his lips together as his forehead creased. "Okay." Matt shut his eyes and when he opened them again, they were white. His whole body glowed. He held his hands out, his palms turned upwards. Greg gulped down the lump in his throat and placed his hands on top of Matt's. Suddenly he was thrown backwards. His body cried out in agony. It was like he was being twisted inside out and back again. The pain ceased and he rolled across the cold wet grass. Rain poured down on him. A loud bang echoed above him. Three small figures and a dragon collided high in the sky. Greg sighed with relief. The four of them were all still fighting he had time. Greg pushed up off the floor and ran as fast as his legs would carry him.

# 34

# Outside View

## *Victoria*

A shadow snaked round Victoria's leg yanking her legs out from under her. Mellissa tried to grab her hand, but a shadow formed behind her. Victoria went to call out, to warn her but the pair were both dragged apart. The shadow around Victoria's leg, jerked round dragging her into the forest. She reached out trying to dig her nails into the dirt to stop her movement but the snake like wisp kept tugging at her. Twigs and leaves scratched at her as she was dragged further into the wood. Victoria curled round on herself hurling ice towards her legs. She came to an abrupt halt as the shadow froze. Kicking her legs she shattered the ice freeing herself. Pushing back up to her feet, Victoria turned to run back to the fight.

Darkness surrounded the area. She couldn't see Kadon or any of the crystal keepers. Light pulsed through the forest. Victoria smiled as she saw Mellissa holding her staff above her head, the heart crystal shining brightly atop it. Radius and Ignis both illuminated light stinging her eyes.

Water slammed into the side of Victoria taking her feet out from under her. She slammed into the dirt jarring her arm. She winced in pain. More water gushed towards her. She rolled out the way just before it smashed into the spot she had just been laid. Jumping up to her feet Victoria came face to face with Kai and Akito. They stood back-to-back with their arms up in a fighting stance. They moved in unison. Pulling back their hands then punching them forward. Water rose up from the ground and blasted at Victoria. Moving swiftly, Victoria slashed her arms down freezing the water. As quickly as she froze it, Kai and Akito defrosted the water and whipped it at her. Victoria darted through the trees dodging their attacks. Kai and Akito ran in opposite directions. Water blasted at her on both sides. Freezing the ground at her feet as she moved, Victoria skated through the trees. Her lungs burned but she had to keep moving, keeping herself a head of her attackers. A bang echoed through the sky. The vibration shook the trees. Victoria looked up as a bolt of lightning crashed into Kadon. Then very quickly after a ray of light followed by flames slammed into him.

Victoria cried out as water slashed at her sides. She dropped to her knees. Kai ran out from behind a tree. "You shouldn't take your eyes off your opponent." He swirled a pair of water whips round. Victoria dove at him, tackling him to the ground. His water whips fell to the ground as puddles.

She pinned him to the ground. "I don't need fighting advice from traitors." As she drew back her fist to punch him something wrapped around her wrist. A water whip. Akito smirked as they yanked on the other end. Victoria was tugged back. Kai punched her in the jaw, causing her to fall backwards into the brush. Akito walked over to Kai and helped him up. Victoria stared up at the sky through the branches of the trees. Her head swam with pain. Kadon flew into her eye line. His eyes were pure black, the swirls on his face slithered as if they were alive. The two stones he wore pulsated as he opened his arms wide. Mellissa flew after him, shining like a bright star. Radius and Ignis flew at Kadon from the opposite direction. The three crystal keepers surrounded him. They all took aim and fired. Their attacks hit in an almighty bang. Victoria frowned. Their timings had been off. As the smoke cleared Kadon grinned from within a sphere of shadow. He threw his arms out to the side and shadows propelled at the crystal keepers. Mellissa's light dimmed.

Victoria's heart felt like it had stopped. They were losing. For all the power the crystals granted them it wasn't enough. She watched the movements of the three figures flying in the air. They were not coordinated. Radius and Mellissa were fighting together but they were not in sync. When Victoria fought alongside Harkura, they could anticipate each others moves. It was the same when she was by Mellissa's side. They all knew each other inside out. But the three crystal keepers hadn't had that time to get to know each other before having to work together.

The pair of water nymphs stood over her, blocking her view. Akito snickered. "So much for the queen's guardian."

Rage rolled through Victoria. She had vowed to stay by Mellissa's side through this all. She was not about to let these two traitors best her. Victoria slammed her hands on the ground. Ice spread through the forest. Akito and Kai screamed as ice spikes shot up from the ground. Victoria rolled up to her feet. Her limbs protested but she pushed through the pain. Ice formed in her hands, and she fired. Kai dove to the side but she hit Akito straight on. Before Akito could counter Victoria spun round kicking them in the stomach. Ice spread from her foot across Akito's body. Putting all her weight into it, Victoria punched Akito in the face. Her head snapped back, and the water nymph crumbled to the ground.

Victoria whirled round firing ice at Kai. He jumped to the right narrowly dodging her attack. His eyes went wide as he looked at Akito on the ground, then to Victoria. Flexing her fingers Victoria summoned more ice. Kai threw a funnel of water at her. With a swish of her arm Victoria froze the blast mid-air. The ice dropped to the ground shattering on impact. Kai scrambled backwards pressing his body to a tree trunk. As Victoria stepped forward, he took a step backwards.

Ignis roar sent a shock wave through the forest. The trees shuddered as Victoria stumbled. Grabbing a tree trunk, she steadied herself. Ignis roared again. This one sounded more shrill causing Victoria to glance towards the sound. Black ooze covered the dragon. Water gushed into Victoria, and she fell on her butt. She pushed herself up magic forming on her fingertips. She went to fire her ice but stopped short. Kai was out of reach, running away through the trees. Away from her.

As Victoria went to run after him the forest shuddered. A loud snap caught her attention. Trees tumbled around her. Pushing ice out behind her, Victoria propelled herself forward escaping the path of the falling trees. She scanned the area. Ignis laid crumpled on the ground at the edge of the forest. Mellissa and Radius materialised beside the dragon. Once Mellissa had hold of both crystal keepers, they disappeared in a flurry of lights.

Victoria's mind raced, as her chest tightened. Where had they gone? Focusing on Mellissa's aura she ran out the forest. Trusting her instincts she went to find her Queen.

# 35

# The Sky Opens

## *Mellissa*

The three of us had been attacking non-stop but Kadon did not seem phased by any of it. Darkness seeped out of Kadon, until black smog was all I could see. Inhaling sharply, I pulled on my magic. Light illuminated my skin. With sheer willpower, I released a pulse of light. Sweat dripped from my brow, as everything came back into view. Kadon hovered in the sky. Ignis roared above him breathing fire. Radius flew up from the ground, twirling his trident around summoning light energy. Kadon waved his arms deflecting both attacks. A smirk spread across his face. "Pathetic."

Running I built momentum and launched myself into the air. My power flared. The hairs on the back of my neck stood up as I channelled lightening. It danced along my arms and up my staff. Aiming at Kadon I fired. Just before it hit, Kadon swirled round catching the electric current, in one hand. He wriggled his arms and black lightening shot out of his opposite hand back at me. I swerved to the left. The lightning shot past me and crashed into the ground below. Soil and stones exploded on impact creating a cavernous hole in the earth. I inhaled sharply as I took in the destruction below. That attack had been meant for me.

"I actually thought you three may pose a threat to my rule." Kadon cackled. "How ridiculous of me." His eyes completely glossed over with shadows as he summoned magic. He opened his arms wide and black ooze shot from his fingertips. Swirling around in the air I narrowly dodged the gunk. My ears rang as Ignis let out an ear piecing roar. The black ooze crashed into him. The dragon hurtled out the sky slamming into the trees at the edge of the forest. A loud snap echoed through the air as trees tumbled. I winced. It was like I was being pinched every time a tree thudded to the ground. Radius' yell drew my attention back to the fight. He soared through the sky, swinging his trident. It shone brightly. As he swung at Kadon's head, black sludge slammed into Radius. He cried out as he plummeted towards the earth.

My heart raced. We were losing. I zoomed over to Radius. Just before he hit the ground, I grabbed his hand and teleported. We materialised next to Ignis. Once my hand made contact with the dragon I teleported again. We landed with a thud. Loosing grip of the other two I tumbled backwards. Crashing onto the grass, I rolled down a hill slamming into a tree trunk. My back ached in pain. I laid out flat, my body stiff as a board. The sky was unnaturally dark. Black ooze rained down on the forest. The green leaves sizzled when the gunk made contact. The trees cried out in agony. "Help us," they yelled.

"I'm sorry," I said through gritted teeth.

Radius slid down the hill. He held his hand out to me. I took it and he yanked me up. "This is it, isn't it? The end." His jaw was tense and his eyes glistened, tears forming. "I hope Harmony and the kids are together."

I dug my nails into his bicep. "This is not it. I will not allow the world to end."

Radius' adam apple bobbed as he gulped. "But even the power of the three life crystals together wasn't enough."

"Mellissa," shouted Victoria's voice. I looked up to see her stood on the hill next to Ignis. I ran up to meet her. Grasping her wrist, I let out a slow breath. "I'm glad you're safe."

"After being yanked away from you I had a little run in with Akito and Kai in the forest, but I also got a clear view of your battle." Victoria panted as sweat dripped down her forehead. She gripped my shoulder tight. "I know what you need to do."

"What could we possibly do that we haven't already tried?" Radius asked.

"Combine the power of the three crystals as one," she said.

Radius swept his arm out gesturing to the black ooze covering the forest. "In case you haven't noticed that hasn't exactly worked."

Victoria shook his head. "You think you are all attacking together but there is a slight gap between each of your strikes. You haven't fought together enough to be truly in sync with one another." Her facial features were tight and focused as she placed her hands on her hips. "What you need to do is what Kadon has." She pointed at each of us. "You need to combine your powers into one entity. All three of your powers in one person."

My jaw dropped. It felt like time had slowed as I thought back to a conversation I had had with Josh in his office. Victoria's idea was one I had already had but Josh had warned me against it. I looked out at the forest towards the battle in the city. I would risk it all if it meant this thousand-year-old war would finally end. I clasped my hand over my chest as I nodded. "Victoria is right."

Radius's eyes went wide like sauces as he shook his head. "No. That sort of power."

"Could destroy the wielder," said Ignis finishing his sentence. The dragons' eyes turned down as he frowned. "But it's the only way."

Radius pounded his chest as he stepped forward. "Very well. I volunteer to take on these powers."

My chest was tight, but I forced my body to move. Tugging at Radius's arm I pulled him back. "No, it has to be me."

Victoria's gaze locked on me; her eyes filled with tears. "Yeah. That was the conclusion I came to."

"But why?" Radius protested. "The queen is young. I am old, let me take the risk."

Ignis lowered his head, and I placed my hand on top of it. He sighed. "The keeper of the heart is the balance between the sun and moon crystal. She is the only one that stands a chance of withstanding the power."

Victoria clasped my free hand in hers. "It's why that good for nothing lizards vision only showed you fighting. It was always meant to be you, our light of hope against the darkness." Tears rolled down her cheeks. "And there is nothing I can do to help you not as your guardian or your friend."

I brushed my fingers along her cheek wiping away her tears. "You're the reason I'm standing here right now. You and Harkura are the ones who have prepared me for this."

Victoria pulled me into a hug squeezing me tight. "I believe in you." I felt her heart beating fast. Her breathing was heavy as she rested her head on mine. My body ached and wanted to crumble onto to ground with her. I took a deep breath and stepped back out of her hold. Rolling my shoulders back, I held my head high and turned to the other two crystal keepers. "Okay, how do we do this?"

"Hold your hands out," said Ignis. I did as I was told. He pressed his claw to his chest and a bright light sparkled. The sun crystal hovered above his claw, and he placed it in my hand. "I keeper of the Sun crystal, relinquish my power to Queen Mellissa." A jolt of energy shot through me, making me gasp. The Sun crystal shimmered in my hand; its warmth wrapped around me. I attached it to the same chain as the Heart crystal.

Radius took my hand in his. He had deep frown lines, and his eyes were creased at the side. "Are you sure about this?" I nodded. He sighed. "Out of the three of us you were always the strongest." He spun his trident round. It shimmered and disappeared leaving behind only the Moon crystal on a golden chain. He put the crystal round my neck with the other two. Holding my hands, he said, "I keeper of the Moon crystal, relinquish my power to Queen Mellissa." Power surged through me again. It felt like I was on fire. I dropped to my knees as I tried to contain it all.

"Mellissa," shouted Victoria. I held my hand up stopping her from coming closer. My pulse raced. I could feel everything the earth, the sea and sky. Every footstep on the land, the beating wings of the birds, the swimming fish in the ocean. Magic soared through me longing to be let loose. I was pure power. I looked up at the sky. Thinking of where I wanted to be and, in an instant, I was face to face with Kadon.

# 36

# Confrontation

## *Gregory*

Greg ran through the city, dodging stray attacks and people locked in battle. The beautiful city was a mess. The castle was a pile of rubble and fires had broken out on the surrounding buildings. Magical beings were locked in battle with one another. They should have had the greater numbers, but Kadon had filled out his army by creating glass creatures. This old air spell made it so this being could regenerate from their smashed pieces. This made Kadon's army unlimited. Greg's lungs burned and sweat stung his eyes. Noise screeched around him but that was all it was noise. He couldn't distinguish one shout from another. The battlefield was not where he was meant to be. He had to get to Mellissa.  Greg cried out as something barrelled into his back. He hit the ground with a thud. Mud splashed onto his face. A pair of hands grabbed at his shoulders. Greg jutted his head back, making contact with something. A women cried out as their grip on him loosened.  Greg gritted his teeth and pushed up to his feet. He spun round just in time to see a lion launching at him. Greg's magic surged out of him as he quickly created a barrier. The lion slammed into it.

"Discutio," shouted Greg. The shield burst outwards blasting the lion. Greg covered his ears as the creature let out a weird combination of a roar and shriek. It hit the muddy ground and shuddered as it shifted back to human form. "Gwendolyn," growled Greg. "I shouldn't be surprised."

His mother jumped to her feet lunging at him. Greg blocked her punches and kicks. She let out a high-pitched scream. "You ungrateful brat."  The skin on Gwendolyn's hand rippled and she partially shifted, turning her fingers to claws. She slashed at Greg's face. He swatted her arms away and shoved her back.

Gwendoyln stumbled into a crouched position. Her eyes narrowed at him, as she pulled a dagger from her boot. She launched forward swinging the blade at him. Greg caught her wrist and kicked her legs out from under her. The knife flew out her grip as she crumpled onto the ground. Greg pushed his hands out wrapping a barrier round Gwendolyn. She clawed at the invisible dome around her, shrieking profanities. Barring her teeth she growled. "I did all of this for you, and I'm repaid for my efforts with constant betrayal."

Greg's pulse quickened as rage flared within him. "I did not betray you. I was never on your side." His fists clenched as he jaw tensed. "I told you what would happen if I saw you again."

Gwendolyn snickered as she crossed her arms. "You won't kill me, Gregory. You don't have it in you. Eventually I will have my way and our history will be rewritten."

"You're insane." Anger swirled around in his stomach. The mere sight of her made him want to shake her and scream. But she was still his mother. Even with all the pain and hurt she had caused him he couldn't bring himself to really harm her. Greg shoulders sagged as his brows furrowed. "You're right I don't have it in me to kill you." Greg's eyes darted to movement just beyond them. He shut down his emotions creating a steel cage round them in his mind. "But that doesn't mean I'll save you from him."

Harkura stood a foot away his hands ablaze and eyes narrowed on Gwendolyn. With a flick of his wrist, Greg lowered the barrier he had created. Gwendolyn shifted into a large brown bear and swiped her claws at Harkura. He swiftly dodged and ran forward raining fire down on her. Greg turned his back on the two engaged in battle. He ran straight into a barrier.

"You're not going anywhere Gregory." Beatrice ran at him. As she did, she shifted into an eagle. She swooped down clawing at his face.

Greg jumped back transforming into a tiger as he did. Swatting the bird with his paw it crumpled into the mud. She transformed back and hissed. "You thought you were so clever wooing Mellissa." Beatrice stood clutching her hand over her chest. Her eyes growing wider as she spoke. "Constantly getting her favour. I'm the better changeling elder. I deserved all the praise. I can't be too mad if she had been into women I'd have done the same."

Greg snickered. "You are just as deranged as my mother." He dropped into a fighting stance, arms up ready. "But I really don't have time for your rubbish Beatrice."

"I'll end you quick then." Beatrice shifted into a rhino and charged at him. Jumping back Greg shifted into a bird and swooped up into the sky. If he couldn't get away from fighting on the ground, he would escape into the air. Flapping his wings he went to fly away when a blast of water slammed into him. Greg crashed onto the ground, his head slamming into the dirt. Shuddering he transformed back. His ears rang as he sat up. Kai stood beside Beatrice with a smirk on his face. "You won't escape that easily."

A wave of water gushed towards him. Yuko slid in front of him, opening her arms wide she sliced through the wave. Water droplets splashed on Greg's face. A hydro blast thundered towards Yuko. She swiftly spun round redirecting the blast. It slammed into Beatrice, and she hit the ground. Her body skidded across the mud.

Kai dived at Yuko. She pushed back against him. He skidded across the ground and snarled. "I was your loyal servant Yuko, but you let us down when you sided with the humans."

Yuko flicked her robe back and crouched into a fighting stance. "I did not side with the humans, I just did not wish to massacre them."

Kai swirled his arms round creating two water whips slashing at Yuko. She hit the ground with a thud. Greg jumped to his feet and went to run to her, but Yuko held her hand up to him. "This is my fight."

Greg nodded and turned to run but his mother dove at him. He kicked her away scanning the area for Harkura. Beatrice was on top of him. Yuko's blast hadn't knocked her out like he had thought. She shifted into a jaguar, opening mouth wide. Bringing her sharp teeth close to Harkura's jugular she went in for a bite. With a yell flame burst from Harkura's body, covering him all over. Beatrice screamed as her body caught fire, she shuddered in the mud shifting between forms.

A roar startled Greg. He turned just in time to see a lion leaping at him. He rolled out the way shifting into a tiger. As the lion pounced at him, he countered. Their claws ripped at each other. He winced as his mother dug her claws into his side. Using his superior size against her, he overpowered her throwing her down. As she hit the ground she shifted back. She cowered on her knees looking up at him with tears in her eyes. "You can't do this I'm your mother."

"I'm done with this." As Greg shifted back his mother jumped up swinging a dagger at him. Before Greg could counter Harkura had grabbed her wrist twisting it round forcing the dagger out her grip. Greg's head span and it felt like everything was moving in slow motion. Harkura caught Gwendolyn's knife in his other hand. Slashing down he sliced it along her neck. She slumped to the ground, blood spurting out onto the grass. Her eyes went wide as she clutched at her wound.

Greg stood there in stunned silence. He felt nothing as the life left her eyes. "Goodbye mother," he whispered. Turning his back on her Greg ran as fast as he could. He formed a barrier around himself forcing his way through the battlefield. He skidded to a halt as he reached the bottom of the hill. Up top were the other two crystal keepers and Mellissa was flying high up in the sky, where the real fight for this world was taking place

# 37

# Last Hope

## *Mellissa*

I radiated light like a shining star. The black goop oozing from Kadon sizzled away in the rays of my light. The trees shimmered greener than before. The battlefield sparkled under my shine. Kadon's eyes narrowed, his head tilted to the side. "What is happening? This power, it can't be."

"But it can." I lifted my arm shooting beams of light up into the atmosphere. Sun light burst form beneath the dark sky. It's rays warming my cheeks.

Kadon's nostrils flared as he snarled. "I am the most powerful being in existence."

I smirked my eyes burning with magic. "Not anymore."

Kadon let out a frustrated yell. Shadows snaked from him and shot at me. I lifted my hand pushing my light out, dissipating the darkness. He gritted his teeth. Swirling the air round, he hit me with a stormy gust. I lifted my arms over my face as the icy wind pierced my skin. Shadow whips caught my ankles, and I was yanked towards him. He pulled his fist back but before he could hit me, I spun round my light sizzling away his magic and kicked him in the stomach. He recoiled back, barring his teeth.

A burning sensation rolled through me. It felt like I was heating up from the inside. I opened my mouth and fire came out. I roared setting the sky a blaze. Water gushed towards me. I caught the stream in my hand swirling it round my arm. Lifting my arm I whipped it back at Kadon. He narrowly dodged. He growled as he flew at me. The air sizzled as the two of us collided. I burned with fire. He sent a wintry chill to put out my flames. The clouds rumbled as Kadon drew water from them and slammed it into me. I lifted my hand and the water droplets floated still in mid-air. Kadon's eyes widened. I lifted my hands and dropped them down rapidly. The rain plummeted and lightning crackled.

Kadon flew in zig zags trying to dodge but I had created an almighty storm. He narrowly dodged a bolt of lightning. Letting out an ear piercing screech, he rapidly spun his arms funnelling the air round. The new air current drew the other elements of the storm into it. "I won't be defeated." He screamed. Pushing his hands out he forced the tornado in my direction.

I didn't flinch from my spot in the air. The oncoming tornado whipped my hair around. His jaw dropped as I swatted it aside, with the back of my hand. I flew up above him. "I'm done with this fight."

My body sizzled with power. I swept my arm down and lightning crashed into Kadon. I created two water whips and with a flick of my wrists wrapped them round Kadon. He yelled pushing against the binds. He screeched and thrust his head forward. Shadows, water, and cold air crashed into me. I shut my eyes and let the magic bubbling inside me soar. I released all the light, water, fire, and plant magic, I had been trying to keep under control. Kadon screamed as I felt my magic slam straight threw his. I opened my eyes to find Kadon in a heap on the ground.

I blinked and was beside Kadon on the earth. Swirling my hands rocks shot up from the ground, either side of Kadon, trapping him in place. With my hand covered with light I yanked the two dark stones from round his neck.

"No," Kadon yelled. He thrashed around on the floor, but he was trapped. I glided my foot across the earth and lifted one arm. The rocks around Kadon shifted, lifting him up to a kneeling position. He sagged forward hanging his head.

He clenched his fists. "Go on then." His head jerked upwards, and he glared at me, his grey eyes now back to normal. "Kill me. Hurry up and end it."

I tilted my head to the side. "I'm not going to kill you. You will be locked up in a cage and never see day light again."

Kadon threw his head back and laughed. "All that power and your still so weak."

"With out the stones you are a normal leprechaun. You are no threat to anyone."

"Does the little queen not have the stomach to do what needs to be done. Pathetic." He smirked. "One day I will get my powers back and you'll be sorry. This isn't the end of our story Mellissa." The smile on his face turned into a frown and his eyes went wide. Blood dripped from his mouth. An icicle stuck out of his chest.

"Victoria." I said as she appeared behind Kadon, her hands stretched out aglow with magic. Her lips were drawn into a tight line and her eyes were tense. An icy chill followed her.

Kadon's eyes were the size of saucers as he spat blood at her. "No this isn't how it was meant to be." He coughed bringing up more blood. His gaze landed on me. "Our destinies are entwined. It should have been you."

Victoria clenched her fist and another icicle shot through Kadon. "No because she is too nice but I'm not." She bent down. Grabbing his hair, she pulled his head back, so his ear was close to her mouth. "I won't give you the chance to hurt her again or anyone else I love." Victoria let go of him. Brushing her hands together as she stood up straight, her eyes empty of any emotion. Kadon's head hung loosely, and his body sagged.

"Victoria," I said again. I stepped forward, reaching out to her. Suddenly it felt like I was on fire. I screamed clutching the sides of my head. My mind felt like it was about to explode. Pain ricocheted through me as I dropped to my knees. Victoria shouted my name as she grasped my shoulders. I shut my eyes tight trying to take back control.

"Mellissa." That wasn't Victoria's voice.

I opened my eyes. Green ones stared back at me. "Greg, how?"

He was knelt in front of me his brows furrowed as his gaze ran over me. "What can I do? Where are you hurt?"

My eyes filled with tears. "It's too late, I can't hold it back."

His hands cupped my face. "No there has to be a way."

"I love you." I shut my eyes and pressed my lips to his. Every bone in my body was screaming in agony. But I kissed him with all the passion and love I had left in me. Magic rolled through me, and I cried out as it tried to break free. My skin felt like it was melting. The different elements fighting against one another. My head was thrown back as I screamed in agony as my magic soared. My vision blurred as I saw stars.

# 38

# A New Life

## *Greg*

Mellissa's lips felt like fire as she kissed him. Her touch burned but he didn't dare let go of her. He felt like his heart was being put threw a shredder. He had arrived too late. She had already taken in all that power; no person should hold alone. Her tears mixed with his as her lips moved against his. She jerked back screaming. Greg tried to keep hold of her but the power inside her exploded out. The wind forced him away. Water gushed round her, and the earth trembled. Magic seeped from every part of her body. Her screams breaking his soul. "Mellisa," Greg shouted, "Give the magic back."

She couldn't hear him she was a ball of blinding light. Radius ran up beside him. "We have to take it back." Radius covered himself in light, his shine dimmer than usual. With his arm over his face, He pushed through the storm of magic surrounding Mellissa. Stretching his other hand out he grabbed at the Moon crystal yanking it from her neck. He dropped to the ground huddling into a ball. "I take back responsibility of the moon crystal." Magic flowed from Mellissa into the moon crystal.

Ignis stomped his foot shaking the ground. Roaring he opened his claw and the sun crystal shot into his grasp. It also began sucking up magic. Greg looked between the two crystals; it was working but it was too slow. His ears were ringing as his heart felt like it was about to burst from his chest.

The two crystals glowed in their keepers' hands. The light around Mellissa disappeared, revealing the girl laid out on the grass. Her clothes were in tatters singed all over. Greg ran to her, sliding down beside her. He was already chanting healing spells before his knees had hit the ground. His hands glowed green as he ran them over her body. All the bruises, cuts and burns gradually disappeared. But she wasn't waking up. Greg tried another spell. His hands went from green to purple. He pressed his glowing fingers to her head, but nothing happened.

Victoria dropped to her knees on the other side of Mellissa. "Greg do something, why isn't she waking up?"

"I'm trying," Greg yelled. His mind raced as he tried every healing spell he could think of. But she was unresponsive.

Tears rolled down his cheeks. He leaned over Mellissa and stroked her cheek. "Please wake up. Mellissa, you have to come back to me."

Victoria shoved him. Grabbing him by the shoulder, she shook him violently. Tears coursed down her face. "Heal her."

"I have," he yelled. Victoria mouth hung open, like she wanted to say something, but no words came. Greg looked at her blankly. He was an empty shell. His heart lay on the ground unresponsive. All this extensive knowledge of healing magic he had, and it was useless.

Victoria let go of him. Her body tensed as she screamed. Punching the soil, she released ice across the land. "This can't be happening."

Harkura came running up the hill. He saw Mellissa on the ground. "No," his voice was barely a whisper. He walked slowly over to them and knelt beside Victoria. She threw herself in his arms as she sobbed uncontrollably.

Greg turned his attention back to Mellissa. He brushed her hair from her face. She looked so peaceful. He pressed his fingers to her neck. She had a pulse. He laid his head on her chest. His heart skipped a beat as he felt the rise and fall of her breathing. "She's alive," Greg shouted. The others gasped peering at her.

Greg hands glowed yellow as he recited the spell to alert him to any unseen injuries. Everything checked out. Her body was physically well. She just wouldn't wake, and he couldn't find a reason why. He laid beside her listening to her quietly inhale and exhale. Mellissa was breathing. That was all he needed because that meant there was hope.

Greg woke to the sound of birds chirping. Sun gleaned through the curtains. Once again, he had overslept. It had been this way since returning to Novosvillas. They had managed to get the UK government to give them access to the land that joined theirs's. Talks with the humans were tiresome but they were moving forward. He brushed his arm over the empty space in the bed. It still felt empty without her there. It had been weeks and things still didn't feel right.

Greg forced himself up. Showered and dressed in jeans and a polo. He headed down to the kitchen where he was greeted by the smell of freshly baked bread. Samson was busily squeezing fresh juice. He smiled at Greg. "Would you like some kiwi juice?"

Greg sat at the kitchen table. "Sure, why not." Samson slid a glass of green juice across the table. "How long till the breads done?"

"Just a few more minutes." Samson hummed to himself as he tidied the mess he had made of the kitchen. Since moving in Samson had taken up baking. There wasn't much else for him to currently do. Urbem Folium was still a mess after the battle with Kadon. Talks with the humans on how to proceed now there was no veil were to go ahead soon but currently their old way of life was gone. It almost felt like their old lives had been a lie. Like some sort of illusion that had been shattered when the veil was destroyed. Greg rested his head in his hands. They needed Mellissa for these talks. He didn't think they would work without her.

Samson placed a plate in front of Greg and a dish of butter in the centre of the table. He then brought a freshly baked loaf of bread over. He sliced it up and put two pieces on Greg's plate. The butter melted on the bread. Greg took a bite and smiled at the warm buttery taste. Samson sat opposite Greg, with his own plate. "So, what shall we do today?"

Greg shrugged. "Same as always I guess."

"I was thinking of trying a new recipe for strawberry shortcake."

The kitchen door banged into the wall. "Is that fresh bread I smell?" asked Victoria marching into the kitchen. She was in a fluffy dressing gown and slippers with a scarf wrapped round her head.

She sat at the table and grabbed a slice of bread smothering it with butter. She took a big bite then gulped down Greg's juice. He narrowed his eyes at her. "Hey that was mine."

She scrunched up her face. "I did you a favour it was nasty."

Samson sipped his juice. "I think it has a rather refreshing taste. What are your plans for the day Victoria?"

"More painting. I'm sure it's something Mellissa would approve of."

Greg smiled as his heart ached at the mention of her name. "Well, I guess I will go relieve Harkura from his watch."

"Matt's also up there with him," said Victoria helping herself to another slice of bread. Greg nodded and got up from the table. He walked down the corridor to the library. He ran his hands along the shelves and picked out a book. It was a fairy tale; he hadn't read since he was a kid. Mellissa would like it. He walked back down the corridor and upstairs to the guest room opposite his bedroom. Harkura and Matt were sat in armchairs either side of the bed chatting about the best way to start a fire. They both looked up at him. "How is she?" Greg asked.

"There is no change I'm afraid," said Harkura.

"Well Samson has been baking again. Go get yourselves some before Victoria eats it all." They both nodded and got up leaving Greg alone in the room with Mellissa.

Greg pulled one of the armchairs closer to the bed. She looked deathly pale all her colour gone. Her chest slowly rose and fell. She looked like she was peacefully sleeping. He sat in the chair crossed one leg over the other. Opened the book and read aloud to her. This was how Greg spent most days now. Occasionally meeting with Yuko and the others to discuss how to move forward with the humans. He had lost count of how many books he had read her. At first, he had refused to leave her side but then the others agreed to taking turns to watch over her, letting him know of any minor change in her condition. It was a miracle she was still alive. The power of the three crystals had almost burned her up from the inside. Radius and Ignis had taken back the power just in time to save her. She had been in a coma ever since. But she would wake one day. Greg had to have faith. And so, he read.

# 39

# Choice

## *Mellissa*

My eyes fluttered open. Handmade butterflies hung from the ceiling. I yawned as I sat up in bed. Sunlight filtered in threw the gaps in the curtains. Books were piled on my desk and clothes were draped over the chair in front of it. Stuffed animals covered my window seat. I stared at my pink walls. I was back in my childhood bedroom at my dad's house. My head spun. How had I got here? I pushed the blankets off and got out of bed. I was fully clothed, in a jade green a-line dress and wearing a pair of strappy gold sandals. What was going on? My brain felt like it was in a haze. I walked across the room and opened my bedroom door. A quite melody played below. The smell of fried eggs and bacon floated up the stairs. My heart pounded in my chest. Someone was down there.

I slowly made my way down the corridor to the stairs. Clutching the banister, I walked downstairs one step at the time. My ears rang as I reached the bottom, like there was something buzzing in my head. I walked into the kitchen and my heart burst with emotion. My dad stood over the hob, spatula in hand. Eggs and bacon sizzled away in a frying pan. The radio playing smooth jazz. Tears rolled down my cheeks as I covered my face with my hands.

"Oh, sweetie don't cry?" said Dad. I felt myself be encased in strong arms. I hugged my dad tight, taking in the smell of his aftershave. He was solid. He was really here.

"I don't understand. I thought I lost you." I spluttered between sobs.

My dad brushed my tears away with his thumbs. "I have been with you the whole time. Watching over you as you fought."

I clutched my forehead as a pain zapped through my mind. The battle with Kadon. I couldn't remember how it had ended. "Dad." I looked up at him, his brown eyes solemn. "You died."

"Yes."

"Does that mean I'm also."

"Yes and no. You have a choice to make." He clasped his hands together. "But before we get into that. There is someone else here to see you." He placed a hand on the small of my back, gently turning me towards the kitchen table.

I had been too focused on my dad to notice a woman sat there. I gasped as I took in her features. She had long dark curls, soft brown skin and big round eyes like mine. "Mum," I said my voice barely a whisper.

She smiled sweetly and her eyes glistened with tears. "I can't believe how grown up you are." She stood holding her arms out to me. I ran over collapsing into her. My mother stroked my hair. "I am so proud of the woman you have become. You are stronger than I ever imagined."

I snorted as I took a step back. My chest was tight as I let out a slow breath. "I'm either hallucinating or I really did die this time."

My mum squeezed my shoulder. "You are not dead yet."

I frowned. "What do you mean yet?"

"We are in the world in between that of the living and dead."

My dad walked over with plates in hand. He placed them down on the table. "How about we talk over breakfast."

We all sat round the table, with a plate of eggs and bacon. I pushed my food round my plate as my parents made small talk. My head buzzed. Images of my battle ran through my head. I massaged my forehead. "How did I get here?" My parents exchanged a knowing look. My dad leaned over placing a hand on my shoulder. "Someone powerful brought us here so we could see you before you leave."

"I don't understand. Leave to where?" I grabbed both their hands. "I want to stay with you."

My mum shook her head. "Honey, you can't stay here, and neither can we." Her lips pressed together. "We are both dead and will return to the afterlife, but you can still go back."

"That is the choice you must make," said dad, "You must choose to wake up." He stood pulling me up with him, into a tight embrace. "I love you sweetie and I couldn't be prouder of everything you have done but I really don't want you to stay here with us." He pressed his forehead to mine. "I want you to live your life to the fullest. Continue to be an amazing Queen. Go have those grand babies of mine."

My eyes filled with tears as I shook my head. "But you won't be there to meet them."

He stepped back towards mum and put his arms over her shoulders. "We will both be watching over you from the other side."

"But I don't know how to wake up. I don't even know how I got here."

"The person who brought us here can help you," said mum, "She is just through that door." She pointed to a door on the wall to the left of us. My forehead creased. That hadn't been there before. I placed my hand of the door handle and looked at my parents stood together. Something I hadn't seen before. They smiled at me filling my heart with joy. They both looked at peace. I opened the door and stepped through.

I quickly shut my eyes as I was blinded by a bright light. A gentle breeze caressed my skin. I wasn't in my dad's house anymore. "Hello Mellissa," said a voice. Opening my eyes I gasped. I was surrounded by lush grass and leafy green trees. A jewel-blue river curved gently through the forest. Sat at the edge of the water was an elf woman. She smiled at me and gestured with her hands for me to come over. Her deep brown curls shone in the light and her mahogany skin glistened.

Placing my hand over the heart crystal I walked over and stood beside her. "You're Freya."

"And you are Mellissa." She patted the spot beside her. "Come sit."

I sat down beside her. Opting to cross my legs instead of dangling them over the edge like Freya was. She was in a princess style dress, the same emerald green as mine. She had the skirts pulled up and draped to the side on the grass. Leaving her legs bare as she circled her feet round in the water. She looked up at the sky and sighed. "I'm sorry Mellissa."

I sat up straight as I stared at her. "Why are you sorry? You never did anything to me."

She took my hand in hers, squeezing it softly. "You sweet girl. Everything you have had to deal with was because of me. The amount of responsibility I burdened you with is unforgivable."

"That wasn't your fault."

"I could have done more in my time. Made different choices. If I had seen what Kadon was sooner, maybe I could have stopped him before he gained so much power." She looked out at the sparkling water wistfully. "But I was young and blinded by love."

I clutched my hand to my chest. "I saw your memories. Kadon was charming at one point. Something changed in him as you grew and when it did you challenged him."

"You are too kind. But that is not my only mistake." She looked me straight in the eye making me shudder. "I never should have made the veil."

"But you did that to protect the humans and your daughter."

"I may have had good intentions, but all that did was lead to my descendants being hunted and murdered." She looked down at her upturned hands. "And you were left woefully unprepared for the war you were going to be dragged into." She cupped my face in her hands softly stroking my cheeks. "Just know I am sorry for the chaos you will have to deal with now that the two worlds are one again." She stood and held her hand out to me. I took it and was pulled to my feet. She brushed her skirt down spreading it out round her legs. "Okay, now you have a choice. You can move on to the afterlife with me or you can wake up." She winked. "But I think I already know your choice. My girl isn't one to give up."

I scrunched my nose. "I don't know how to wake up."

She put her hands on her hips as one eyebrow rose. "That's because you're not hearing everything properly." She tapped the side of my head. "That should be better."

My head suddenly felt light. The haze in my brain had lifted and the buzzing was gone. A big grin spread across my face. I could hear him. Greg's voice. He was reading to me.

Freya had a massive smile plastered on her face. "You got yourself a good one in him." She winked and then she was gone. I shut my eyes as white light surrounded me. Opening my eyes I whispered, "Greg."

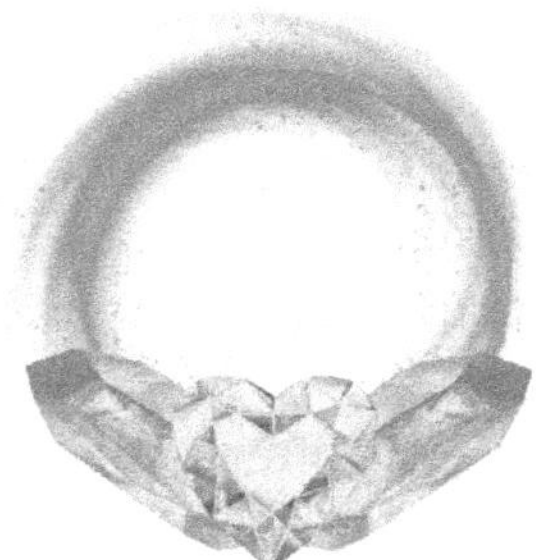

# Epilogue

## *Mellissa*

My heart raced as I stared out the carriage window. The forest was a vibrant bloom of colours. Sunlight shone brightly on the treetops. There wasn't a cloud in the sky and the smell of wildflowers floated on the gentle breeze. I took a deep breath trying to calm my nerves. Harkura and Victoria were across from me looking stunning in their formal wear. Victoria was dressed in an emerald gown with a corset bodice that laced up at the back. Her hair pinned up into a bun, her fringe pushed to the side and a golden headband shimmering atop her head. Harkura was in a smart jade green suit with gold accents. Their outfits matched perfectly.

I fiddled with the beading sewn onto the skirt of my dress. Harkura took my hand and smiled his indigo eyes sparkling. "Don't worry everything will be fine."

My forehead creased as I frowned. "Are you sure? We should have done this closer to home so much could go wrong."

"Extra security is in place just for today."

"What if anti-magic protesters show up?"

Victoria sighed. "Thats what the security is for. Along with the cars full of guards upfront and behind us."

"And of course you have us." Harkura straightened his back as he tugged at the sides of his suit jacket. "No protester will get near you with us around."

"I would rather not get into a fight when I'm looking this good." Victoria winked. "But I'd do it for you. However." She pointed at me. "There will be no need because today will go exactly to plan."

A smile crept onto my face. "I guess we are due for one of our plans to work out."

"Yes, we are. Now stop messing with your dress before you ruin it." Victoria leaned forward untangling my fingers from my skirt.

I pouted. "This journey seems longer than before."

"We are almost there. Look." Victoria pointed out the window.

The tree line was thinning and giving way to houses. My jaw went slack as I gazed out the window. "Why are there so many people in the streets?"

"To get a glimpse of the queen, silly."

My stomach fluttered with anxious butterflies. "This was a bad idea."

Victoria shrugged. "There is still time to back out. Harkura and I can get this carriage turned around."

"Thats not what I meant. I just didn't expect so many people to be on the streets. We should have just done this at the castle."

"You are the one who insisted on the church across from where we went to high school."

"Yeah, because this village is where we met and where I lived with my dad. He took me to that church as a child. It makes me feel like he is here with us."

Harkura squeezed my hand. "Then this wasn't a mistake. This is the perfect venue."

As the carriage travelled through the streets of the village I grew up in, crowds of people lined the roads. They waved and cheered as we went past. They held up signs of congratulations and joy. I waved back as we passed. Barriers had been put up with police stationed along them, keeping our path clear. But not one person caused a scene. There were no anti-magic protesters in sight. Everyone was happy and joyful. My heart was warm and full.

Victoria batted her hand in my direction. "No tears. It will ruin you're make up."

I gently patted at my damp eyes with my fingertips. "I'm just so happy."

"Come here." She pulled a tissue out her golden clutch bag and dabbed at my eyes. "You're still presentable."

The carriage slowed and came to a stop. We were outside the church. It was just like a remembered with its steeple spires and grand bells. The footman opened the carriage door. Victoria got out first followed by Harkura. He turned back holding his hand out to me. Sliding my hand into his I stepped out of the carriage. Victoria rushed round me, fanning out the skirt of my dress. She grabbed a bouquet of white roses from the front of the carriage and handed it to me, keeping a smaller matching one for herself. She straightened the gold crown on my head and smiled. He icy blue eyes glistened. "You look amazing. You ready?"

"Yes."

Harkura linked arms with me. I lent on him for support as we walked up the church steps. Its windows of many hues sparkled in the sun. Victoria followed behind holding the train of my dress. Which was white with a lacy bodice and layers of fabric made up the skirt. Sparkling beads had been sewn on in the shapes of different flowers.

We made our way into the church foyer. A man stood by the doors and nodded at us. He held his hand up gesturing for us to wait. He stepped inside. Calming music played and I could hear chatter from inside. Victoria stepped in front of us and peered into the main hall. Everything went quiet. All I could hear was the hammering of my own heart. The man reappeared and a fanfare began to play. Victoria went in first. It felt like an eternity passed but really it couldn't have been more than a minute or two. Both doors opened wide revealing the long aisle and rows of people sat in pews. Victoria was just reaching the end of the aisle.

The opening to the bridal chorus started to play. Everyone stood and turned their gazes to me. Harkura escorted me down the aisle, which seemed longer than when we had visited and planned this all. He became my strength; without him I would have fallen flat on my face. I was a ball of nervousness but also giddy with excitement. Up ahead I saw him, Greg. Stood with Samson facing the front. But then he turned, and our eyes met. His green eyes shone as he grinned. I felt like I might melt right there halfway to the alter. As we reached the end of the aisle, Harkura bowed before placing my hand in Greg's. His touch sent tingles up my arm. Greg stood tall, his shoulders back and his eyes on me. I beamed up at him. This was it. The start of the rest of our lives.

# ABOUT THE AUTHOR

Whitney Morris has always had a passion for storytelling. Growing up she loved to escape to into the fantasy worlds of magic from her stories. She is a cat lover with one of her own, is crazy about owls, and is addicted to chocolate.

Whitney loves books, and she and her husband are raising their four children to be fellow bookworms in South Yorkshire, England.

The Life Crystal Chronicles is her first YA fantasy series.

Find Whitney on social media

| | |
|---|---|
| Instagram | @wrlmorris_author |
| Facebook, BookBub Twitter & Pinterest | @wrlmorris |

**Other books in the series:**
Crystal Heart
Glowing Heart
Raging Heart

Final Heart